G000257773

LAHORE

Advance Praise for *Lahore*

'As the men fought over religion and maps, the Partition heaped unspeakable atrocities on women. Manreet's book is a faithful, unforgiving look at what was and also what shouldn't have been. *Lahore* is breathtaking in scope, painful yet gentle to the touch.'

Taslima Nasreen, author of *Lajja*

'Vivid and atmospheric. By deftly weaving the personal and the political, Manreet Sodhi Someshwar transports us to the uncertain months leading up to the tragedy of Partition.'

Aanchal Malhotra, author of *Remnants of a Separation*

'A timely reminder of what differences and divisions can do … An engaging read that tries to humanize the politics of the Partition. Current, relevant and important. This is a voice which makes you question, rethink and reimagine the past as the future and the future as the past. A voice to pay attention to in these times of rising intolerance and right-wing extremism. A voice of reason and reckoning.'

Sabyn Javeri, author of *Hijabistan*

'Tension pervades this first part of Manreet Sodhi Someshwar's Partition trilogy. It wafts through the corridors of power, penetrates bonds between friends and lovers, and befouls the earth itself. Without releasing the reader from its ominous undercurrent, Manreet deftly weaves the big strands of history with the finer threads of human feeling, reminding us of a calamity that tore apart not just nations and states but also the heart and spirit of a people.'

Manu S. Pillai, author of *The Ivory Throne: Chronicles of the House of Travancore*

Praise for *The Radiance of a Thousand Suns*

'Searing personal memories of the Partition and the anti-Sikh pogrom.'

Scroll

'Underneath a heavy coat of concealer, the bruises are still fresh. *The Radiance of a Thousand Suns* is a moving tale of dislocation, of identity in alien nations, of the double-edged sword that is memory, and of the onerous legacy of a father's unfinished work.'

Hindustan Times

'[A] formidable narrative testimony to our lived experiences of mass atrocities and collective trauma ... her prose powerful and shattering ... Manreet subverts the nation-state's archive.'

Outlook

'At a time when the political landscape is shifting towards a singular narrative, it feels like very relevant reading.'

India Today

LAHORE

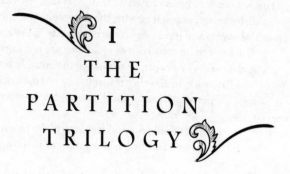

I
THE
PARTITION
TRILOGY

MANREET SODHI SOMESHWAR

HarperCollins *Publishers* India

First published in India by
HarperCollins *Publishers* 2021
A-75, Sector 57, Noida, Uttar Pradesh 201301, India
www.harpercollins.co.in

2 4 6 8 10 9 7 5 3 1

Copyright © Manreet Sodhi Someshwar 2021

P-ISBN: 978-93-5489-195-3
E-ISBN: 978-93-5489-069-7

This is a work of fiction based on historical fact. All situations, incidents,
dialogue and characters, with the exception of some well-known
historical events and public figures, are products of the author's imagination
and are not to be construed as real. They are not intended to depict
actual events or people, or to change the entirely fictional nature
of the work. In all other respects, any resemblance to actual
persons, living or dead, is entirely coincidental.

Manreet Sodhi Someshwar asserts the moral right
to be identified as the author of this work.

All rights reserved. No part of this publication may be reproduced,
stored in a retrieval system, or transmitted, in any form or by any means,
electronic, mechanical, photocopying, recording or otherwise,
without the prior permission of the publishers.

Typeset in 11/15 Berling LT Std at
Manipal Technologies Limited, Manipal

Printed and bound at
Thomson Press (India) Ltd

MIX
Paper
FSC FSC® C010615

This book is produced from independently certified FSC® paper
to ensure responsible forest management.

For
Tayaji, Rajinder Singh Bhalla,
Whose Laur is mine too.

And Panjab,
Undivided.

The struggle of man against power is the struggle of memory against forgetting.

Milan Kundera

Awwal Allah noor upaya,

Kudrat ke sab bandey,

Ek beej te sab jag upja,

Kaun bhaley kau mandey.

Kabir, Gurbani

About The Partition Trilogy

Set in the months leading up to and following India obtaining freedom in 1947, The Partition Trilogy is an exploration of the events, exigencies and decisions that led to the independence of India, its concomitant partition, and the accession of princely states alongside. A literary political thriller that captures the frenzy of the time, the series is set in Delhi, Lahore, Hyderabad, and Kashmir. Covering a vast canvas, Jawaharlal Nehru, Vallabhbhai Patel, and Dickie Mountbatten share space in the trilogy with the ordinary people from the cities that were affected by the partition and the reorganization of the states.

Backed by astute research that ensures the authenticity of the political thread, this trilogy will take readers back into a world of great political upheaval and churn. In its fresh, incisive, and insightful portrayal of a cataclysm that haunts us to this day, The Partition Trilogy is both spellbinding and believable – a remarkable feat.

Cast of Characters

His Majesty's Government (HMG)

(London)

King George VI, King of the United Kingdom and British Dominions, and Emperor of India

Winston Churchill, Prime Minister of the United Kingdom from 1940–45

Clement Attlee, Prime Minister of the United Kingdom from 1945–51

British Empire in India/The Raj

Lord Louis (Dickie) Mountbatten, last Viceroy of India (1947), and the first Governor General of independent India (1947–48)

Edwina Mountbatten, wife of Louis Mountbatten, and the last Vicereine of India

Pamela Mountbatten, younger daughter of Louis and Edwina Mountbatten

Mizzen, Sealyham terrier belonging to Edwina Mountbatten

Neola, a mongoose gifted to Pamela as a pet

Lord Wavell, second-last Viceroy of India

Lionel (Pug) Ismay, chief of staff to Lord Mountbatten

Eric Miéville, Mountbatten's principal secretary

George Abell, Mountbatten's private secretary

Alan Campbell-Johnson, Mountbatten's press attaché

Ian Scott, Mountbatten's deputy private secretary

John Christie, Mountbatten's joint private secretary

V.P. Menon, reforms commissioner in the Raj

Evan Jenkins, Governor of Panjab

Olaf Caroe, Governor of the North-West Frontier Province (NWFP)

John Colville, Governor of Bombay

Roy Bucher, general officer commanding-in-chief of Eastern Command

Douglas Currie, military secretary responsible for the movements of the Viceregal household

Conrad Corfield, political adviser responsible for the princely states

Cyril Radcliffe, Inner Temple lawyer, and chairman of the Boundary Commission

Political Leaders of the Subcontinent, Their Families, and Staff

Gandhi/Mahatma/Bapu, leader of the Indian National Congress

Jawaharlal Nehru, Prime Minister in the interim government

Motilal Nehru, Jawaharlal's father, twice president of the Congress

Indira (Indu) Gandhi, Jawaharlal's daughter

Rajiv and Sanjay, Indira's sons

M.O. Mathai (Mac), private secretary to Jawaharlal

Vallabhbhai Patel, home minister in the interim government

Jhaverba, Vallabhbhai's wife

Manibehn, Vallabhbhai's daughter, assistant, and housekeeper

Dahyabhai, Vallabhbhai's son

Vithalbhai, Vallabhbhai's elder brother

Vidya Shankar, Vallabhbhai's private secretary

Mohammed Ali Jinnah, leader of the Muslim League

Fatima Jinnah, Jinnah's younger sister

Liaquat Ali Khan, finance minister in the interim government

Begum Ra'ana, Liaquat's wife

Abdur Rab Nishtar, Muslim League member

Maulana Abul Kalam Azad, education minister in the interim government,

Morarji Desai, Congress member

Krishna Menon, president of the India League, and close friend of Jawaharlal

H.S. Suhrawardy, premier of Bengal

Khan Abdul Ghaffar Khan, charismatic Pashtun leader, and a close friend of Gandhi

Amrit Kaur, Congress member, and a close associate of Gandhi

Sarojini Naidu, Congress member, and writer

Acharya J.B. Kripalani, Congress president

Baldev Singh, representative of the Sikhs to the Viceroy's Executive Council, and defence minister in the interim government

Giani Kartar Singh, Sikh leader

Master Tara Singh, Sikh leader who opposed the partition of Panjab

Bhim Sen Sachar, Sardar Joginder Singh, and Sardar Ujjal Singh, legislators from Panjab

Khizar Hayat Tiwana, premier of pre-partition Panjab

I.H. Khan of Mamdot, leader of Opposition in Panjab Assembly (pre-partition)

Princes

Hamidullah Khan, Prince of Bhopal, and chancellor of the Chamber of Princes

Jamsaheb, Maharaja of Nawanagar

Hari Singh, Maharaja of Kashmir

Mir Osman Ali Khan, Nizam of Hyderabad

Hanwant Singh, Maharaja of Jodhpur

Others

(Lahore)

Mehmood, coolie at Lahore Junction

Beli Ram, coolie at Lahore Junction, and resident of Kesari Hata

Shammi Joseph, rickshaw puller, and resident of Kesari Hata

Lata Lily Joseph, Shammi's wife

Billo, 'mad woman' of Kesari Hata

Kishan Singh, clerk at Lahore Junction, and resident of railway quarters

Iqbal Singh, Kishan's older brother based in Lyallpur

Parminder (Pammi), Narinder, Surinder, Kishan's three daughters

Nishtar Singh Arora, Kishan's next-door neighbour

Ahmed Niazi, Kishan's other neighbour

Asad Niazi, Ahmed's son, and Pammi's college-mate at Dayal Singh College

Balwant Rai, Kishan's boss

Mangat, Ahmed, Hari Kumar, Kishan's colleagues

Sepoy Malik, soldier who fought in Jang-e-Azam (WWII)

Tara Malik, Sepoy Malik's beloved

Kanwal Malik, Tara's father and shopkeeper in Anarkali Bazaar

Jujhar Singh, Sikh organizer

Hakam Singh, leader of a Sikh squad

Bagga, demobilized soldier, and leader of a Muslim gang in Lahore

Others

Walter Monckton, English lawyer, and constitutional adviser to the Nizam of Hyderabad

Shamsher Singh, Kishan's cousin, and chaprassi at Viceroy House

Khaliq, Jawaharlal's driver

Madha Rat, barber in Bakrol

Amu mian, servant in Bakrol

Prologue

Delhi is the Indian Rome, some historians say.
Those myth-makers are Westerners.

There is a certain symmetry, one can grant. Rome has seven hills; Delhi has seven cities. Each new sultan, emperor, king built himself a new capital on the plains, each built to last, hubris the one defining constant. A poet sums it up well:

The one who occupied this throne before you
As assured of his immortality he was as you.

What remains of those seven cities – Indian historians count many more; the earliest from 3000 BCE – is ruins, mostly. Omen enough, one would think, for the British, never as prescient as poets.

Dismissing the augury, however, King George V lays the foundation stone for his imperial city during his 1911 tour of India – officially, the Delhi Durbar. The plan is to be around for the next 400 years, at least. They have been around for that much already. Time in which the colonial British Empire in India has amassed eleven provinces and 565 princely states. (The provinces are directly under British rule; so are the states, but they have nominal princes.) The plan is for George RI – *Rex Imperator*, aka King-Emperor – to hold onto the *I*, a suffix he has earned as the Emperor of India.

But, along comes Hitler to bust said plans.

When our story begins, in February 1947, Britain, bankrupted by WWII, is about to pull out of India. Churchill, who won Britain the war, even calls it 'Operation Scuttle'. But he's been booted out of office – for heroes fight wars, but seldom rebuild countries – the freedom movement in India is on the boil, and WWII has exposed the hypocrisy of British rule in India. The Labour government under Attlee wants its hands clean.

As the British scuttle, what is happening to India?

Let's take a look.

1
Laur (February 1947)

'R un!'
    'Wha-aat?'

'Run, fool!' Mehmood rasped, shoving his friend forward. The slogans had got shriller and more combative, the procession swollen with factions shouting conflicting demands. A clash was imminent.

'What, Mehmood?' Beli Ram grumbled.

They had been walking down Railway Road when a Muslim League protest march made its way from Anarkali Bazaar, waving green flags, holding aloft posters of Jinnah, demanding Pakistan. At Lohari Gate, younger men and some women – likely students – had joined the marchers, making very different demands: 'Reinstate civil liberties!', 'Hindus–Muslims–Sikhs unite!' The burka-clad League women beat their chests in syapa, 'Khizar sarkar hai-hai!' The female students chanted, 'Long live Congress–League unity!' and the male students repeated after them loudly. Now, they were all trying to out-shout each other – total tamasha. And here was Mehmood ruining—

'Mooove!' Mehmood hissed again.

A scream rang out, followed by scuffles, and shouts of 'Grab the motherfucker!', 'Grab him now!'

Mehmood craned his neck to where a huddle had formed in the procession – manly arms raining fists down.

A man was dragged to the side, his white Gandhi cap aloft in the hand of another, who thrust it at his fellow marchers and yelled, '*See!* See the work of Congressmen … Harassing our women in plain sight!' A thwack landed on the captive's head. Reeling, he struggled to free himself. 'Let me go! I did nothing!'

As Mehmood hovered at the edge of the crowd, he was reminded of his visit to Karachi's Clifton Beach: One minute his feet were on the sand, the next, a breaker had snatched the ground from under him, toppling him over. The bright noon sun glinted off the blade of a spear.

'*Kill* the infidel!'

The demand rang loud, puncturing the momentary stasis. A whistling above them. A flaming arrow descended upon the procession. The stink of oil and resin spread in the air. Another arrow followed. This found a direct hit, the crowd parting, distancing itself from the human firecracker that spun and shrieked as flames rose from his skullcap and coat-clad sleeves.

'Hai! The Hindus are dropping bombs on us!'

The marchers ran pell-mell. Mehmood and Beli Ram were lifted with the surging crowd, before it became a stampede. As Beli Ram lurched to the ground, Mehmood hoisted him up by the collar of his kurta, pushing him to the side, where a narrow alley branched off ahead.

Upright, Beli Ram tried to weave his way through the agitated crowd. Assorted cries filled the air. Mehmood was close behind; he could hear him cussing as they tried to cut through the mob. Surely, they would get crushed. Beli Ram blindly struck for the right, where the alley's dark mouth lay. Elbows in his face, prods in his back, his sweater ripping as he flailed through and stumbled out, one foot plonking into the drain that ran through the middle of the alley. Lifting his foot out, he limped forward – his eyes scanning for an exit as feet thundered close behind. The narrow lane was cold and dark in the shadows of the houses that bordered it. He shivered.

Was Mehmood still behind?

Beli Ram scrunched his eyes at the stampede. Two women were buffeted along by the mob. He thought he sighted his friend, but a rushing river of people separated them, a tributary of which was in the alley now, threatening to drown Beli Ram. He stumbled forward, seeking an open doorway he could take refuge in. But all doors, even windows, of the double-, triple-storeyed houses were shut as if against marauders. Feet thundered in his ears – or was it his thudding heart? A shove from behind sent him staggering. He stretched out his arms to steady himself. But his limbs were tossed about and his bones protested, as he was squeezed from all sides. He remembered being caught in a herd of hurrying buffaloes as a child, their sweaty, fleshy flanks suffocating him. Beli Ram tried not to panic. His feet left the ground. The horde shifted, shuffled and flung him against the wall of a house. He stuck out his hands and clung to the rough bricks.

His breath came rapidly. Sweat trickled into his eyes. But he would not let go of the chafing bricks. With his back firmly against the wall, Beli Ram inched forward, his wool sweater snagging on the uneven surface. Scraping his way along the wall, his hand came up against a damp disc, then several, and now the overpowering smell of cow dung enveloped him. A churning sound and the tinkle of bells came from a door that stood ajar, a few feet away from where he crouched. With an eye on the mob hurrying forward, Beli Ram slid against the cakes drying on the wall and scuttled his way to the door.

Stepping inside, he lost his footing as the ground suddenly dipped. It was dark. Beli swore as his head smacked against a sack. A heavy odour of mustard and piss assailed him. Gagging, he tried to stand up. His hands came away wet from the floor. Strange sounds filled the air: lumbering, squeaking, tinkling … He was trying to make sense of his surroundings when something bore into him, ramming him onto a sack. A rope smacked his face. No, it was a—

Beli Ram's eyes picked their way through the darkness. A beast was treading in circles around the room, snorting warm air into the dankness. Blindfolded, it was oblivious to him and to the hungama outside, as it spun and turned an oil press. The big bull was approaching; its curving horns set to gore him. Beli dropped to the floor, plastering himself against the inside wall, and felt the bull's breath wash over him. Narrowly escaping its flicking tail, he slipped out of the room.

The number of people in the alley had swollen. Beli licked his dry lips. All available space on the outside wall of the oil press was dotted with drying cakes of cow dung. In an alcove, a ladder inclined against the wall.

Beli Ram sprinted forward. He climbed up shakily, his feet slipping on the thin bamboo. On the roof, he crouched low to scour the lane and the main street where he had been separated from Mehmood.

They had been walking back from the railway station – skirting around the crowd of men carrying posters of Jinnah and shouting their demands for Pakistan – debating whether to go for biryani at Kareem's or the samosas at Motiram Halwai's, when their business had been hijacked by an unruly mob. What was happening to people? Going berserk at lunch hour? If they had filled their bellies in time, these men would be snoring by now, on cots under the winter sun.

And where *was* Mehmood?

Men continued to tumble through the narrow alleyway. Some fell, others clambered atop them. A banner that had slipped from someone's grasp crumpled under hurried feet. A scuffle. Several hands trying to pry free a green flag held aloft by an arm. The man with the flag managed to break free and, sighting the ladder, started to clamber atop. Arms lunged at him, grabbing his pyjama-clad legs. Still clutching the flag, he hit out with one foot, sending an assailant teetering. Beli Ram watched, his throat constricting. The Muslim League man was nearly at the rooftop, in which case his pursuers would follow him up and find Beli Ram too. There *was* no other place he could run to. Of the adjoining rooftops, one was too far, the other too high …

The ladder creaked as the men in the alley pulled it away from the wall. For a moment, man and flag perched on a step, the ladder was an erect column. Until it arced away. Screams and splintering as the bamboo crashed onto the escaping men. Howls, cusses. The flag was now in the hands of a man who was ripping it with manic energy. As its erstwhile bearer scrambled to get away, another man pounced on him. The League man turned sideways, his face shocked as he faced his pursuer. The throng of men pulsing around them was sprinkled, their faces and clothing smeared by a sudden drizzle. Only, the drops were red. It was an unusual rain, something the men seemed to register as the man who had been carrying the flag suddenly slumped forward, a red line on his neck sputtering little jets of blood.

Beli Ram doubled over, his stomach heaving up to his throat. Where *was* Mehmood?

2
Laur (February 1947)

The goondas in the lane below had just killed a man. For the sin of carrying a League flag? But Mehmood was not a Leaguer. And if ever he carried a flag, for whatever reason, he would have sense enough to ditch it in the nearest gutter at the first sign of trouble. That thought fortified Beli Ram momentarily.

When the shouts died down, he peered over the alleyway.

The mass of men had reduced to a trickle that snaked down the alley, avoiding the man lying spreadeagled on the brick-paved road, his blood pooling into the central drain. Further down, the bordering houses were taller, rendering the alley even darker. In a dim entrance archway, something shifted. Beli Ram leaned over the rooftop, craning his neck. A red coolie's kurta merged with the shadows.

Mehmood!

Beli Ram collapsed in relief.

'That was a close call, eh?'

Beli Ram, reeking of cow dung, tried again to get his friend to speak. But since they had skulked their way out of the alley and started walking back towards Kesari Hata, Mehmood had stayed as silent as a stone. Now he padded on, his leather jutti scrunching, a shawl draped over his lungi–kurta.

'Tell you what? Let's pick up freshly fried samosas from Pandu Halwai and I'll make garma-garam cha, and we'll have the best lunch ever!'

'You think I'm worrying over a missed meal?' Mehmood's intent gaze was elsewhere as he worked the right tip of his moustache.

'No?' Beli Ram rubbed his chin. The mice scampering in his tummy since early noon were rampaging elephants now, but Mehmood acted as if he had eaten an entire cow at breakfast and not the tea and kulcha they had both bought from outside the railway station. His friend could be strange that way. Ahead, Shammi Joseph wiped the seat of his rickshaw, which was parked beside the chabutara of his house.

'What, Shammi,' Beli Ram hailed him, 'done for the day already?'

Shammi turned his head. He had thick lustrous hair, one perpetual lock dangling over his forehead. Truth be told, he was so dashing that many of the young women of Kesari Hata had been in love with him until he went and married a much older Hindu widow. She converted right after their marriage. Tongues in the neighbourhood had wagged about the scandalous widow, the scandalous Christian church, and shameless Shammi. What really rankled the community was the fact that a Hindu widow with no prospect of remarriage could have set up home again with a virile young man. Every Sunday, when Lata Lily Joseph – dressed in a satiny salwar–kameez – stepped out for Mass with her husband, the women of the Hata, roosting on rooftops or chabutaras, went collectively cockeyed.

'Didn't you hear of the riot near Lohari Gate?' Shammi shouted. His voice, perennially hoarse, sounded like a frog's croak. Small mercies; one man should not have all the luck in the world. 'Miscreants killed people and set fire to shops – I was at Anarkali when an agg da bamba raced down shrieking!'

'Fire engine!' Beli Ram squealed.

'We were there, and had a narrow escape,' Mehmood added. 'Any idea who the goondas were?'

Shammi shrugged and moved to the rear of his rickshaw, continuing his wiping. He spoke louder. 'The talk in Anarkali is the usual nowadays. The border between Pakistan and Hindustan, and where in Panjab it will be ... Laur will be in Hindustan, Kishore Lala said, because the real estate in the city is in the hands of Hindus. But Chaudhry Shakur, the wholesaler, said Muslims are the majority in Panjab, and so on they went, back and forth, others adding their voices, and in the end, no one was listening to anyone.'

'It is Attlee's recent announcement that has created this problem,' Mehmood snorted.

'But the goras departing is good riddance, no?' Beli Ram asked.

'Depends which king comes to power in Dilli – Jinnah, Nehru, Gandhi?'

'Na,' Shammi clucked, his head bobbing up from behind the rickshaw. 'Things will change, our padre says. There will be elections and we will elect our own government. No more kings.'

'Be it so, yaara,' Mehmood hailed Shammi as they neared. 'But tell me, the daily protests, the riots between brothers – why are all these occurring if not for the kingdom of Hindustan? This story is as old as Mahbharat.'

Shammi paused, arms resting on the folded canopy of his rickshaw. 'In this battle, let us stay safe. If there's life, then there's the world.' He crossed himself.

'True,' Beli Ram agreed and prodded his stomach. 'But to stay alive, you have to eat!' They had reached the rickshaw now and Beli Ram, staring at Shammi's blue sweater-clad chest, thrust his neck forward. 'Why this jewellery?'

Shammi Joseph plucked the locket dangling from a long chain around his neck and held it up for the two friends to view. 'Cross. Cross of Yeshu.'

Beli Ram patted the air. 'Aaho, that I know, but why are you wearing such a big cross like some padre?'

'Our padre says it's best to distinguish ourselves as Christians, so that in the fight between you people, we don't get killed.'

'Fight? Between us?' Beli Ram looked from Mehmood to himself, frowning.

'Aaho. Have you missed the protest marches taken out daily by menfolk of your religions? Why, even women are joining them nowadays, without burkas even!'

'That!' Beli Ram snorted. '*That* is the fight between the Muslim League and the RSS.'

'Exactly,' Shammi nodded. 'Muslim and Hindu. Pakistan and Hindustan.'

ഉ

In the dying rays of the February sun, the two friends proceeded down the lane. Beli Ram clucked as he examined his ripped sweater, hugging his arms close to his chest. With the sun gone, it had got chilly. Beside him, Mehmood adjusted his safa – firming the two short turras that unfurled from each side of the turban. Chabutaras had sprouted men – gossiping in groups or shouting across the narrow lane to one another. In the daytime, those terraces and rooftops were occupied by womenfolk, who sat chopping vegetables, oiling hair, doing embroidery or chatting amongst themselves as children played in the lane. They were cooking dinners now, and the smell of woodsmoke and cooking oil was in the air. The ancient banyan too had its own gathering of men – some perched atop the concrete plinth, some reclining on a jute cot. Beli Ram acknowledged the elders with a bowed head and a right arm that darted outwards in a 'Pairipaina'. Except for a few grunts, the men stayed mostly silent amidst the gud-gud of hukkah. When they had walked ahead, Beli Ram could still feel their eyes on his back. To break the tension, he said, 'Say, Mehmood, don't you think Shammi's padre is overreacting?'

Mehmood twirled the other end of his moustache. 'What do you think of the silent uncles?'

Beli Ram shrugged.

'Come on, Beli, spit it out. You know they were looking askance at me because nowadays, when they see me, they see a Muslim – not your childhood friend. Have you noticed how many of these men wear the white Gandhi cap when they step out of the Hata nowadays? As if in competition with the skullcaps selling wholesale in Anarkali!'

'But, yaar, will wearing either cap make the chilli redder?'

'What?' Mehmood tossed his chin.

'Aren't Hindu, Sikh, Mussalman, Isai, Parsee like the spices in Panjab's masala box? Assorted?'

Mehmood wove an arm around Beli's shoulder and grinned. 'Beli, my friend, you're speaking sense when the rest of the world is behaving as if bitten by a rabid dog. So your sense has become nonsense, see!'

They had reached Beli Ram's one-room-with-courtyard house. As he reached for the key in his pocket, Mehmood said, 'Let's go visit Kishan Singh soon. He is bound to have some news that will shed light on the situation.'

Kishan Singh was a railway clerk whose home was in the railway quarters, close to Lahore Junction. In the evenings, he liked to sit in his garden and listen to the radio. He also read several newspapers – *Dawn*, *The Tribune*, *Siasat* – and was up to date on current affairs. Besides, his brother or cousin or somebody worked in Dilli in the Viceroy's mansion as a durwan, was it?

'Take it from me – all of this is the angrej's mischief. Like Shakuni mama, always driving a wedge between brothers.' Beli Ram opened the lock, unhooked the chain, and flung the wooden door open.

'Are you saying you are *not* interested in a visit to old man Kishan?'

Beli Ram refused to rise to the bait. Mehmood knew he had a soft spot for Kishan Singh's elder daughter, but really it was all a dream. What were the chances of a match between a poor illiterate Hindu coolie and the college-going daughter of a middle-class Sikh man? Visiting him was a good idea, though. And if he managed to catch sight of Pammi, even better. Beli Ram extended his arms in elaborate welcome, and ushered Mehmood into the courtyard. Mehmood took the cot that was reclining against a wall, set it down and made himself at home.

As Beli Ram made to shut the door, his gaze extended to where the men sat smoking and gossiping. Hukkah smoke drifted up to mingle with the dusk air as the giant banyan hulked over them. Beli Ram narrowed his eyes, then shook his head. *Fool!* he remonstrated himself. But he couldn't escape the niggling feeling that a woman was sitting in the tree's branches, swinging her legs. A churail. The story went that some nights, one could hear the tinkling of her anklets and her cackle too. Legend had it that many years ago a woman of Kesari Hata had died during childbirth and her spirit had made its home in the banyan. Her in-laws were cruel and this was her revenge, targeting the males of her family. In the end, the story went, she drove them mad or out of the lane.

Beli Ram shivered and shut the door.

3

Delhi (February 1947)

The interim government of India had been formed on 2 September 1946. Earlier, Britain, drained by WWII, had elected the Labour Party to power. Clement Attlee, the Prime Minister who booted out Churchill – of 'I hate Indians' fame – was also the Labour expert on India. As if rectifying his predecessor's boorishness, Attlee hastened to announce the date for transfer of power from His Majesty's Government to responsible Indian hands – no later than June 1948.

One of those 'responsible Indian hands', the home member in the interim government, Vallabhbhai Patel, stood at the window of his official residence studying the pre-dawn mist blanketing the garden. 'You think someone's there already?'

'Sau taka,' Manibehn replied, adjusting the folds of her shawl around her khadi saree.

'Guess we'll just have to dodge them then,' Vallabh said.

'Yes, Father. They're aware your first meeting is at 5 a.m. They'll wait.'

'But my morning walk cannot!' He swivelled from the window and buttoned up his jubba, the khadi waistcoat spun by his daughter. 'You realize, Mani, that at seventy-one, I have lived more than three times the life of an average Indian? Some days, I feel myself an earthen vessel close to cracking.'

'Which is why the exercise,' Manibehn smiled, handing him the thick khadi shawl she had spun him especially for the Delhi winter.

Draping it over his shoulders, Vallabh said, 'Though, what could be better for me than to find release while doing what I have accepted as my dharma, hmm?'

'It's been a long road, Father—'

'But we aren't there yet!' Vallabh finished. He had had a late start in life, beginning school at the age of eight, passing his matriculation at twenty-two, graduating as barrister in England at the age of thirty-seven, joining the Congress Party at forty-two. Like the proverbial tortoise ... Except, he had heard that Robert Clive's tortoise, Advaita, was alive in Alipore Zoo in Calcutta, and, at 200 years of age, had outlived his master – the founder of the British Empire in India – by a century and half. As for Vallabh, he was still battling the British, thirty years on. At the door, slipping his feet into the customary country-made chappals, he stepped out.

A supplicant, seated on the porch, started as he saw a man slice through the mist as if hurrying to catch a train pulling out of a station. A woman scurried behind him. How was the supplicant to know that Vallabh, in the extensive time spent jailed by the English, had developed the habit of pacing back and forth because the grounds available for exercise were limited! He brought such briskness to his walking routine that an intelligence officer of the Raj, observing him in jail, had recorded that he was 'walking faster than a man in normal health'.

Vallabh hastened through Lady Willingdon Park. Trees stood as still as sentinels, observing his quick march. The ancient among them, the gnarled many-limbed banyan, had seen the march of history. The domed stone structure now coming into view was from the fifteenth century, when the Turks had ruled over Delhi. Scattered in the lush greenery were monuments that marked the passage of the Afghan Lodhis, who yielded to the Mughals, who lost to the British.

A harsh cry shattered the stillness. His step did not falter, but he cast an eager glance around. There, atop the cupola, a peacock silhouetted against the awakening sky. Vallabh glanced at Mani, who had also stopped to stare. 'A mating cry,' he said, 'but the peacock is known to use it even when he merely desires the company of a peahen!' Now the peacock unfurled his tail, the rays of the rising sun lighting the iridescent colours, a living rainbow perched atop the dome. A series of shrill calls floated over the garden.

'Success!' Manibehn nodded.

Vallabh smiled one of his rare smiles and continued pacing the walkway.

'Father, you know I can deal with the supplicants on my own, but there is a petitioner who came in yesterday whose case you should know about.' On his nod, she continued. 'It is a Muslim petitioner from Old Delhi. Their three-storey house has been in the joint family for generations, he says – an ancestor who came from Persia to work in the court of Emperor Jahangir. Now, one of his Hindu neighbours is threatening to kill him and his family if they do not vacate their house within a week and go to Pakistan.'

Vallabh paused. 'I should meet this Hindu man, if only to learn the whereabouts of this Pakistan. Where it begins and where it ends ...' He resumed his pacing.

Manibehn knew better than to pester him for an immediate answer. Since 1928, when she took upon herself the role of taking care of her father full time, she had seen it as her calling. Homemaker, secretary, nurse, companion … The daughter had even accompanied her father to jail on occasion.

'You know, Mani, since they landed on our shores in 1600, there has never been more than 1,00,000 British in India? Never exceeding that count over their 350-year presence in the subcontinent. And yet, they became our rulers.'

Manibehn was listening to her father, but one part of her mind was also on the first meeting of the day, which was to be with Margaret Bourke-White, a photographer from *Life* magazine. She had washed the apples, peeled the oranges, chopped the pistachios and readied dates for serving. Toast and marmalade—

'How did they conjure up this magic, Mani? It is a question worth asking.' Vallabh squared his shoulders as he spoke, with Manibehn walking behind him. 'India's defining feature has also been its greatest vulnerability: our diversity. The Raj would not be the Raj without the active collaboration of the Mir Jafars and Jagat Seths of India. Now the British are set to roll up their bedding and depart. But they need that final push. The revolution is close to achieving its objective of a free India, but not wholly there – as you reminded me earlier. Churchill has talked of dividing India into Pakistan, Hindustan and Princestan, the emissaries of the government from London know doublespeak, and the Muslim League … Well, what can I say of Jinnah …'

Nearing the end of his walk, he had reached Aurangzeb Road, across which lay the circular, white house that was his residence. As they reached the gate, Vallabh said, 'Vidya Shankar will seek you out regarding that Muslim petitioner.'

Manibehn nodded – Father's private secretary would know what to do – and hurried up to the house. Plaintiffs thronged the porch already, and soon, visitors would arrive, spilling onto the lawns.

Vallabh watched his daughter and sighed softly. With quiet efficiency, she oversaw his engagements daily, providing tea and sundry refreshments to visitors, keeping the house humming. She spun the yarn for his dhoti and kurta – even the shawl he had wrapped around himself as protection against the chill – took notes at his official engagements, and nursed him when his spastic colon, worsened by extensive jail stays, flared up. If he was the face of the revolution, she was the quiet revolutionary. The revolution had denied her marriage even.

He started to pace the lawn, fresh dew moistening his sandaled feet. His mind went back to his prior train of thought. *What shape would the free nation take* … As he walked back up, he caught the gardener frowning over a flower bed, hands on his waist. 'What happened?' he called out.

'Look, Sardar, look!' The gardener flung his hands in dismay towards the neatly laid flower beds, with trampled-upon flowers. 'See how your unruly visitors roam about and ruin my work. *Who* walks on a flower bed?'

'Forgive them, my friend. They are just eager for azadi. Never before have they been allowed onto the lawns of such a bungalow.'

The gardener shook his head ruefully. 'Their azadi shouldn't ruin my garden.'

That Vallabh agreed with. Their work was cut out for them. Freedom was coming – and the price was still being paid.

4

Delhi (March 1947)

'The resignation of the Tiwana government has set light to the tinderbox that is Panjab.' Vallabh gazed at the reports on his desk. 'The Muslim League's agitations have paid off, but at what cost? Governor Jenkins was unwise to ask the Khan of Mamdot to form a government. A clear signal to the Hindus and Sikhs that the days of coalition are over ...'

'Master Tara Singh sees it as the return of Muslim tyranny,' Vidya Shankar added. 'As you see, Sardar, he's called for the formation of Akali Fauj—'

Vallabh raised his furrowed brow to gaze at his personal secretary. 'The private armies already exist – Muslims, Sikhs, Hindus, all have been raising them for a while now. But the Master brandishing his kirpan on the steps of the Panjab Legislative Assembly is like waving a red flag before an enraged bull ...' He read aloud from one of the papers on his desk. '"Kat ke denge apni jaan, magar na denge Pakistan." Do or die. It's an ultimatum. Which the Muslim extremists will answer.'

'Sardar, now that Governor Jenkins has assumed direct charge, perhaps things will calm down?'

'One can hope, Shankar, but Panjab's unity is dead.' Vallabh squared his jaw. 'Get me V.P. Menon.'

'The *Raj's* reforms commissioner?'

Vallabh nodded. 'Tell him, it's urgent.'

Vidya Shankar appeared to hesitate. 'Sardar, may I speak freely?' At the home minister's nod, he continued. 'Mr Menon has the Viceroy's ear. And Lord Wavell's sympathies, as we know, lie with the Muslim League.'

Vallabh did not speak. Upon appointment as the home minister in the interim government, he had realized the need for a private secretary. Morarji Desai had suggested the name of Vidya Shankar. Vallabh had grilled the young Indian Civil Service (ICS) officer for an hour and a half, assisted by Manibehn. Shankar was efficient, organized, quick on the uptake and, as Vallabh was learning, loyal.

'Aurangzeb or Clive?' Vallabh asked.

Vidya Shankar started.

'That was the choice I was given when I took office as the home minister in the new twelve-member Constituent Assembly. Whether to live on Aurangzeb Road or Clive Road? Between the two conquerors, do I choose the old Mughal or the new English?' Vallabh snorted.

'In the end, it was the house itself that settled the question. Manibehn figured the rooms – entrance foyer, bed, living, this office – would serve well. The government provides a gardener, a couple of servants to help Mani run the house, and a guard, yes, in civilian clothes to man the gate. See him there?' He pointed to the window which overlooked the garden and the gate beyond. 'It provides employment for one man – though I doubt the household or I need protection. It is India that has to be secured.'

Vallabh looked intently at Vidya Shankar.

'My new role has brought me new associates, Shankar, both English and Indian – many of whom were responsible for sending us Congressmen to jail. Now, those men are my subordinates. They have to work for me and I have to make them follow my orders. I cannot let our past history or rancour come in the way. There is only one goal; that of building a free India.'

Vallabh paused, a faint twinkle in his eye. He then nodded towards Vidya Shankar. 'To address your specific concern. It is precisely *because* Menon has access to the Viceroy that he has a superior understanding of the Raj's intentions. As for his sympathies … Well, they match yours.'

∽

As she served him a simple lunch of dal, vegetables, and rice, Manibehn updated her father. 'You have an appointment with V.P. Menon for 2.30 p.m. Perhaps a nap after lunch to—'

'Panjab is in flames, Mani. Reports, phone calls, telegrams are coming in by the hour as the situation deteriorates. See for yourself.' With his left hand, he pushed a sheaf of papers for her to read.

Manibehn glanced at the top sheet. 'Lahore silk market set ablaze'. Then sifted through a few more.

'Amritsar becomes an inferno'.

'Gangs roaming streets with knives, lances and lathis in their hands'.

She looked away. Refilling her father's glass of water, she sat down.

Vallabh pushed his plate away, right hand atop. He had eaten less than half his usual lunch. 'Not just Lahore and Amritsar, the madness has spread to all major cities of Panjab. Rawalpindi, Jullunder, Sialkot, Multan ... The League has been spoiling for war for too long. They refused to accept Jawaharlal as the Cabinet leader in the interim government, openly proclaiming they were in only to get a foothold to fight for their cherished goal of Pakistan. They agitated against Tiwana's government because they do not believe in coalition building and now ...' Vallabh swallowed hard, 'now we have civil war on our hands!'

Manibehn sat back in her chair. Her years of sitting in on her father's political meetings, taking notes, getting acquainted with Congressmen, had given her an unparalleled political education. As she smoothed the cover of the dining table with one hand, she said, 'Attlee's statement of 20 February has meant one thing only to the League: partition. Even Bapu said that the wording was ambiguous enough that it could lead to the demand for Pakistan from those provinces that wanted it.'

Outside the room, the usual bustle of the home minister's home office was amplified by the telephone ringing non-stop. To avoid adding to the din, Manibehn had instructed the cook not to use the pressure cooker in the kitchen. However, it seemed as though the birds too had followed her instruction. Birdsong, that usually floated from the open windows through the day, was missing. As if the mynahs and sparrows too were stunned by the gathering storm.

She cleared her throat. 'So, are we looking at a divided India?'

Pushing his chair back, Vallabh arose. His face did not give anything away, but there was a stillness in her father's piercing eyes that Manibehn had seen before. She was just four years old when Mother had passed away, and she had heard of that incident when Father got the news as he was cross-examining a witness in a courtroom in Anand. Apparently, he read the telegram that was handed to him, put it in his pocket, and continued. In the end, the witness broke down. Only later did Father inform others of the contents of the telegram: the announcement of his wife's death. Manibehn imagined that when he read the telegram, her father's eyes had that same peculiar stillness she had just witnessed.

'Jinnah's mad dream might be coming true,' Vallabh said as he walked back to his study.

5
Laur (March 1947)

S epoy Malik's unit was one of the last to be demobilized. He returned home having won a Great War for Great Britain. But Lahore in late 1946 was seething. An ancient *Great War* was stirring in the breasts of his city folk, Lahore its battlefield. Somewhere down the line, the battle against the British had become the battle between the Muslim League and Rashtriya Swayamsevak Sangh (RSS). It was as if the Allied troops had started clashing with each other. Jinnah's call for Direct Action Day, issued from his posh Malabar Hill mansion in Bombay, in the holy month of Ramzan, was transcribed by his lieutenants on the field as the launch of jihad for the establishment of Pakistan. The large-scale butchery that followed was labelled the Great Calcutta Killings. (Note the English fetish for 'Great', which they routinely exercised after their – great? – escape from a swampy isle to the wide world.) When news of the murder of ordinary Hindus – peasant, rickshaw wala, tea seller – reached Panjab, political leaders demanded 'blood for blood'. Calcutta's cyclone made landfall in Lahore, and set off an earthquake.

Panjab: Where the Mughals, Mongols, Arabs, Afghans, Persians, Pashtuns, Brits, Greeks had deposited over millennia like silt, clay, sand, and gravel in its alluvial soil; where Alexander was so folded in the mitti to give rise to perpetual Sikandars; where no epic battle was forgotten, least of all the famed one between brothers ... Sepoy Malik had expected to return to his Lahore of pleasure and pastime, but the city – *founded by Loh, the son of Ram! Ainvayi! Says who?* – was buzzing to a very old battle cry.

Which the sepoy was ignoring.

After all, he had returned, and mostly intact. The visible impairment was his limp, which caused him to swivel with the right hip with every step forward. But he could walk, which couldn't be said for some of the other men who had signed up as volunteers from his neighbourhood. The dead couldn't have much use for walking, tipped as they had been into unmarked graves in the foreign soil of Europe. With no burial rites, no sacred fire, no prayers to assist the soul on its journey, it was unlikely any would have reached Paradise even. But Sepoy Malik was back in Lahore, to the relief of his parents. Even though his father had sent him off with a gruff, 'Take a bullet in the chest, never in the back, and return an afsar.'

He had shown up unannounced at the wooden door of his home. And all his mother could do was alternate between tears and smiles, gabble about his stick-thin body, touch him again and again, as if convincing herself that the diminished war-returnee was indeed her son. In between, she rustled up a meal for him. To his surprise, it was choori. A childhood staple he had not had in years.

Bowl in hand, she sat beside him, feeding him every bite of the thick wholewheat roti mashed with jaggery and ghee, feasting on the sight of him. When his father came hurrying home, he hugged him so tight that Sepoy Malik wondered if the old man wanted to crush him to death for not returning an officer. In the strength of his old father's embrace lay his unbridled emotion, masked otherwise by a gruff demeanour. Swept into his father's arms, Sepoy Malik was reminded of the story from the Mahabharata when the blind King Dhritarashtra crushed a metal likeness of Bheema, mistaking it for the Pandava who had killed so many of his sons in battle. Later, his mother informed him that his father had slept with the letters he had written home over the four years from battlefields, beneath his thin pillow. Now that he was home, she gathered them to stow in a trunk.

Sepoy Malik glanced through the letters, embarrassed at the emotion in them. *The bodies strewn over the fields, one atop the other atop another, remind me of ripe guavas that fell when I climbed the tree and shook it, squashed in parts, leaking.* The letters were censored, he knew, and he was careful to avoid writing anything which would indicate his location or the number of troops, or the name of his regiment even. In another letter, he had written how the boys had coined a name for the enemy's airplanes – Garuda, for what else could explain the mighty machines that swooped in the air like Lord Vishnu's eagle? *Having seen this war, the other men say, all that is written in the Mahbharat and Ramayan is true.* As he skimmed through the missives, the battlefield did not seem distant and he recalled it with a feeling like loss. The unmarked sandy desert of Egypt, with no cover, no shelter, nowhere to hide, the zeppelins hovering in the sky, raining bombs; the rugged mountainous terrain of Italy, cannon balls hurtling through air, smashing all upon contact; the machine gun he had wielded, which fired 700 bullets per minute, and reduced men to hole-riddled rag dolls. With the sudden clarity that the battlefield provides – kill or get killed – he realized the war was alive within him.

He sprang up from the string cot to the handpump and sloshed water on his face. It was dusk – his mother was cooking by the wood fire, his father seated on a low stool, drinking tea, and they were conversing. Their voices floated over to where he stood.

'Oh, lucky one,' he heard his father console his mother, 'no man can return to Panjab whole. Only the broken-limbed come back from war. And our son's only got a little limp.'

Even his beloved Tara shared his mother's misgivings. Her response had been mixed, though he had returned with his crown jewels intact, ensuring, in addition, that the English King kept his. Still, doubts were cast due to the visible injury.

His return baggage included his uniform, one medal, one holdall, one trunk. The trunk was military green, rugged looking, with brass corner protectors, leather straps, and a big brass lock. The other items were apparent, but *what* was inside the trunk? To everyone's dismay, Sepoy Malik refused to open it for inspection and, as the days wore on, people stopped asking. It was empty, they opined, what could a man bring from war? And considering he had lost a leg, a tin trunk was little consolation. Besides, everyone was caught up with azadi and Pakistan and Gandhi and Jinnah and becoming more-Muslim, more-Hindu, more-Sikh, more-whatever. The medal did elicit some chatter when folks viewed it on display in an alcove along with a snow globe he had brought home. But the globe promptly distracted them; they shook it and watched, open-mouthed, as snow fell upon fir trees and sloping red-roofed houses. Until, one day, to his mother's horror, the globe disappeared.

The young sepoy was attempting to regain the confidence of his beloved Tara, who remained unconvinced that Malik had functioning apparatus between his legs. Months of wooing had yielded little. He found reasons to cycle past her home, even

as his limp made the cycling wobbly, hoping to catch sight of her on the rooftop, hanging clothes or gathering them. In the bazaar, their fingers brushed as she checked glass bangles at a roadside cart with her friend Pammi and he strolled past. Even the snow globe failed to work its usual charm; she had seen one at a neighbour's, who had returned from France as an officer and his showed the city of Paris, complete with a toy soldier.

In desperation, he turned to the trunk.

6

Delhi (March 1947)

Over the past few days, Vallabh had met with V.P. Menon daily – at times, twice a day. He had also met with the legislators from Panjab: Bhim Sen Sachar, Sardar Joginder Singh, and Sardar Ujjal Singh. Horrific stories of destruction and the loss of life and property they narrated brought the ongoing carnage in Panjab province smack into the home member's office. 'The League has lost East Panjab,' they petitioned the Congress Working Committee, 'the time to act is now. Partition the state, save the Hindus and Sikhs!'

Now, as Vallabh paced the floor of his study, he turned to enquire, 'We've had this discussion before, but remind me again, Menon, why partition makes sense.'

V.P. Menon was not an ICS officer, having started work as a secretary. But what was more valuable to Vallabh was Menon's chops as a Raj insider. He was the principal typist of the first draft of the Montagu–Chelmsford Report, had spent years in the Reforms Branch, including helping implement the Government of India Act and the elections of 1937. Their association had begun in August 1946, when Menon had suggested to the Viceroy that perhaps they reach out to Vallabh to ascertain his view on the interim government being planned. Wavell was keenly aware that Jawaharlal's stand on the role of the Viceroy within the government would make the plan stillborn. In Menon, Vallabh had found common ground – a son of the soil like him, political pragmatist, and a blunt speaker. So well had the two bonded that it was heard that Wavell was now worrying that 'little Menon' had become the Sardar's 'mouthpiece'.

Menon scooted his stocky frame forward on the sofa, and crossed his hands before speaking. 'First, we are looking at civil war in the cities of Lahore and Amritsar. The fear is that it can spread to all of Panjab and other provinces. Second, the severance of the Pakistan area will enable the emergence of a strong central government. And finally,' his eyes followed the pacing Sardar, 'once the League has Pakistan, it will lose its capacity to obstruct Congress in the rest of India. Which means,' Menon paused and Vallabh glanced at him, 'Congress would be free to abolish the separate Muslim and other minority electorate.'

Vallabh nodded. 'The sad truth is that even if we were to sign off on partition today, the Raj has been working on it for a long time.'

'Certainly,' Menon nodded. 'The partition of Bengal in 1905 was one green flag. Followed by the India Councils Act of 1909 that laid the foundation stone for separate electorates.'

1905 was also the year his son, Dahya, was born, Vallabh recalled. When he was still a pleader in Borsad hoarding money for a passage to the UK to pursue barristership. Instead, Vithalbhai had demanded Vallabh let his elder brother go in his place – the passport being in their common name of

V.J. Patel. Vallabh had acquiesced, even guaranteeing to cover Vithalbhai's expenses in England. Which he did, keeping his own ambition at bay. Then, in 1909, Jhaverba passed away. Not only did his partner in life disappear suddenly, she left behind two young children. Yet, what continued to occupy him, besides the care of Mani and Dahya, was the desire to join the ranks of barristers educated in England – that one sure path to fame and money. Which he was able to pursue, leaving his children in a boarding school in Bombay, until his return in 1913 as a new barrister in Ahmedabad. His high fees paid for the upkeep of his Bombay-based children and his lavish lifestyle; dismissive of local cleaners, he sent his stiff collars to Bombay's cleaners. English became his preferred language—

A servant padded in with a tray that he placed on the table in front of the sofa. Nodding to the Sardar, he stepped away. Vallabh sighed. Those days could be another life altogether, the demands of Congress or the nation farthest from his mind … even Bapu, whom he first met in 1916.

'You know, Menon,' Vallabh said as he approached the sofa, 'once upon a time, I used to think that the summum bonum of my life lay in imitating the foreigner, in speech, dress … all things that mattered. So fully did I switch to English that I, a ploughboy from Borsad, had difficulty speaking my mother tongue!'

Hearing which, Menon's jaw hung loose. The Sardar he had heard of was the son of peasants, who understood the peasants better than Gandhi himself. And he understood them so well that he had won the 'battle' of Kheda, when he rallied the farmers to successfully revolt against the English in the first large-scale demonstration of Gandhi's satyagraha.

Vallabh took the cushioned chair across from Menon. 'The influence of the English must never be underestimated. I was fortunate that fate smacked me right onto the path of Mahatma Gandhi. But in their years in India, the English have honed divide and rule to a fine art. The Government of India Act was meant to transfer power to Indians; instead, it cemented separate electorates for different communities.'

'So they can continue with the narrative,' Menon pushed his thick-framed spectacles up his nose, 'that the natives would kill each other unless the English were there to govern them.'

'Today, I have four legislators who have travelled from Panjab with first-hand reports of precisely how Muslims are killing non-Muslims. Erstwhile brothers drinking each other's blood.' Vallabh probed the corners of his mouth as he locked eyes with Menon. 'The Mahabharata is our story, but in this modern version – our Shakuni has an English avatar.'

Vallabh started to pour Menon coffee. 'Developed any taste for tea?'

Accepting the cup and saucer, Menon laughed. 'Since the British brought tea to Kerala, we love our chaaya and coffee.'

Vallabh smiled. 'I am too fond of tea. You know,' he took an appreciative sip, 'at one time, I stopped tea and rice, both items I enjoy a lot, because I wanted to eat exactly what Bapu did.'

The fragrance of coffee and tea wafted through the room, riding the chilly spring air. Menon saw a faraway look on the Sardar's face. With his broad forehead, penetrating eyes, big nose and impressive jaw, he reminded him of a Roman senator in contemplation.

'Now, Bapu is miles away in Bihar …'

The Mahatma was trying his best to put a salve on Hindu–Muslim tension in Bihar and Bengal following the violence unleashed by organized Muslim mobs in Noakhali. But his peace mission was failing. To avoid forcible conversions, and driven by fear of life, Hindu refugees were pouring into Calcutta. The rattle of Menon's cup–saucer being returned to the tray roused Vallabh. He sighed.

'… And I am drinking enough tea to flare up my ulcer.'

As he made his way to the Congress Working Committee where Jawaharlal, Maulana, C.R. and Prasad were already in conversation with the Panjab legislators, Vallabh remembered an incident from many years ago.

∽

The iron poker was red-hot in the fire, its pointed end aglow. His hand bandaged in a scrap of cloth, the man clutched the rod and withdrew it from the fire. He turned to the one seated in front of him. The fire crackled, flames leaping with a gust of wind.

Young Vallabh watched him, unblinking; the poker set to sear his flesh.

The sky outside, visible through the open window, grew darker as rain clouds advanced. Madha Rat stood still, with the poker in his hand, face flushed from the heat rising from the rod, his eyes bulging.

'Go on, do it!'

A loud clap of thunder echoed through the haveli.

'I don't have all the time in the world. The test awaits.'

The arm holding the poker twitched. Beads of perspiration shook, then trickled down a hairy limb. Sweat made his face livid. 'I can't do it.' Madha Rat tossed the poker onto the ground.

'Why?' The young man looked at him askance. 'You are a barber; you can lance it – like taking a blade to the hair on the neck.'

'Na!'

'I was told all of Bakrol turns to you when a tooth is to be pulled out.' Vallabh eyed the barber with exasperation, but Madha Rat seemed committed to non-cooperation. The Pleader's Test was around the corner and he had not a minute to waste. Precisely the reason why he had come here to this haveli to study in peace and quiet. Which he would be doing, but for the boil. He raised his arm and peered at his armpit. Packed with pus, red-rimmed, the boil was right at the spot where it made any movement torture. A barber with shaky hands was like Yama at his doorstep. But the pus needed to be drained if he wanted relief. With a wave of his hand he requested the poker from the barber.

Madha Rat, relieved, placed the poker back in the fire. 'It needs to be searing hot,' he added helpfully.

At twenty-five, Vallabh was rather old for the Pleader's Test. But he was working according to a plan. Having passed his matriculation at nearly twenty-two, with neither the money to attend a law college nor the six years it required, he had decided to self-study, with books borrowed from local lawyers. A Pleader's Test would allow him to become a lawyer. After which he would begin to earn and save money for his one ambitious project: to become a barrister educated in London. Attending school in dusty Karamsad, young Vallabh had learnt that fame and money came early to barristers educated in England. His family did not have the means, but he had the will. He longed to go overseas to see the people of the country who, living 7000 miles away, were able to rule India for so long. The Pleader's Test was the first step.

He beckoned for the glowing poker. Madha Rat handed it over and hovered close by. The sky was dark, fat raindrops kicked their heels on the wooden roof above, the kerosene lamp cast the room in a jigsaw of light and shadow. Vallabh raised his arm, eyed the boil and, with a steady hand, tipped the glowing poker straight into the boil.

Afterwards, he made his way up the dark, narrow staircase to his room on the second floor. The steps creaked in unison with the wooden haveli, which hummed a melancholy tune as its wood frame shifted with the wind. In the room, he lit a kerosene lamp with one hand. Placing two bolsters on the floor mattress, he sat down to study.

In time, another set of footsteps sounded on the wooden staircase.

'Amu mian,' he called out. Vallabh had come to the haveli to study in peace, and it was the servant who ensured the examinee didn't have to bother with anything else.

He darted into the room, tut-tutting, sat beside Vallabh and began to unpack a cloth bag. 'I met Madha Rat in the bazaar. Apparently, he lost his nerve?'

Vallabh snorted.

'But you didn't.' He asked Vallabh to raise his arm, peered at the lanced armpit, grunted, and removed a sock from his bag. As Vallabh watched, Amu mian poured dry rice grains into the sock from a long-handled iron ladle used for tempering. 'Hot,' he added as explanation.

'As if my armpit wasn't seared already!' Vallabh said.

Amu mian tied the long sock at the mouth. 'Madha said three–four men are usually needed to hold the patient, who loses his mind screaming! You were there alone ... What was he to do?' The servant laughed as he placed the rice-filled sock against the inflamed armpit.

'Ahhh,' Vallabh let out a yelp. Soon, the warm compress started to comfort the throbbing armpit. Heat kills heat – there was some truth to that adage.

Amu mian folded a piece of cloth and began to bandage the armpit. 'Keep it on for a while. I'll get you some food.' He gathered the cloth bag and stepped out of the room.

∽

Forty-seven years ago, Vallabh had lanced his boil, and what he recalled most clearly was that the anticipated pain had been worse. Sometimes, the best cure for a diseased limb was amputation.

7
Laur (March 1947)

Kishan Singh picked up the *Hindustan Times* which he had briefly discarded, studied the front page again, particularly the maps that showed how the provinces of Panjab and Bengal could be divided; then he folded the paper and put it back on the glass-topped table. From the covered front porch where he sat, he could see the dark sky beginning to colour. Soon it would be morning and all of Laur, indeed all of Panjab, would hear the news. That the Congress had proposed, he picked up the newspaper again and read, 'that Panjab's predominantly Muslim portion be separated from the predominantly non-Muslim portion.'

Over the still slumbering morning, he heard Lala Amar Nath's tinny voice reciting some bhajan as he went about his morning ablutions. His other neighbour, Ahmed Niazi, had trooped off to the mosque even before the call of the muezzin, as was his daily practice. Technically, he, Kishan Singh, could be singing gurbani – adding his prayers to the religious medley weaving its way out of their neighbourhood. Which was predominantly Muslim or non-Muslim? The two neighbours to his immediate left and right were Hindu and Muslim, across was a Muslim, flanked by a Muslim and a Hindu, and beyond the Hindu house was that of another Muslim and then a Sikh and then … Oh, Kishan Singh swatted the air with his right hand. How would this division be done in their colony? Would the Niazis have to exchange houses with the Hindu family across, so the street between them could act as the dividing line? But what if some family refused? Would the line abandon its straight path, run a circle around that house, and then proceed forward? In which case, how many squiggles and circles and triangles would it draw as it sealed the Muslims from the non-Muslims? Would the gates of people's houses become barriers, checking the entry of others? Muslim in, Hindu–Sikh out? But what if his Muslim friends came visiting and he wanted them in, or indeed had invited them over? Would they need permit cards from Jinnah for visiting Kishan Singh's home? And Kishan Singh similarly would carry a Nehru-signed card? But … what about his workplace? Lahore Junction had officers and clerks and coolies who were Hindu, Muslim, Sikh – much like the passengers its trains carried. This was all madness!

Since Kishan Singh did not know what else to do, he stepped into his little garden to clear his head. Sure, madness had gripped Laur, but it was the job of leaders to tamp it down, not get infected by the madness in turn. He walked to the gate and sighted the milkman parting the mist with his cycle as he rode down. In the distance, a horse's hoofs sounded. Dew sat in drops on leaves, the sun was a fiery orange in a misty sky, and a koel cooed.

Wait, koel! Identify yourself. Muslim/Non-Muslim?

A laugh sputtered out of Kishan Singh. This was all so absurd it had to die down.

∽

That afternoon, Kishan Singh's office at Lahore Junction had an unexpected visitor. 'Motia aleo!' Hearing that endearment – who else would call him 'prince of pearls' – Kishan Singh wheeled around from his desk to find his elder brother bearing a sack of farm-fresh vegetables and another sack of sugar. 'I heard the rate of sugar in Laur's bazaars is a rupee and half for one seer. Open-air thuggery, I say!'

Kishan Singh decided to head home early and sought permission from his senior, Balwant Rai, who waved him on. They hired a rickshaw home as Iqbal Singh quizzed his brother on the situation in the city. 'Even we in Lyallpur are hearing of the protests and killings. So I thought to check for myself.'

'It is always wonderful to see you, pahji.' He steadied the sack at his feet, the other was slung in the folded hood at the rear.

'The fact is,' Iqbal Singh continued as he smoothed down his long white beard, 'we need the angrej sarkar to run this country. Otherwise, we will be at each other's throats in a second in a fresh Mahbharat! All these people who marched for the resignation of Khizar want a Muslim government. Now Congress is staking a Hindu one in east Panjab. In which case, where do the Sikhs go, hmm?'

Kishan Singh nodded dutifully. His brother, like the majority residents of Lyallpur, had sympathies – no, affection – for the English. The Empire had granted soldiers returning from WWI a barren tract of land. Within a generation, through sheer hard work, the demobilized soldiers had converted Lyallpur to flourishing fields. Now, it was a prosperous region, with a large Sikh presence. Kishan was a toddler when his elder brother was recruited. Sepoy Iqbal Singh had returned after two years, having seen action in France. So impressed was he with Europe that he insisted Kishan pursue his studies and leave farming to elders like him. For that, Kishan was grateful. The only way he could see himself in the fields was as a scarecrow. Papers, files, books, and tables were his natural environment, and, as senior clerk in the Railway's Parcel Office, life was good.

'Hmm?' Iqbal Singh prompted.

'Yes, yes,' Kishan replied. 'Governor Jenkins is in charge now.'

'The problem is our leaders. Tara Singh is barely taller than his kirpan, and others like Baldev Singh are in the Congress's pocket. We need a Sikh who understands the concerns of his quom and speaks the language of the English. How else will we make the government appreciate our demands? Any surprise both Jinnah and Nehru speak like the angrej! If they will grant Pakistan, then they will grant Sikhistan too. The English play fair and square. Question is, who will put our case forward to the King?'

Kishan Singh was glad they had reached home. While his brother went to the toilet, Kishan went to rustle up tea and something to eat. Since his wife passed away five years ago, he had acquainted himself with the kitchen. Kishan was committed to the education of his three daughters. Parminder was in first-year BA, Surinder in Class 10, and Narinder in Class 8. Pammi shouldered the responsibility of the kitchen and her sisters, but Kishan Singh liked to make himself useful in the house. He had wanted to help his wife too, but she would shoo him away from 'women's chores'. Once, when she was kneading atta, he had demanded to be shown where in the flour it said, 'For bibi only.' Kishan Singh smiled at the memory as he strained tea into two mugs.

His brother sat in the lawn, enjoying the mellow sun, stroking his long beard as Surinder and Narinder faced him, hands clasped in front, nodding. At his approach, they seemed to find release. He heard them mention homework as they scurried back inside.

Despite his sixty-odd years, Iqbal Singh radiated vigour. In contrast, Kishan Singh's beard was grey and he tied it in a neat knot daily. Kishan also looked older. Was it to do with the fact that his brother spent his days in wide open fields, while Kishan was cooped up in an office? Or that Iqbal Singh approached life, as he had done war, with clarity and determination, while Kishan seldom had definite answers. Which was why Kishan Singh scribbled poetry, none of which he shared with his elder brother. Being called a 'communist' – because he did not spend enough time in the gurdwara or with the Granth Sahib – was enough; poetry would out him as a pansy. As he served him tea and fresh roti, Kishan realized his brother might have preferred lassi with roti.

Iqbal Singh blew on the tea before slurping it. 'What about your railway union?'

'The Railway Labour Union is keeping a distance from the League and the Congress. For us, things are as usual. Of course, one can't help overhearing the discussions all around: Division, Pakistan, Jinnah ...'

'The Raj and Governor Jenkins just have to stay firm—'

'But independence is coming, virji.'

'Perhaps. But what kind? You think this big country, which the angrej has administered for 300 years, we will learn to govern right away? Slowly, slowly, the angrej will hand over its reins to us … time enough for Jinnah, Gandhi, Nehru, whoever to learn.'

'So, no Pakistan?'

Smashing a whole onion with his right fist, Iqbal Singh peeled it. 'There's as much Pakistan as there is Sikhistan! Hindu, Muslim, Sikh are scattered all over Panjab. This is our land, the land of Nanak and Ranjit Singh. But yes, if I lived in Laur, I too would be worried.' Tearing off a bite of the thick roti in which Kishan Singh had sprinkled salt and some red chili powder, he began munching.

At the sound of the gate being unlatched, the two brothers looked up. A young woman in a salwar–kameez, her head covered in a chunni, books clasped in the nook of her left arm, stepped in.

'Pammi puttar!' Iqbal Singh hailed as he stood up.

'Sat sri akal, tayaji.' Pammi bowed as she brought her hands together. Iqbal Singh blessed her head with both palms, 'Keep living.'

'Sat sri akal, chacha!' Pammi's companion hailed from behind the gate. He had a thick mop of hair and shiny eyes. He was dressed in a pair of trousers and a blazer – a pucca student. Kishan Singh beckoned him over. 'Come, Asad puttar.'

'Another time, chacha. Ammi will be waiting.' He bowed and walked to the two storeyed-house next door.

When Asad had left and Parminder was indoors, Iqbal Singh frowned as he slurped his tea. 'Does this boy accompany our Pammi to college and back daily?'

'Not daily, only evenings or when there is an extra class. With the violence in the air, it's just safer if she has him for company.'

'Hmm.'

Iqbal Singh finished his tea, rubbed his big hands as he scrutinized the Niazi house next door.

'Asad is a decent boy. His family has been our neighbour for years now. Nice peace-loving people. We exchange greetings and sweets on Diwali and Eid.' Kishan Singh realized he was prattling.

'Keep it limited to mithai only. There is no marriage between our two kinds.'

'Marriage?' Kishan Singh frowned. 'Virji, you're running ahead.'

'Na. A boy who spends so much time with a girl his age has only one thing on his mind. Besides, our Pammi is a beautiful girl. How old is she now? Eighteen? Why don't you find her a suitable groom?'

Kishan Singh wanted his daughter to study, graduate, find a job. 'She is still in first year BA—'

'So find a boy who will let her study after marriage. Remember you have two other girls! For a widower, this is not an easy matter, I realize.' He stroked his beard. 'Say yes and I will tell your parjai to start looking.'

Kishan Singh could hear his daughters giggling inside. One of them squealed, likely Narinder, before a hurried shushing followed. That would be Surinder. She had her mother's sober demeanour and worried over her board exams constantly. He tried to steer the conversation away. 'Let the problem in Panjab settle ...'

'What is to settle? Hindu, Mussalman, Sikh – we are all Panjabis, separate but together. Always have, always will be. Which is why we need the angrej to keep a hand on us.'

Separate, how? Kishan was named after a Hindu god, his brother had a Muslim/Urdu name. And didn't Guru Nanak take the best of both Hinduism and Islam to create Sikhs? A flock of birds chirruped as they flew overhead. Iqbal Singh belched loudly and said, 'Waheguru!' Around them, the setting sun had set the sky aflame.

꙰

The next morning, as Kishan Singh began to read the day's newspapers, the chanting from Lala Amar Nath's house had company of Iqbal Singh's recitation of the bani. Kishan folded the papers neatly, reserving his reading for the evening, and went to the kitchen to assist Pammi with preparing breakfast.

8
Delhi (March 1947)

The interim government was paralysed.

The Congress and the Muslim League were in a deadlock over their separate visions for a free India. Jinnah wanted his Pakistan and the provinces to go with it therefore: Panjab, the Afghanistan-bordering NWFP, Kashmir, Sind, and Bengal. Gandhi wanted his united India. His lieutenants, Jawaharlal and Vallabhbhai – increasingly aware that India was haemorrhaging in Bengal and Panjab – were debating whether a surgical scalpel would help. But Jinnah was in no mood to prune his Pakistan. Even though Hindus in Bengal wanted nothing to do with his Pakistan. Nor did the Hindus in Panjab. Where the Sikhs in turn were getting squeezed in the Hindu–Muslim pincer.

As for the British, having ransacked India of manpower and materials, most recently for WWII, which broke the Empire's back, they couldn't now wait to transfer power to 'responsible' hands. One of which was Jawaharlal Nehru, whom the British had frequently incarcerated in their jails for unlawful behaviour. Almost ten years of his life spent imprisoned, he was now Prime

Minister in the interim government. In testament to English irony, the jailed was to kick out the jailer.

But the truth, Jawahar knew, was muddier. Having wrapped up their world war, a very broke Britain had handed India its war's woes: a shortage of foodgrain, near-famine conditions in parts of the country, rising prices of essentials, demobilized soldiers, communal flare-ups ... At his desk since 4 a.m., Jawahar was writing to Lord Wavell, enclosing copies of the resolutions passed by the Congress Working Committee. But hopes for a settlement with the Muslim League had been dashed again—

'Pandit ji,' Mac popped his head in through the ajar door, 'Maulana Azad is here to see you.'

Jawahar waved to his personal assistant to let Maulana in. In charge of education in the interim government, Maulana Azad was erudite and wise, a scholar of Islam, and an ardent nationalist. Jawahar and he were jailed together in Ahmednagar Fort in adjacent rooms. They would spend time discussing an array of matters, political and social, before Maulana, particular about his meal time, retired. Just a year apart, they were old friends, but the direction that freedom struggle was taking had created recent differences.

Maulana walked in, dressed in his customary long black sherwani and fez cap. They greeted each other and Maulana pulled up a chair to sit down across from Jawahar. 'You look agitated,' he observed.

'Liaquat's latest salvo? A 25 per cent tax on all business profits of more than one lakh rupees! What the hell is he thinking?' Jawahar rose and started to pace the small room that served as his study, hands clasped behind his back.

Maulana Azad probed his well-maintained goatee as he watched his friend's progress. 'Liaquat Ali Khan might be finance minister in the interim government, but he's batting for the Muslim League. When they tax the industrialists who finance us, they cut the Congress off at its knees. Besides sparking an internal war in Congress between our left- and right-wing factions.'

'Jinnah's unmitigated nonsense has led to this state of affairs. He wants the whole of Panjab and the whole of Bengal, and will drag all the non-Muslims screaming and kicking into his Pakistan, if he could!' Jawahar blew air out of his mouth.

Years spent together in prison had given them a body language common to those thrown together in captivity. Maulana stood up. 'Let's walk in the lawn.'

'Yes ... The house is small but the lawns are spacious.'

The two men headed out via the main hall, which was used as a reception. Indira was talking to Mathai and watched them leave. Jawahar was happy that Indu was there to act as hostess – there were people to meet, meetings to attend, dinners to be given as interim Prime Minister. He had requested her assistance, and she had arrived with her two young sons without demurring. Shy and reserved, she was playing her role as official hostess with quiet efficiency.

Outside, Jawahar fingered his kurta pocket and brought out a tin of State Express 555 cigarettes. He offered it to Maulana, who declined. Jawahar lit up, and they fell in step.

Picking up the earlier thread of their conversation, Jawahar said, 'Since Jinnah declared Direct Action Day last August, the League has been hell-bent on getting Pakistan through violence. First, the killings in Noakhali. Now the atrocities being committed on Hindus and Sikhs in NWFP and Panjab ... Muslims are not believers in ahimsa, apparently.' He snorted.

'Not to mention that the League is running a civil disobedience campaign in both those provinces,' Maulana added.

Jawahar puffed on his cigarette. 'The situation in Panjab is electric. Baldev was here yesterday. He's receiving missives from Sikhs daily, in person or otherwise. The idea of living under Muslim Raj is anathema to them. Master Tara Singh wants Sikhistan, a separate homeland to be carved for the 6 million Sikhs out of Panjab—'

'Perhaps we revisit the Cabinet Mission Plan?' Maulana asked as he twirled his handsome whiskers.

Jawahar stubbed the cigarette under his foot. Maulana had led those negotiations on behalf of the Congress, which made him partial to it. Where Vallabhbhai wanted a strong centre, Maulana was happy with a loose federation of Hindu and Muslim provinces. But the same plan had placed the Sikhs in a particularly difficult position when it lumped Panjab in the Muslim-majority group. 'You know,' Jawahar started to walk and Maulana fell in step with him, 'tricky as Bengal is, Panjab is trickier. No other province was so closely involved in the war effort. It was the main supplier of foodgrain and soldiers. Nearly a million Panjabis served in the armed forces. And the communal issue is three way ...'

'The war also drew support for the Muslim League in Panjab. While Congress stayed neutral, Jinnah saw the opportunity to throw his weight behind the Crown. Now Wavell rewards him for his loyalty by propping up the idea of Pakistan.'

'We can hope the new Viceroy will be different.'

'Lord Mountbatten?' Maulana shrugged. 'From one lord to another ...'

Jawahar gazed into the distance. The sky was a clear blue, so unlike his troubled mind. In the garden, the Ashoka trees were laden with lush orange flowers. A-shoka. Sorrow-less. It was spring, freedom was near, and yet ... 'A million men who saw war in the theatres of Europe, Africa, Southeast Asia – skilled in warfare, now demobbed and back in Panjab, where communal rhetoric is raging. What are those soldiers thinking?'

'Or doing—'

A sudden cry, and Indira came running down the walkway, waving her arms frantically. Behind her M.O. Mathai stood in the doorway, his face dark. The men took to their heels. Indu was pale and shaking as Jawahar held her upper arms and tried to make sense of her frenzied speech: '... from Panjab ... horrifying massacre ... women ... well ...'

Back in his office, Jawahar held his breath as Mac tried to get Governor Jenkins on the line. After he finished talking to the Governor, an ashen Jawahar turned to update Maulana.

Thoah Khalsa, a village in southeast Rawalpindi, home to a large and prosperous Sikh community, was attacked by Muslim mobs in the thousands. The Sikhs defended themselves for three whole days before hoisting white flags from their rooftops. But the massacre and looting didn't stop. As their men fought, the women jumped into the village well with babies in their arms. In time, the well was so full of submerged bodies that the remaining women tried to jump again to drown themselves. Again and again.

As of today, not one Sikh or Hindu was alive in the village.

9
Delhi (March 1947)

At the dining table, Indu watched her father push his food around as though it were not his favourite yakhni but some dreary jail meal. A spare eater, he nevertheless relished his choice foods. Lost in thought, head bent over the food, his aquiline 'Kashmiri' nose – which she had inherited from him – was oblivious to the fragrant aroma of the spiced creamy curry. She recalled when he had launched the Quit India resolution from Gowalia Tank in 1942 and the very next day the police had arrived to arrest him. Anticipating them, Papu was about to sit down to a last meal he loved: a bowl of cornflakes, eggs, bacon, toast, and coffee. Seeing the spread, the inspector had announced that there was no time for breakfast. 'Shut up!' Papu had said. 'I intend having breakfast before I go.' He was imprisoned in Ahmednagar Fort for 1041 days thereafter.

At the memory of his last detention, Indu straightened up and wondered how to get Papu to eat his food. Rajiv responded to distraction: stories, sightings of birds, even an ant crawling on the floor. Perhaps she could use the same ruse with her father ... 'Papu,' she said in a deliberately jaunty tone, 'the new Viceroy is expected to arrive soon.'

Jawahar stopped playing field hockey with his food and looked up. The stomach-churning news coming in daily was enough to shake his faith in the sanity of the human race. 'Yes, I met Mountbatten in Singapore after the war. He took me for a drive down the city streets in his open car – to the horror of his staff! I believe they'd told him to stay away from me, a rebel with prison dust still clinging to his shoes. He's expected within a fortnight now and I look forward to continuing our dialogue.'

A faint cough sounded. Jawahar puckered his brow.

'It's Rajiv,' Indu said. 'I'm afraid he's caught some seasonal bug.'

Jawahar nodded. 'It'll be hot soon enough.' The crisp winter air which reminded him of his beloved mountains was already curling with heat. 'The children slept early?'

Indu shook her head. 'Not early enough!'

Jawahar pushed his plate away and reached for the sherbet jug. 'What news of Feroze?'

'The *National Herald* occupies him ... which is good.'

As he poured himself a glass of the rose-flavoured syrup, Jawahar watched her, his eyebrows raised.

'Well, you know, Lucknow is a nice town, but ... so dreary!'

'Where one often comes into contact with persons with a perpetual hartal of the mind.'

'Isn't that so! There is a peculiar deadness to our provincial towns, and they seem to be getting more narrow-minded. The RSS is drawing large crowds to its rallies in Allahabad, Cawnpore, Lucknow. I was given a vivid description of one such show by one of the Malaviya boys. Thousands of uniformed volunteers, a disciplined crowd that sat cross-legged on the floor, warnings not to move or talk or interrupt, pin-drop silence as

Guru Golwalkar spoke. So horribly reminiscent of the German model!'

Indu had personally borne the brunt of that 'narrow-minded' mentality in 1942: News of her marriage to Feroze, a Parsi, had generated controversy and animosity on account of the 'mixed marriage'.

Jawahar took a satisfying sip of the cold sherbet and sat back. 'The Brown Shirts and Khaki Half-pants have a common ideology of racial purity and superiority. RSS leaders, Golwalkar included, openly proclaim their admiration for Hitler and Mussolini. Any wonder Khizar banned both RSS and the Muslim League National Guards in Panjab in January. There, the RSS has 50,000 local members – more than the Guards even. And both these militias are behind the Hindu–Muslim riots—'

Feet padded down the hallway as a young Rajiv, dressed in his nightclothes, hopped onto his mother's lap. Indu wrapped her arms around the two-year-old, who watched Jawahar with bright eyes.

The grandfather opened his arms wide. 'Come to Nanu!'

Rajiv coughed and wiggled against his mother.

'Come,' Jawahar urged, half standing up.

Indu patted her son's hair, questioning him with her chin. Rajiv pointed a chubby index finger in the direction of his grandfather. 'Nanu's drinking blood!'

Jawahar dropped down in his chair and laughed loudly. As Indu grinned, Rajiv hid his face in his mother's bosom. When he had finished laughing, Jawahar quipped, 'History repeats!'

'How so?' Indu asked, as she rocked her son softly.

'For that, I'll have to tell you a story.'

'Pray, do.'

One afternoon, at their Allahabad home, after lunch, Ma told young Jawahar the next story from the Mahabharata: How the mighty Bheema had killed Dushasana, much as he had vowed – 'I will drink my brother's blood' – and torn into his entrails. The retelling made Jawahar's siesta feverish with warring characters from the Mahabharata wading through a blood-soaked battlefield, visions of Bheema's bloody mouth, vultures feasting on carrion ... One vulture flew close to Jawahar, inching horizontally along the bed, advancing upon him, so close that he could see its eyes, brown as honey, its golden-brown feathers soft as down, its beak curved like a scythe, from which hung flesh, dripping globules of blood on the white bed sheet. Drip. Drip. Drip—

He screamed. Then raced out of his room and down the corridor, trampling the shadows of the Ashoka trees in his path. He paused outside his father's study to seek shelter. But found a raucous gathering of men inside, not unusual in Anand Bhavan. But the men were drinking blood from goblets as they laughed, his father leading them! Panic-stricken, Jawahar raced to the kitchen, where he dived into his mother, hiding himself in the folds of her soft muslin saree. Mother's hands in his hair, ruffling, soothing; vapours laden with spices wafting in the air, a ladle clanging against a vessel; his aunt's tinkling laugh as she teased him.

He looked up urgently, saree folds clutched tightly in his small fists, 'Ma, father's drinking blood!'

Aunt laughed louder.

Jawahar turned indignantly towards her. *What did she even know?* The warm moist air in the kitchen was so far removed from the heavy air of the study, where men talked war and drank blood. Panicking afresh, he clutched Ma's face with both hands.

Lowering her head, she kissed him on his forehead and whispered, 'It's a new drink.' She smoothed his hair, then pivoted his chin with her hand to view his face. 'Wine, it's called.'

∽

'Wine, sherbet,' Jawahar laughed. 'The bloody red liquid is fated to terrify young boys in our family!'

'I can imagine. Dadu was quite formidable either way,' Indu chuckled. She was thirteen when he had passed away, a committed nationalist who had twice served as president of the Congress Party. But she remembered him best as a genial patriarch and loved the story which linked him inextricably to her birth. When she was born, the womenfolk clucked in dismay at the arrival of a girl. Which irritated Motilal, who had brought up his two daughters much the same as his son. 'This daughter of Jawahar,' the grandfather proclaimed, 'may well prove to be better than a thousand sons!'

Jawahar took a sip of his drink, looking visibly relaxed. 'I remember feeling foolish and relieved in equal measure. Your Dadu usually drank whiskey, and I was used to seeing the amber libation. But Ma fixed it all with a bowl of freshly fried pakoras, which I ate in the kitchen, relieved that my father had not developed a liking for blood like Bheema.'

Rajiv had dozed off by then and, cradling him, Indu walked softly to her bedroom. Left seated at the dining table, fifty-seven-year-old Jawahar could not shake off the story of his childhood. Nowadays, the stories of the Mahabharata, narrated by his mother and aunts, which vivified his childhood, returned to him in sleep. The Great War. From 3500 years ago. Was it a presage? The violence stirring the countryside in Bengal and Panjab was no more sporadic, its barbarity was epic even ...

His heart thudding, Jawahar breathed in deeply, trying to calm down. There was no soft muslin saree to hide himself in; there was no boy any more – only a grown man with a boy's nightmares.

He pushed his chair back to walk around the room.

In his peregrinations through India, he had learnt how every incident, story and moral from the Ramayana, the Mahabharata, and other epics was engraved in the minds of the masses. He had seen his mother's mother daily recite the verses of the Gita from memory as she pottered about her kitchen in Lahore. Illiterate villagers knew hundreds of verses by heart, their conversation often full of those references. A peasant once surprised him by giving a literary turn to a simple talk about present-day affairs. 'The wheel will not stop turning,' the peasant replied when Jawahar asked him how long he thought they could maintain the peaceful protests against the Raj, repeating what Bhishma had said to Karna on the battlefield.

Why then were they forgetting the lesson at the heart of the Mahabharata?

When the mighty Duryodhana, the last of the Kauravas, lay dying on the battlefield, he turned to the eldest Pandava, his cousin and bitterest enemy, Yudhishthira, and said, 'Go, take your empire! What will it bring you but sorrow and tears?' To inherit a land and people devastated by war was no victory. The bloody battle between brothers over a kingdom had led to complete annihilation. The tribal in Orissa knew this as well as the peasant in Bengal as well as the Kathakali dancer in Kerala as well as the grandmother in Panjab ...

Indu was at the table again, her chin questioning him about the leftover meal. He shook his head and she started to clear the table. Around him, the house lay still, having surrendered to sleep.

The Mahabharata was as much about war as it was about dharma, that amalgam of duties and responsibilities. Hadn't a vigorous Jat, wedded to the soil from generations immemorial, the same soil which provided the epic battlefield of Kurukshetra, summed up for him the essence of the Mahabharata in one phrase: Thou shalt not do to others what is disagreeable to thyself? But the stories of lynching, burning, rapes and loot coming daily from the villages of Panjab flew in the face of such earthy wisdom—

'Papu,' Indu appeared in the door, 'shall I get you a glass of warm milk?'

'My valise,' he beckoned with his left hand, heading to his room. 'I need to pack.'

'Where for?' Indu hurried behind.

'Panjab. I must visit the province and talk to the people and the officers on the ground. I refuse to let Panjab become a battlefield! There has to be a cure for this madness.'

10
Laur (March 1947)

In Shalimar Gardens, Sepoy Malik waited impatiently as Lauris around him enjoyed the pleasant evening. Men had cast off their sweaters and walked with a swagger, women released from their shawls blossomed like roses, children's voices rang high, attar was in the air, and everyone was engaged in the business of pleasure. He craned his neck from behind the rose bush, wondering when Tara would arrive … if she would arrive … Had their puppy love survived all these years of separation? Would it now survive his injury?

Three years ago, before he could enrol in college, he had enlisted as sepoy. With a monthly salary of twenty-five rupees, plus seven for overseas posting, it was his chance to gain money and izzat to approach Tara's wealthy father. In the meantime, his friend Asad had reached second year of BA. Some days ago, the sepoy had waited outside Dayal Singh College to catch up with Asad, and he had met Pammi there too. Tara and Pammi continued to be thick friends even though Tara had failed matric. Not that she was bothered about it. 'My in-laws want to see my report card, is it?' she had retorted, as Pammi recounted when he enquired about her friend. Tara's heart was never into studies; what she really wanted was to get 'love-married'. The recollection brought a smile to his lips—

'Sikandar!'

Asad hailed him with an upright arm. Beside him were Pammi and Tara. He hadn't been able to see her at leisure since his return, managing only to catch fleeting glimpses on rooftops or bazaars. But Asad bhai had been helpful. Pammi had extra classes on Thursday, and perhaps Tara could make some excuse to join them as they walked back home? Which they would conveniently do via Shalimar Gardens? The plan had worked, for here was his Tara. In a pink salwar–kameez, her face framed by her long tresses, she was the most radiant rose in the entire bagh.

'Sorry, yaar,' Asad said as he neared, 'we got held up because of Nehru. Apparently, he's in Laur and the whole city seems to have descended on the roads to catch a sight of him!'

He clasped Asad in a tight hug.

Pammi smiled and said, 'Hello.' He hadn't realized how lovely her voice was, like honey. And had she grown prettier in the three years he was away? Or was he just giddy with joy about finally getting to meet his beloved and so was feeling benevolent towards all? Still, Pammi's glinting nose pin drew attention to her delicate nose and large eyes. She was like a lily to Tara's rose.

'We'll circle the charbagh and be back!' Asad slapped him on his back and Pammi, after giving Tara's hand a quick squeeze, fell in step with Asad. He watched them go, suddenly feeling shy.

'So, sepoy?' Tara raised her brows, a smile struggling to break free from her rosebud mouth.

'Shall we?' He pointed to the bench he had carefully selected earlier. Hemmed in by two large rose bushes, it was almost hidden from the view of the strolling public.

Tara sat down, arranging her net chunni with care. As he took the few steps to reach the stone bench, he tried to make his gait look natural, keeping the limp at bay like it was some enemy combatant.

'So, tell me.' Tara's head was at half-tilt, her almond-brown eyes like some Diwali sparkler. He watched her hands spin and dance in the air, her voice washing over him until the tap was turned off. He started.

'War got your tongue?'

'Tara ji—'

'Don't ji me!' She looked away in a huff. But she turned back quickly enough. 'Oh, Sikandar, did you miss me?'

Sepoy Malik bunched his mouth. 'Hmm ... In the war, I saw different kinds of bombs. There was one that made a lot of sound as it approached. I named it Tara.'

She slapped his arm.

'It also lit up the night sky, and if you weren't careful, it blinded you before killing you.'

Tara crossed her arms and frowned. 'Well, Mr Agg-da-bamba, all you know is how to screech! And you're never on time; the house has already burnt down when the fire engine arrives.'

Sepoy Malik let out a hearty laugh, then held his earlobes in apology.

'So, tell me,' Tara continued. 'Did you miss me or you just couldn't tear your eyes away from the mems?'

Sepoy Malik recalled the march down a Paris street when a white woman had rushed up to him and planted a kiss on his cheek. He had definitely missed a step or few! Never mind that the woman was old enough to be his mother. Some of the sepoys talked about catching action when off the field – apparently their brown–black skin did not repulse the white women of France.

He looked at her intently. 'No white mem can match my memsaab.'

'I'm not *your* memsaab.'

When he continued to gaze at her, she protested. 'Stop looking at me like you'll eat me.'

A coloured ball rolled their way and soon, a boy came looking for it. Sepoy Malik stood up and kicked the ball gently towards the child, who scooped it up and ran away. As he turned, he saw Tara's eyes gazing intently at his right leg. Shame and anger filled him, and he sat back heavily. She flapped a hand in front of him. He continued to stare at the ground. She waved a hand again. He clasped it roughly and held it between his hands. It felt like butter. Their eyes locked. Beads of sweat sprouted on her temples, her mouth quivered—

Footsteps stalled near them. Tara's hand flew out of his embrace. Asad stood watching them, smiling.

'One more round?' Sepoy Malik asked.

Pammi looked unsure. 'We'll get late. Bapuji worries if I am not home before dusk …'

'Okay, do a half-round and come back,' Tara pleaded. 'Please, Pammi!'

When the two were out of earshot, Tara turned to Sikandar. 'I cannot be your memsaab … If things were difficult before, they are impossible now. You are a Leaguer, I am a Sanghi.'

'We're both Malik. Were. Are.'

Tara made a face. 'You're Jat; we're Arora.'

'You won't need a surname change even.'

Tara shook her head.

Was she worried about his injury, how it might have impaired him ... Was that why she was raising the objections obliquely. Hadn't she once said that to marry him, she would convert happily. Of course, they were younger then ...

'Tara,' he said, his voice hoarse with emotion, 'I'm okay, you know ... despite ... despite what it looks like ...'

'Oh! Sikandar,' Tara placed her palms on his chest. He grasped her wrists. 'Pitaji is identifying grooms for me. Sona didi got married last year, and she is pregnant already. Jijaji seems nice, but didi says he hardly talks to her, busy as he is assisting his father in their business – they have a wheat mill. Jijaji's chachaji is into yarn and hosiery, and Pitaji thinks his son would make a suitable groom for me. I could be married off by shravan ...' Her mouth wobbled.

'Shhh ...' Sepoy Malik crooned. 'Not so fast, not so fast. We'll find a way.' He could see Asad and Pammi returning. The last rays of the sun cast long shadows of the hedges and bushes onto the lawns and walkways. How quickly time had passed. 'Listen, we have to meet again!'

With a nod to indicate their approaching friends, he placed Tara's hands back in her lap. She took one edge of her chunni and wrapped it around one finger.

'When do I see you again?' he asked urgently.

'Why? One meeting with no gift is sufficient lesson for a girl.'

She had returned to her teasing ways. 'Want to see a *real* souvenir from the war?'

'An explosive one?' Her eyes were agleam.

'Sau feesadi!'

'Wedding.' Tara smiled. Seeing his crestfallen face, she laughed. 'Not mine, idiot! A relative is getting married soon. Meet me there.'

Sepoy Malik frowned. 'At a *wedding*?'

'I'll send the details through Pammi.' She stood up, straightening her chunni. 'A large gathering is easy to slip out of unnoticed.'

11
Delhi (March 1947)

The stage was fitting for a majestic wedding, of European royalty with Mughal monarchy. Louis Mountbatten, wife on one arm, ascended the sweeping steps to Durbar Hall. The gold-and-scarlet turbans of his bodyguards stirred in the breeze, their sabres glinted, the trumpets blared, and, inside, gilded thrones awaited. Under a crimson canopy of thick velvet, Mountbatten took oath. As it concluded, a boom reverberated down the Hall, repeatedly – the canon outside sounding its thirty-one-gun salute, alerting the denizens of the Empire. The pomp and pageantry under the gold dome might have made Shah Jahan envious, but Louis Francis Albert Victor Nicholas Mountbatten, just crowned Viceroy of India, was the King's emissary sent to dissolve the British Raj. On a strict fifteen-month lease, he was here to transfer power. The splendour of the Viceregal anointing was the vestigial exhalation of an Empire clattering down.

Now Dickie surveyed the gathering in the Durbar Hall that had witnessed his swearing-in ceremony. A motley crowd of his countrymen in robes and wigs, Indian princes in all their regalia, Congressmen in coarse khaki – each with their own expectations of the Viceroy. Folks back home were frenetic at the impending loss; Dickie was acutely aware of the thanklessness of his job.

'They don't want me out there,' he had confided to his aides as they mounted the aircraft to India. 'We'll probably come home with bullets in our backs.'

He faced them, dressed in his white admiral's uniform – decorated with a cornflower-blue sash, gold aiguillettes, multiples medals. He had intended to do justice to the ceremony through the full splendour of his naval uniform. In his previous job as Supreme Allied Commander of the South East Asia Command during WWII, Dickie Mountbatten had received the surrender of the Japanese in Singapore. In his new job, he was tasked with publicly terminating the very job. He had to find a way to impress his authority upon people, yet carry them along. It was a tricky balance. Which he meant to establish at the very outset.

Dickie stepped up to the microphone.

It was a breach of protocol, a break with tradition, against the advice of his staff.

He started to address the gathering.

'This is not a normal viceroyalty on which I am embarking. I am under no illusion about the difficulty of my task.' As the last Viceroy, he was to transfer power as Attlee wanted, but also to find a way to not entirely decouple Britain from India, much as his cousin, King George VI, Emperor of India, desired. 'I shall need the greatest goodwill of the greatest possible number, and I am asking India today for that goodwill.'

The Durbar Hall was meant to be seen at, not heard in. Dickie was not sure if the acoustics had delivered – his intended audience hadn't stirred. But he had caught the attention of two men: Nehru in a Gandhi cap and Liaquat Ali Khan in a fez. And that of Edwina. As Dickie finished, with his request for India's goodwill, his wife had cocked her head at him, ever so slightly. If he had managed to surprise her, he had certainly confounded the press, whose flashbulbs were popping. Good!

And thus, on the morning of 24 March, seventy years after his great-grandmother's coronation as the Empress of India at another Durbar Hall in Delhi, the last Viceroy began to dismantle the Crown in his own style. Fitting for a great-grandson who had knocked the spectacles off the imperial nose whilst his christening.

∞

At his desk after the swearing-in, Dickie took stock of the situation.

When Edwina had first heard of the Viceregal offer to her husband, she had noted in her dairy: 'Possible new horror job.' Upon arrival in India two days ago, the outgoing Viceroy, Lord Wavell, had greeted the Mountbattens. After which, he had escorted Dickie to his study to appraise him on the new job: an impossible task.

On Dickie's prodding, the much-decorated war hero, who had lost his left eye in WWI, had confessed, 'I have tried everything I know to solve this problem and I can see no light …' Thereafter, Wavell debriefed Dickie on the several efforts made by his team to reach a solution that would satisfy the major stakeholders – the Congress and the Muslim League. Wavell had been in India since 1943 to resolve the political deadlock. With that aim, he had convened the Simla Conference in June 1945, which Jinnah and Gandhi had attended. However, Jinnah's insistence that the Muslim League be considered the sole representative of all Muslims had led to the Congress blowing its fuse. 'We've reached a complete impasse here,' Wavell had concluded.

Dickie squared his shoulders. A naval man, he appreciated being informed of the depth of the problem he was wading into. But Wavell's next revelation had reminded him of being aboard the *HMS Kelly* as it took a bomb in her magazine and went down quickly. From his safe, the Viceroy had withdrawn a manila folder and planted it under Dickie's nose. It was labelled: 'Operation Madhouse'.

'Old chap,' Wavell had said, 'I call this "Madhouse" because that is the nature of the problem. I see one solution; it is a terrible one but the only one I have.' Then he went on to provide details. It entailed the British evacuation of India, province by province, women and children first, followed by other civilians, then soldiers.

'Gandhi did say that we leave India to god, or anarchy,' Wavell had ended.

God or anarchy.

Now, Dickie mulled over his options. In WWII, as commander of the newly commissioned destroyer *HMS Kelly*, he had promised his crew that he would never give one command: Abandon ship. 'The only way we leave this ship is if it sinks under our feet,' he had declared. Since his boyhood, Dickie had been enamoured with a naval career, inspired by the feats of his father, Prince Louis of Battenberg, the First Sea Lord of the Royal Navy. A post his father was ousted from when his German family name became a handicap following WWI. His father had changed their name from Battenberg to Mountbatten, but never recovered from the fall from disgrace. Which left young Dickie consumed by the desire to one day occupy that very same post, the First Sea Lord of the Royal Navy, and wipe the stain off.

To that end, he had trained himself to work harder than any other man, superior or subordinate. Fascinated by the increasing role of technology in warfare, he studied signals, dabbled in physics and communication, and surrounded himself with inventors, scientists, technicians, and anyone else who could feed his scientific curiosity. Churchill had selected him to lead Combined Operations, a commando force created to develop the tactics and technology that would eventually bring the Allies back to the continent. As SEAC commander, he had taken the Jap surrender. After which he had waited for his next naval command. The sea awaited, the title of First Sea Lord still beckoned, the stain on his father's reputation still to be erased. But they had kept him on the Active Flag List and despatched him here instead.

Dickie rubbed his forehead. He had not been keen on this new role of Viceroy, a digression for a navy man. Besides, what was he to execute exactly? Nobody knew. Churchill had condemned it 'Operation Scuttle', an attempt by the Labour government to make use of brilliant war figures in order to cover up a melancholy and disastrous transaction. Even the King, his cousin, had pondered: 'Are you to lead the retreat out of India or work for the reconciliation of Hindus and Moslems?'

Damn!

Which brought to mind his last visit to his mother when he had said goodbye at Broadlands. 'Damn! Damn!' she had exclaimed, still strong at eighty-three, still bitter at the ignominious end to her husband's illustrious career. 'You will be there for years ... if you come back at all.'

In some ways he felt himself aboard a sinking ship ...

But when the *Kelly* rolled over, he was still on the bridge, fighting his way to the surface as she went under. With a few survivors, he had held onto a life raft, even as German planes raked the waters, leading the men in singing '*Roll out the barrel*'.

Doubtless, he was afloat on a full sea ... The solution therefore could only be to execute his mission like a true naval man. As he had once admitted to a querulous Churchill: 'I suffer from the congenital weakness of believing I can do anything.'

Dickie jumped up and started to survey his study. Wood-panelled, dark and ponderous with the weight of failed past negotiations. Stepping out, he went in search of Edwina. She would know how best to execute his plan.

The Viceroy's study, headquarter of his command operations, would be painted a light shade of green, a comforting aqua, reminiscent of his beloved seas. The wood panelling favoured by his predecessors was too heavy for the sailor within him.

12
Laur (April 1947)

Beli Ram squatted in the corner, where a small, raised platform with a bucket served as his bathing area. He crunched the twig of neem releasing the bitter taste. Last night, he had returned home late. Panjab Mail was held up in Ambarsar or somewhere else for hours, and, by the time it reached, it was ten hours behind schedule. But the Mail meant lots of passengers with lots of baggage and the chance to earn some well-needed money. Exhausted, he had slept soundly and woken up later than usual. Though, looking at the sun, it would appear like it was noon already! Yet, the womenfolk's chatter had not yet erupted in the lane. Breakfast done, husband and children sent away, house cleaned, they started their business of roosting on chabutaras around ten. He shifted the twig to the other side of his mouth. The bright sunshine was exhausting him already. Soon, the barest movement and he would be bathed in sweat. An orange. He felt a yearning for an orange – its juicy, sharp sweetness would freshen him up.

The twig end had split into bristles and he started to brush his teeth. He had filled enough water from the well yesterday – he peered into the brass bucket: Perhaps he could get a quick bath out of it too? He spat. Snapping the twig, he bent it and scraped his tongue. Filling a steel tumbler with water, he rinsed his mouth, once, twice, and washed his face and hands. Rolling his shoulders back, he stood up. The towel was draped on a string in the courtyard and he wiped his face. The sun had made the coarse cotton bristly.

'Mothers, sisters, daughters, ladies ... The fruit peddler is here!'

The rai with his fruits and vegetables. Saliva pooled in his mouth. Beli Ram fingered the pocket of his kurta for coins and headed to open his front door. Outside, the rai had taken his customary position at the entrance to the lane. His basket of wares gleamed in the morning sunlight. Beli Ram shut the door and walked down. He cleared his throat loudly to alert any women who might want to cover themselves, for once the menfolk left, women sat at ease – chattering amongst themselves, forsaking chadars and chunnis, especially in this heat. Billo, the cat-eyed older daughter of Moolchand, was on the rooftop talking loudly to herself.

'Motia aleo,' the rai greeted him warmly, 'what can I offer you?'

Beli Ram eyed the watermelons, guava, papaya, ladies' fingers, spinach, karela. 'No orange?'

The peddler raised his eyes skywards. 'The unseasonal rains have ruined the crop. Maybe we will get some later. But here, try the guava. Look how it glows with health.' He held up a guava in one hand, its skin a smooth golden with rose blushes.

But Beli Ram could taste the missing orange juice in his mouth. He stood undecided.

No rain, no rain this time!

Billo grinned from her rooftop at the rai and Beli. Her uncombed hair fanned out like some halo. The men ignored her.

'Perhaps you would like a slice of watermelon, huh? Or papaya?' The rai's eyes twinkled as he waxed eloquent about the qualities of his wares, his head bobbing.

'Oye!'

Both men turned at the loud hailing. Mai Peeto, the matriarch who owned the well, beckoned with an outstretched hand. A large woman, she was perched on her string cot beside the well. She frowned. 'You, rai, go away! We are not buying anything today.'

'Mother,' the rai smiled, 'I have just arrived. Let me enjoy the shade for a bit, and perhaps some other sisters might want to buy a fruit or two in the meantime.'

'No, no,' the woman shook her arm. 'We have all decided we will not buy anything from your kind. Now go; go away! Sell your wares in a Muslim mohalla.'

The rai's smiling mouth, sprouting from amidst his abundant free-flowing whiskers, clamped shut. Briefly. Then he rallied again. 'Mother, I am a poor peddler. I have children to feed back home. My fruits and vegetables,' he indicated his basket with both arms, 'are fresh and cheaper than what you will find in the bazaar. Sisters,' he raised his head to address other women who sat listening on raised platforms outside their homes, 'the vegetables await. The finest karela, the colour of green velvet. Or perhaps you would like to cook potato with variyan today?'

A child had hurried up, one fist clenched. He pointed to a pomegranate.

'Padshaho,' the rai plucked a rosy-red pomegranate and handed it to the boy and took the coin. As he fiddled within his waist bag for change—

'No!' The boy's mother had showed up. Shaking her head, she returned the fruit.

Mai Peeto hollered from her spot, 'All the women in the mohalla have taken a vow never to buy anything from a Muslim. Your kind are killing our men in broad daylight. Mother of Roshan, tell the rai now!'

The face of the mother clutching her son's shoulders was pinched. Beli Ram felt sorry for her. The problem was that everyone needed water, which was why Mai Peeto could bark orders from her cot. If the rai had oranges, he would surely have bought one! *Aaho*, the voice within him sniggered, *and I would have showered with that orange's juice too*!

The rai tried again, his peddler's voice, loud yet pleasant, rolling out the virtues of his wares once more. But he was shut down as a chorus arose from the lane, other women joining Mai Peeto.

'Muslims are butchering Hindus and we are to buy your fruits!'

'Go, and never come back!'

'Sisters, the bazaar has better fruit – you may pay a bit more, but let's support our Hindu brothers.'

The rai locked eyes with Beli Ram, sighed, and picked up his basket. Carrying it on his head, his arms cradling it, he walked away. Billo had quieted down on the rooftop and watched.

'Dafa ho!' a woman hollered at the rai's receding back.

Really, women, Beli Ram wanted to chasten their meddling selves, the man has left, what more do you want?

∞

After a breakfast of fennel tea, and thick roti sprinkled with salt and red chilli powder, Beli Ram stepped out for work. The treatment that the women had meted out to the rai troubled him. The peddler was a stranger, sure, but he had been coming to the Hata since forever. Why this hysteria over some fruits and vegetables? Normally, these women would haggle until their throats went hoarse. But a rai who sold wares cheap right outside their doorstep was sent packing today. Next, would they complain when Mehmood came visiting? He shook his head. There was no understanding women!

As he reached the end of his lane, a voice hollered from above.

'Oye! No oranges for you.'

Billo. Beli Ram continued walking, but the woman's demented cries trailed him.

'Only red rain … feast for vultures …'

Where would the rai have gone? To another mohalla close by … Bani Hata? Beli Ram would pass through the Hata on his way to Lahore Junction. He wanted that guava now.

Around him rickshaws trilled, horse carts clattered, cyclists wove around pedestrians as Beli Ram waddled on, feeling perspiration trickle down his back. Bani Hata's gate lay ahead. He sidestepped fresh cow dung only to have his foot land on a pulped papaya. Arms flailing, he tried to stay upright. Which he managed, but his right foot was a mess – the jutti coated with orange flesh and the black seeds of the gutted papaya. As he got his bearings, he noticed the floor was littered with fruits and vegetables, which a couple of cows were munching upon. Beli Ram frowned. Had a vegetable cart toppled over this morning? Or had the goods rolled off an overloaded cart headed to the bazaar?

Ahead, a few rickshaws were parked, a man sold peanuts in paper cones and a man sat on his haunches, head in his hands, his lungi touching the dirty ground beneath. Around him

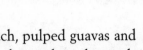

were strewn green leaves, strips of spinach, pulped guavas and pomegranates. Beli Ram hurried forward, avoiding the rinds and peels and torn flesh. Reaching the man, he put a tentative hand on his shoulder.

Sure enough, it was the rai. His whiskers had drops nestling in them, his eyes were dim.

'W-what happened?'

The rai sniffled. 'As I was heading to Bani Hata, some miscreants plucked my basket and pelted my fruit and vegetables all around. See,' he thrust his arms forward. His basket lay upturned, some spinach still clinging to it.

'But why?'

'They were teaching the Hindus a lesson, they said.'

13
Delhi (April 1947)

At 6.30 in the morning, Dickie Mountbatten and seventeen-year-old Pamela rode out of the Viceregal mansion. As per the Viceroy's explicit command, there was to be no escort for this time. However, the security of the Viceroy was not to be taken lightly and two armed bodyguards rode behind at a discreet distance. Sunlight skimmed treetops and the air was refreshing. In an hour, the crispness would curl as heat fried the air. The Ridge above Delhi was one of the delights of the capital city, thickly forested, relatively cool and, at that hour, trilling with birds.

'It makes me absolutely sick to see the house full of dirty Indians!' Pamela announced as they rode on.

Her father looked at her with raised brows.

'Un-huh,' she said. 'That is exactly what I overheard one of the English ladies telling another.'

Dickie acknowledged her with a grunt and concentrated ahead. Riding unescorted was not the only departure the new Viceroy had initiated. As part of his terms of agreement for the office, he had insisted that he not be bound by the rigid formality of former Viceroys. 'My wife and I would wish to visit Indian leaders in their homes, unaccompanied by staff,' he had stated. And in India, Edwina and he had promptly set about on their stated mission. Parts of India were experiencing conditions of near-famine and, for the first time in history, the Viceregal household was put under rationing. The fact that British rule in India might end up being viewed as bookended by famines – a terrible famine in 1770 immediately following the establishment of rule by British East India Company in Bengal – troubled him. The unusual rationing had led to expected grumbling ...

Edwina had mentioned, with a wicked grin, that some staff members were reportedly angling for invitations from the household of the Viceroy's chief of staff – apparently, at the Ismays', meals still promised a full belly in return. Nonetheless, meeting people was one way to get to know them, and the Viceroy and Vicereine had been hosting garden parties, luncheons and a few large dinners, with Edwina's one explicit rule that ensured at least half of those present were Indians. Clearly, if Pamela's hearing was sound, which he knew to be the case, some British guests were viewing this with hostility.

'Thank you, Pamela. Your mother's and my policy is that the Viceroy's House is wide open, socially and politically, to people who would otherwise never have found their way here before ... particularly Indians.'

'And I wholly approve.' Pamela threw back her head and prodded her horse into a gallop, as the grounds opened up in front of them. Dickie followed. He caught up and they rode along at a steady trot. A man with a bundle on his head, dressed in a white cotton dhoti and kurta, barefoot, sped by, stirring little eddies of dust. Clearly, he was in a hurry to get somewhere before the full heat of the sun was upon him. No wonder most Indians were early risers, accomplishing half a day's work before breakfast! Sardar Patel, Nehru, Gandhi – all were up before 4.30 a.m., he was informed.

'Daddy, how are you finding it thus far?'

'SEAC – even in the hectic days of Kohima and Imphal – was a rest cure.'

He was referring to the South East Asia Command he had helmed during the war, and it was Pamela's turn to raise her brows. 'What did you make of Mr Gandhi? He really is a remarkable old man and a great character. All that nonsense back home of him being a funny little man in a loincloth! Really, we English can be quite ignorant.'

Dickie grinned. 'Well, he did wear a loincloth when he visited. With a shawl though. I am afraid the air conditioning in my study might be too cold for him.'

'Did you read what the papers have been saying back home?'

'What particular part?'

'The bit about the black hand on the white shoulder.'

'Caused quite an outrage, hasn't it?'

Her father seemed rather pleased at the idea. It was the day of his first meeting with Mr Gandhi on 31 March. After which Mummy and Daddy had posed with him on the Viceregal lawns for the customary photographs. Thereafter, they turned to go inside the house. Mr Gandhi – affable, frail – was used to his great niece being one of his crutches as he leaned on her for support and walked. Instinctively, his hand reached for her mother's shoulder, and a lingering cameraman got the perfect shot. It didn't bother Mummy at all – indeed she welcomed it, probably, for there was a genuine warmth between them right from that first introduction. But what an uproar it had created!

'I have no patience as you know with people who express such sentiments. And your mother is a woman who knows her mind.'

'Mummy will have nothing to do with the Pukka Sahib sort of British in India.'

'Are you still getting lost in the house?'

'But of course! It's enormous. You spend so much time in your study you have no idea how immense it is. It takes ten minutes to walk from my bedroom to the dining room. Bicycle is quicker. Our first tour of the house took over two hours. Mummy is convinced it was built for the express purpose of losing people in. But she is determined to learn everything about the house ... The estate and the servants and I dare say she scared off the comptroller!'

'I do hope it's not too wearing for Edwina.'

'You know the size of the domestic staff? Upwards of 5000! That will wear anyone down!'

They paused at a hilly spur, green cover ahead, the orderly city behind. A persistent cheeping of house sparrows alerted Dickie to a thicket where birds hopped busily from branch to ground to branch, pecking busily.

'Look!' Pamela squealed, pointing above. A clutch of ridiculously green parrots, red-ringed, scarlet beaks, perched in a tree ablaze with orange flowers. A tintinnabulation of persistent cooing, urgent calls, and shrill screeching.

Quite extraordinary, really; I must learn to identify the bird calls and the foliage, Dickie thought. The sun was glinting way above the horizon now; time to head back. They rounded their horses. The family sat down for breakfast at 7.15 a.m., after which they would each head off on their respective tasks. As Pamela and Dickie joined the track, a camel lumbered by, its rope lax in the hand of a man who plodded ahead. The Indian wore an elaborate, multicoloured turban – its various hues synchronous with the multiple coloured threads draped around the camel's neck, complete with bells, tufts, and mirrors. Pamela watched them wide-eyed.

His day ahead was packed with meetings and briefings. Communal rioting was spreading, as if by chain reaction; the princes were seeking his direct intervention on their behalf; the Congress and the Muslim League were seemingly keen only on resisting each other … At the end of all the sessions, he would end up feeling a bit like a boiled egg.

'Humour your daddy,' Dickie urged, 'tell me something pleasant.'

'It really is such fun out here, seeing all the birds and animals. Besides, in this furnace-like heat, the swimming pool in the house is lovely to bathe in.'

14
Laur (April 1947)

As his rickshaw cycled down Railway Road, Kishan Singh read *The Tribune* with interest. The editorial quoted another editorial from *The Times*, London.

'The Muslim League attempt to seize power in Panjab, admittedly a nodal point of Pakistan, has broken down in the face of Hindu and Sikh opposition. If persisted in, it seems likely to reinforce the growing demand for the division of the province into Muslim and non-Muslim areas.'

Usually, he was able to finish reading all his papers before heading to work. But there was so much news nowadays, so much of it conflicting, that some days, after he had read all the papers, he felt less enlightened than before.

Pammi had laughingly suggested: 'Stick to one paper, Bapuji, it will save us money also!'

Which was true. The price of everything was rising … except of human life. The war had brought back many soldiers, who roamed the streets with visible injuries or visible arrogance, sharpening their moustache tips and, Waheguru knew, what else?

He folded *The Tribune*, clamped it under one thigh, and opened *Dawn*. Something about the newspaper didn't seem right. With narrowed eyes, he scanned the front page, skimming over the headlines, racing down the columns, then up to the title – there! A quotation from the Quran was prominently printed to the left of the title. On the right was an advertisement for men's hair dye. Kishan Singh folded the newspaper. *Dawn*, a mouthpiece of the League, had just made its allegiance very public.

The twin turrets of Lahore Junction looked down upon them as they approached the railway station. After paying the rickshaw, Kishan Singh walked to the red-brick building. Inside, a voice hailed, 'Adaab, Singh saab!' It was the coolie, Mehmood, sipping his tea.

'Adaab,' said Kishan Singh and walked up to him. 'Here,' he handed him his copy of *Dawn*. 'Newspaper is fresh; I haven't even read it. Perhaps you can sell it back.' He lifted his chin in the direction of the bookshop located on the platform ahead.

Mehmood acknowledged this with a tip of his head. 'Mr A.H. Wheeler will sponsor my tea today!'

∽

At lunch time, news arrived of an attack on passengers at Gorazai railway station in Rawalpindi. Details started to trickle in. The attackers were green-uniformed Muslim Leaguers … The victims were Hindus and Sikhs … Twenty were killed.

Kishan Singh tried to work amidst the growing hullabaloo. Since Balwant Rai was away in some meeting, the staff huddled around tables, exchanging stories of what they had read or heard or cooked up.

'The League will not rest until it has its Pakistan,' Mangat clucked. 'Jinnah wants to be king like Gandhi.'

'Gandhi and king!' Ahmed guffawed. 'He can't afford one set of decent clothes even.'

'Gandhi is an ascetic, a mahatma,' said Hari Kumar. 'Keep him out of it.' Kumar was a serious young man, with a neatly trimmed moustache, who always dressed in ironed pant–shirt. An active member of the railway union and a committed communist, he marched in the streets demanding Hindu–Muslim unity.

'Lo!' Ahmed slapped his hands in merriment. 'Keep Gandhi out. My brother, we would, but Gandhi gets in everywhere. In his langot, he keeps inserting his spindly self in our affairs. Bhai, can I send him a pair of salwar–kameez? In khadi, okay? Not my size, of course,' Ahmed's hands showcased his tall frame, 'but my younger son's! How sharp will your Gandhi look then, hmm?'

Kumar's jaw clenched. Would he rise to the bait? Kishan Singh watched from the corner of his eye. No. After a pointed glare at Ahmed, Hari Kumar returned to his work. He banged the typewriter's keys with controlled fury.

'Still, it's sad seeing innocent people dying because our leaders cannot see eye to eye,' Mangat sighed and walked back to his desk.

'Not eye to eye, it is the time for *an eye for an eye*,' Ahmed declared. 'The one who shows weakness gets eaten; that is jungle raj. British Raj is ending, so who will get power now? The one who grabs it! In that department, the descendants of mighty Ranjit Singh are falling short. Bhai, what happened to the famed valour of the Sikhs, hain? They have grown prosperous and fat like they were some lalas!'

Hari Kumar clanked the typewriter lever loudly. A non-verbal khasma-nu-kha.

Ahmed was throwing glances at him as he spoke, Kishan Singh knew, wanting him to wade into this communal bickering. Ahmed would be happy if Kishan Singh punched him. The two could then pummel each other to settle the question: Which was the more martial race – Sikhs or Mussalmans? Kishan had no desire to fight, not only because he did not know how to throw an effective punch, but also, what was the point? If slugging it out was proof of ability to govern, why not hand over the administration to wrestlers? Such foolish thinking annoyed him. But Ahmed was hankering for a fight – and some days, Kishan entertained the thought that if he was built like Iqbal virji, he would have no problem resolving the matter.

∝

On his way home, Kishan Singh stopped at Anarkali to pick up some bottled pomegranate juice. The girls loved it, especially Pammi, and, in this heat, the drink would be refreshing. He exchanged a few words with Kanwal Malik, the owner. His daughter, Tara, was Pammi's good friend, although she had not cleared her matriculation. Malik sounded worried. 'Uncertainty is bad for business. Besides,' he lowered his head to whisper, 'I heard reports of Hindu shops being attacked and the police simply looking away.'

Carrying that depressing piece of news and two bottles of soda, Kishan Singh walked to his colony, only to find that he could not enter. A barrier had come up, which some young men stood guarding.

'What is the meaning of all this?' Kishan Singh asked the young male standing closest to him.

'This is to safeguard the colony,' he said, his youthful face pimpled. 'Only residents will be allowed in. Are you a resident?'

'If you don't know that, how will you guard the colony?'

The boy blushed. 'I'm only visiting my cousin who lives here. Asad bhai!' he yelled.

Asad detached himself from a group of men. 'Adaab, chacha,' he raised the wooden barrier with some difficulty. 'You see, we're still perfecting this.'

Kishan Singh could see the pulley system they were improvising to lift the heavy wooden barrier. 'But what's the need for all this?'

'Need, chacha?' Asad's head recoiled, his thick hair bouncing. 'All mohallas are building barricades and gates to keep strangers out. There is looting and killing happening daily, and that is the work of miscreants from outside. We'll start collecting money to put up an iron gate soon. That will properly secure us.'

Before Kishan Singh could enquire if Asad and the other boys had consulted their elders, a strapping man loomed over them and clamped Asad's shoulder with one big hand. 'Work awaits, boy.' His voice was firm and clear, and even though he spoke quietly, Kishan heard it as a command. Asad scurried off to join the other boys. Kishan stepped away from the hulking presence. The man did not reside in the colony; he didn't seem like a relative of a resident either. He was directing the construction of the barricade like he was on some battlefield. He even looked like a soldier. Where had he come from? And why?

Something else gnawed at him as well, but he could not put a finger on it. With these niggling thoughts, Kishan Singh reached home.

'Sasrikal, Bapuji!' Pammi, delighted with his offering of soda bottles, relieved him of them.

And he realized what else was troubling him. When Asad saw him, he greeted Kishan Singh with adaab instead of the usual Sat Sri Akal. Was it intentional on Asad's part? Or had the presence of the Mussalman soldier simply suppressed the customary Sikh greeting?

Or was *he* just splitting hairs? Kishan Singh pondered over this as he removed his turban.

15
Delhi (April 1947)

'You're doing much better with this business than I am, frankly.' Dickie sipped on orange juice and watched the swimming pool with crinkled eyes. Morning was the only time the sun wasn't beastly enough for the outdoors. And breakfast was the only meal they could certifiably have together.

'That's because you have the tougher constituents, darling,' Edwina smiled. As her husband had started meeting the various Indian leaders, she had initiated her own tea and luncheons with prominent women: Amrit Kaur, who was very close to Gandhi; Manibehn, daughter of Vallabhbhai Patel; Begum Ra'ana, wife of Liaquat Ali Khan; and Sarojini Naidu, who was also her mother's childhood friend! Edwina enjoyed an instant rapport with Amrit Kaur, but not so much with Fatima Jinnah, the sister of the Muslim League leader.

'Not a hearty fact,' Dickie said drily. Following the swearing-in, he had begun executing his mandate by meeting important Indian leaders and representatives of all the main stakeholders in India – Christians and Parsees, in addition to Hindus and

Muslims; businessmen and academics. The Viceroy's study hummed like a command centre: Each meeting took place there, lasted an hour, and was recorded immediately after. What Dickie had gleaned from the series of meetings was the location of power centres: the trio of Gandhi, Nehru, and Sardar Patel for the Hindus; and Jinnah alone for the Muslims.

'Which of them is being the hardest on you, Daddy?' Pamela asked as she buttered a slice of toast.

'It would be simpler to talk about the one I think I will enjoy working with. Pandit Nehru. He struck me as most sincere. Of course, we are acquainted from before – Singapore – which helps, but I daresay he has an open mind …'

Edwina smoothed back her hair. 'He strikes me as sophisticated and worldly wise. And he's so erudite, having written all those books.'

'Hmm … In our preliminary discussions on the future shape of India, I get the sense that there is room for manoeuvre. Though, of course, he won't contemplate partition of any sort.'

Pamela nodded. She had gone with her mother to a party hosted by Pandit Nehru and met his daughter, Mrs Gandhi, too.

'Wavell's assessment was different – he called Nehru quixotic and emotional – so we shall see. But I am happy to report that the Spirit of the Hive is alive and functioning in Viceroy's House!'

'Spirit of the Hive?' Pamela cocked her head at him.

Dickie sat upright and began arranging orange segments on a plate. Edwina seemed lost in her thoughts. He stacked several in close proximity to the centre, a core, from which thinner circles radiated outwards. 'A beehive,' he pointed an index finger at the plate, 'is an efficient working organization. See the core here? That's the heart of the hive. In my case, it's my immediate staff – Ismay, Miéville, Abell, Ian Scott, Christie … you know them –

and our daily staff meetings, where we review the events of the past twenty-four hours and deliberate over future policy. We work as a team; I am the team leader. Which means I can run my ideas past these men, all old India hands, who know their areas way better than I could ever hope to.'

Dickie looked pointedly at Edwina.

With a lazy smile, Edwina leaned forward, plucked a segment from the outer circle and popped it in her mouth. 'Didn't Abel begin with a first posting in Panjab?'

'Yes. As a young ICS officer, two decades ago. He's worked with Governor Jenkins, Viceroy Wavell, and now, myself. A wise man and an experienced Panjab hand.'

A series of short barks interrupted them. The Sealyham had sighted something in the bushes and was yapping at it.

'Mizzy!' Pamela hailed. 'Mizzzeee.' The barks had grown frenetic. The Sealyham was bewildered by the new fauna he was encountering in the Viceroy House's untrammelled gardens. Pamela pushed her chair back, 'Can I be excused?' On a nod from her mother, she went to join the dog in one of the manicured gardens that stretched outwards from the pool.

A khidmatgar stepped up noiselessly to serve tea to the Viceroy. Dickie frowned at the cup.

'I'll give you an anna for your thoughts,' Edwina chimed.

'Make it a 4 anna at least,' Dickie grunted. 'Many would pay a king's ransom to hear the Viceroy's thoughts.'

'Not the Vicereine; she has his ear.' Edwina leaned forward to place a hand on his right forearm.

'Jinnah ... I'm afraid the Ice-man is also a No-man.'

Edwina patted his arm, offered him the teacup, and settled back. She remembered what her husband had said after meeting the Muslim leader the first time. 'My god, he was cold!' Dickie's proverbial charm hadn't thawed Jinnah the least.

'He says "No" to everything, every option, every plan, every solution, *except* the one that gives him an independent Pakistan. A child couldn't be worse. If I cannot reason with him, how do we hold a discussion? Indeed, I get the impression he was *not* listening. Another "No".'

'Hmm … Well, if it's any consolation, his sister is equally frosty. And bent upon getting that Pakistan. I shared with her my visit to Lady Irwin College where a class of fourteen Hindu and two Muslim girls had elected one of the Muslims as head girl. A cheery prospect, I thought, in these tense times. Miss Jinnah demolished my credulity. "We have not been able to start our propaganda in that college yet," she said!'

Dickie nodded before waving to Pamela, who was heading back with Mizzy in her arms. 'Another day awaits.' Placing his napkin on the table, he stood up.

'You've established a good rapport with Mr Gandhi, darling. That's important.'

Dickie frowned, whether at the sun that shone like a plate in the sky or at his thoughts, Edwina couldn't decipher.

'An old poppet,' Dickie said with affection before kissing bye to his wife and daughter.

Edwina and he had enjoyed meeting Gandhi, whom Wavell had dismissed as a charlatan. But Dickie was committed to spending time with the ultimate leader of the Congress to gauge him better. On 1 April, Gandhi had suggested that Jinnah be invited to form an interim central government, a crucial step to maintain the unity of India. It was April Fools' Day, which made Dickie wonder how seriously he ought to consider it. The idea was bold and imaginative but, his advisers told him, it had been aired in the past as well and been soundly rejected by the Congress. Gandhi's two lieutenants, Nehru and Patel, had sympathy for their old man, but they were being pragmatic.

Patel, especially, Dickie found, was a realist, wholly concerned with ground reality.

∽

That evening the Viceroy hosted a garden party. It was an entirely pleasant affair – the heat of the day had dissipated, garden lights twinkled, guests mingled, many of them Indians who had never set a social foot in the Viceroy's House before. Dickie watched Edwina indulgently. She looked so elegant in her floral-print dress as she conversed with Pandit Nehru, whose head was bowed in avid concentration.

Soon, a dance recital was in the works; chairs were assembled for people to sit on and watch. As the audience settled, Edwina appeared from the kitchens where she had gone to oversee something. Not a chair was vacant. Dickie was about to stand up when Nehru shot up and offered his chair to her. Smiling graciously, Edwina accepted.

A gong sounded, music piped up, drawing attention to the stage where dancers in brightly toned dresses wove their sinuous limbs rather intricately. Quite charming, except Dickie could not help noticing the smiling Nehru, sitting cross-legged on the floor at his wife's feet.

16
Delhi (April 1947)

Jawahar paused at the door to Vallabhbhai's home, the striking orange flowers of the palash tree arresting him momentarily. The morning sun had lit a fire in its branches. He reached out to pick a flower that had fallen to the ground. Ma would soak the flowers in water for the rich yellow colour to play Holi with.

'Jawaharlal?'

His host, having lost him, stepped back onto the porch where Jawaharlal had stopped. 'Ah,' Vallabh said, 'I see you are admiring the gardener's work. My green thumbs are grey going through files.'

Jawahar smiled. Five years ago, the Quit India movement had brought senior Congressmen to the confines of various jails. A time of great uncertainty, as war spread through the world radiating out of Hitler's Germany with Japan threatening to invade India. The British or the Japs, both were inimical to India's interests. Vallabhbhai and he were imprisoned in Ahmednagar Fort jail, along with Maulana, Pant, Pattabhi, and others, the age of the group ranging from the early forties to the late sixties. A mile-long wall of stone surrounded the sixteenth-century Fort, where a woman warrior, Chand Bibi, had made a heroic stand against the Mughals. The heart of the Fort was an open quadrangle, lined on all four sides by single-storeyed barracks. Inside the barracks, the rear windows were bricked up. So the quad was where the motley group of Congressmen, not allowed newspapers or letters, gathered.

'But you are keeping up with your exercise?'

'I pace, morning and evening. Runs in the family; my father was a pacer as well.'

'You made good use of the 200-foot path.' Jawahar grinned.

'Ah! Ahmednagar. Back and forth, back and forth. I think I covered four miles every day. And thought.'

'And gardened.'

'A little,' Vallabh acknowledged. 'You were the star gardener though, coaxing that barren leafless soil into a blooming bower!'

Sowing, digging, planting, pruning, weeding ... in the hot sun with his hat on, in the pouring rain with his raincoat on. Thinking. Reading. Writing. Jawahar completed his book, *The Discovery of India*, as he marked three birthdays imprisoned in the Fort. 'It was a way of biding time.' He pointed to the creeper. 'Remember Shakuntala's bower?'

Vallabh laughed, his head thrown back. In the Fort prison, near the entrance to his room he had grown a morning glory creeper on a string trellis. It formed an arch of pink and blue flowers, its limbs rooted in two earthen flowerpots where roses bloomed. Appropriately, he named it after the legendary beauty from the Mahabharata, who was wooed by a mighty King in a beautiful bower, whose son gave the land its name, Bharat.

'As you said, we were biding time. And now, the time has come.' Vallabh extended his arm. 'Shall we?'

They sat down to a breakfast of dates, toast with marmalade, apples and oranges. 'Not the type you favour,' observed Vallabh, aware of Jawaharlal's liking for a typical English breakfast of eggs and bacon.

'After Bapu's goat's curd, any alternative is better.'

The men chewed silently. They were due to meet the Viceroy in an hour, and each man was marshalling his thoughts. Violence between Hindus and Muslims was escalating in the countryside, and the Viceroy had suggested to Jinnah that he join the Congress leadership in an appeal to all Indians to desist from provocative acts that might lead to bloodshed. Jinnah had agreed. A draft was prepared, but when it came to signing, Jinnah had refused. Apparently, he was offended that, on behalf of the Congress, the appeal was to be signed by its president, Acharya Kripalani. 'An unknown nobody,' Jinnah had dismissed. The thought made Nehru fume.

Vallabhbhai, reading him correctly, said, 'Jinnah is being petty as usual.'

'Petty, and a busybody. It is for the Congress to decide who should sign on their behalf.'

'He wants to be seen as no less than Gandhi's equal.' Vallabhbhai's smirk indicated the yawning gap he saw between the two leaders. 'Perhaps Lord Mountbatten will make him see sense.'

Jawahar probed the date in his hand. Jinnah and Gandhi both came from the peninsula of Kathiawar in Gujarat, both were British-trained barristers, both were Congressmen – once. Jinnah was the older member of the party, the one who had welcomed Gandhi upon his arrival in India from South Africa, who had stressed in 1915 that the greatest problem facing them was to bring about unanimity and cooperation between the two communities, so that the demands of India to the British may be made unanimously. Now, in 1947, with independence in sight, the same Jinnah, as leader of the Muslim League, seeking a separate homeland for Muslims, was quibbling over an appeal to avoid bloodshed. 'Common sense, more like,' Jawahar said. 'Some people seem intent on a hartal of the mind.'

Manibehn arrived with a bowl of pistachios and tea. Vallabh stood up, took the tray from her and started to prepare tea for his guest.

'All those years of hartals, general strikes, stopping work, fasting and prayers, prison and resistance, and finally, freedom appears on the horizon. Fifteen months, if Mr Attlee is to be believed.' He handed a teacup to Jawaharlal.

His mouth set, Vallabh let one hand fall to his side, then clasped both behind him, and walked over to the window, outside which a bougainvillea grew. Even as Attlee had announced freedom, he had rung a death knell to the unity of India. A probable partition was on the horizon. Not a new thought at all. The end of the war had brought a new Prime Minister in London, but Attlee and his men were rolling out the plan which Churchill had always wanted. Dividing India into Pakistan, Hindustan, and Princestan. Now that holding India by force had become an impossibility, the British would not leave India and Indians to manage their own fate.

'The Raj has always stacked up the League against the Congress – as if a minority could balance the vast majority. Jinnah throws these tantrums because he knows he has an appreciative audience. But,' Vallabh turned to look at Jawaharlal, 'can we blame the British for doing what they excel at? Divide and conquer. Since the Battle of Plassey.'

Jawahar snorted. 'It was neither a battle nor was there a Plassey. Only in the British lexicon can bribing be the equivalent of fighting. And Palashi get mangled to Plassey.' He touched the leathery leaves of the palash in front of him, after which was named the village on the Hooghly, where Robert Clive in 1757 had begun the British Empire in India.

'The British idea of fair play,' Vallabh said in a droll voice.

'Clive laid the foundation of British India through treachery and forgery. It was an unsavoury beginning and something of that bitter taste has clung to it ever since.' One of the early consequences of that rule was a famine that ravaged Bengal and Bihar, killing over a third of the population.

'And yet, look how the British hold themselves up as custodians of law and justice!'

A raucous twittering filled the air as a bunch of sparrows alighted on the bougainvillea. Vallabh returned to the table. 'The British have disguised their politics as concern for the minority, abetting Jinnah and the League in its demands for Pakistan. Now, if that is a solution, I could apply it to Great Britain. And, within one week, I would bring such disagreements to the fore that England, Wales, and Scotland would squabble like rabid dogs.'

Jawahar nodded as he sipped tea. 'The Viceroy requested my estimate of Jinnah.'

'And?'

'I let him know that Jinnah's success, which has come late to him in life, is his capacity for a permanently negative attitude. He knows Pakistan would never stand up to constructive criticism, and has ensured it should never be subjected to it.' Placing the cup on the table, he sat back in his chair. 'The important thing is that the British have announced pack up, and the Viceroy appears a man we can work with. He specifically stated in his first meeting that his intent is not to wind up British Raj as the last Viceroy, but to lead the way to the new India as the first. Even Bapu thinks we can trust in his honesty of purpose.'

'Perhaps,' Vallabh shrugged. 'He is a Tory admiral though, and, as his chief of staff, he has brought Ismay, one of Churchill's favourite generals.'

'I think we have room for manoeuvre.'

Jawahar had told the Viceroy frankly that Wavell's decision to invite the Muslim League to join the interim government had been a serious blunder. The League was determined to sabotage any economic planning from the centre, aware that the success of such planning would ipso facto undermine the case of Panjab for Pakistan. He had put forward to the Viceroy his previous proposal of a tripartite administration of Panjab on communal lines, with a central authority on major non-communal subjects as a way to break the deadlock.

'And bitterness is not an answer. Instead, we need astuteness and patience. We have not fought for so long to yield it all to the Raj's machinations. Churchill, even in Opposition, had exhorted Wavell to keep a bit of India … even as much of it had to be yielded. Acting worse than any housewife bargaining with a baniya for that additional free sheaf of coriander. Fitting for a nation of grocers.' Vallabh smirked.

Jawahar handed the three-petalled palash that looked like a crown to Manibehn, who was helping a servant clear the table. The two men left the room. Cradling the flower in one palm, Manibehn stacked saucers and heard her father use one of his favourite proverbs.

In Kheda, Borsad, and Nadiad, indeed in various parts of India, she had heard him speak at rallies and connect with the people through his use of everyday proverbs. He was a man of the soil like them, they understood him and followed him as their Sardar. When did they begin to address him thus? Was it in 1928, when he led the farmers of Borsad in their strike against the tax hike? Was it when he was the leader of the farmers' milk cooperative against the British? Or earlier, when he first started working with Bapu? Not that the genealogy mattered. Sardar: Chief, in Hindi, Urdu, Persian, Gujarati – in most Indian languages – and its meaning was clear. She watched the figures recede as her father's words played in her mind.

'The dog walking under the bullock cart can claim that he is pulling the cart. We should let Mountbatten believe he is the architect and we the masons completing the building in sync with the architect's plans.'

17
Laur (April 1947)

Great planning had gone into arranging their meeting via notes Tara had written – and Pammi had passed on through Asad – to Sepoy Malik. Now, he brought to it his military skill of stealth and reconnaissance as he surveyed the wedding – of a wealthy relative with a large landholding by the banks of the Ravi river – from a carefully chosen spot. Tara snuck out at the pre-arranged time. It was a moonless night. Leading her to a disused boat shrouded by tall weeds near the riverbank, he showed her the special gift he'd carried with him. After Tara's lacklustre response to the snow globe, Sepoy Malik was hoping this would do the trick. He'd thought of showing her his rifle, but guns were commonplace in Panjab.

Olive green, plumper than the fattest bitter gourd she had ever seen, it was what he called a 'Mills bomb'. A souvenir of the war he had fought, so potent that when the safety pin was tugged, he indicated a latch, it could kill a room full of men.

'How many men did you kill?' Tara asked.

'You don't want to know. But here,' he pulled out of his pocket the medal, strung on a black thread, the brass dimly glowing in the darkness, and proceeded to put it around her neck. 'With this, I wed thee,' he proclaimed in English.

She tittered. 'You have returned an angrej, is it?'

'I have returned after licking the angrej's enemy! In my spare time, I picked up gitter-mitter,' he said, hoping to make her laugh at their colloquial for the English language.

She felt the cold medal against her neck. 'Say more, in Angreji.'

'Care for a fag?' Malik drew a tin of cigarettes from his shirt pocket, the tremble in his hand hidden by the dark. Extracting one, he lit it with deliberation using a lighter, before blowing out a thin jet of smoke. During the war, cigarettes were plentiful.

From the look in her eyes, he knew he was making an impression. English phrases and words tumbled out of him, disconnected, disjointed … but who cared? In the three years he'd been away, Tara had blossomed like the kachnar flower; he spoke to impress, she listened to be impressed.

'Stand firm. Dig for victory. The need is great, time is short.'

A draw from the cigarette.

'Rats as big as cats. Yes, sir! Whiz bang. Flaming onion. Bum fodder.'

A spiral of smoke.

'Careless talk costs lives. Mr Hitler wants to know! Whirra whirra whirra phut phut phut!'

With his free hand, the gabbling sepoy took her palm and placed it on his groin. It throbbed and grew beneath her hand. He babbled on, his eyes on her. His hand above hers, he guided her.

'We're up against it! To victory, together!'

The heat in the boat dispelled the vapours arising from the water's chilly surface. Too many layers of clothing came in the sepoy's way; silk and brocade and embroidered beads slid and crinkled and detached as young Malik flung away the cigarette and latched on a dewy mouth—

He found himself being pushed away; the gabbling had stopped, the magic suspended.

A song from the trenches rose in Sepoy Malik and burst through in its mangled melodious form, his dulcet voice elevating the ditty to exotic high art.

Just think of th' boys at th' front,
No beer, no whisky, no cunt;
They shit in their trenches
Think of their wenches,
Cheer up, m' boys, fuck 'em all!

Tara leaned in until their foreheads touched. 'Say, Sikandar, in my three years of waiting, how many white women did you kiss?'

The smell of roses filled his nostrils, his eyes were glued to Tara's cleavage, where moisture shone like silver. And yet a hand sprang to his throat as Malik swore, 'By god, Tara! The only way I slept was by imagining us like this.'

Momentarily shy, Tara's eyelids dipped. And the sepoy leaned in for a kiss.

'Keep singing,' Tara muttered.

A breast to caress, a beating heart, a taut abdomen slick with sweat. As long as the sepoy sang, he had treasures to dig.

'Fuck 'em all. Fuck fuck fuck 'em all!'

Later, head averted, she assembled herself back so she could be seen in a gathering without drawing comment. He waited, picking out her form in the darkness that his eyes had got used to. Having exhausted his fount of English, he was now quietly content. The cricket's chirruping sounded clear in the misty night. Returning the medal because his mother would miss it, Tara hastened away. Until she looked back, a lock of hair sprung loose like another invitation, massaging an upright Mills bomb in her palms. 'I will keep this as souvenir.'

'Oye!' Malik stirred from his languor. He had not meant for her to take it. 'Watch out, Tara, it's dangerous!'

'Not more dangerous than me.' And Tara was off, her laughter tinkling on the mist-shrouded banks of the Ravi.

18
Delhi (April 1947)

At 10 a.m. Dickie Mountbatten began his meeting with the provincial governors who had arrived from across India with first-hand reports for the Viceroy, and to discuss a possible political plan going forward. Bombay, Madras, Panjab, Sind, United Provinces, Bihar, Orissa, Assam, Central Province, the North Western Frontier Province – only the Governor of Bengal was missing because of ill health. The men sat anti-clockwise in order of precedence around the large oval table.

Dickie started with an appeal for loyalty to the letter and spirit of the British Government's decision to exit India. And, to alleviate any pending doubts, reiterated that June 1948 was a firm departure date. To further set the tone of his reign as Viceroy, Dickie repeated the remark Pamela had overheard.

'Gentlemen, I invite your cooperation in sending home anybody who expresses sentiments of this type. And do not tell me that Wavell would never have done it. Well, I'm not Wavell ... and I will not stand this.'

Dickie spoke soberly as he sat upright in his chair and addressed the seated governors. 'I realize this is early stages, but from my preliminary talks with various representatives of the Congress and the Muslim League, I can see little common ground on which to build any agreed solution for the future of India. I can say that the *absence* of common ground is emerging. A truly united India looks doubtful ... Apart from Gandhi, all the other leaders seem to tacitly accept that a partition in some form is a ground reality.'

In the sombre, panelled Council Chamber, the air conditioning at gelid, Dickie Mountbatten was at the helm. 'It is clear that we need an alternative to the Cabinet Mission's Plan – partition with certain powers reserved to a central authority, perhaps.' With that he opened the floor for the governors to initiate their updates.

Assam began with its account and everything was quite benign. But before Dickie could begin to exhale, the report from Bengal stated that the province, with Muslims and Hindus in roughly equal numbers, was in great agitation. Even if partition was considered, East Bengal would become a rural slum, a concept unacceptable to many Muslims. Additionally, the relationship between Jinnah and the Muslim premier of Bengal, Suhrawardy, was fractious. In turn, Suhrawardy was ready to play with the Hindus.

British rule in India had begun with Bengal with a hero of the Empire, Robert Clive, winning the Battle of Plassey. Calcutta, India's largest city, became the capital of the British Indian Empire. With a population of 62 million people, it was the largest province, despite an earlier partition in 1905 for administrative reasons by Viceroy Curzon. Bengalis, deeming that split to be along religious lines, had protested with demonstrations and strikes, until it snowballed into a wider Indian protest about

British rule. More recently, Jinnah had declared, 'We shall have India divided or we shall have India destroyed', and called for a Direct Action Day to showcase how they would get Pakistan if denied to them. The Great Calcutta Killings that resulted had spread to Bihar and Panjab like conflagration.

'I've learnt from my briefings,' Dickie wagged his head, 'what starts in Bengal never stays in Bengal.'

Next, Sir Olaf Caroe, looking rather tense and tired, began his update on the situation in the North-West Frontier Province. 'The province is an anomaly: More than 90 per cent Muslim, it returned a Congress government in the elections of 1945. If India were to be partitioned, NWFP would stew with controversy. The Muslim League will want it for Pakistan, the Congress will insist it stay with India. I think we need fresh elections in the province.'

'But does not the premier, Dr Khan Sahib, enjoy the confidence of his people?' Dickie asked.

'The premier, and his more famous brother, Khan Abdul Ghaffar Khan – a charismatic Pashtun leader and a close friend of Gandhi, so much so that he is called the "Frontier Gandhi" – do *not* want an election. They lead the pro-Congress "Red Shirt" group, on account of their brick-coloured garb. But the tide is turning, I'm afraid.'

'How so?'

Caroe rubbed his hands. 'How so, how so,' he muttered. 'Let's see ... The ongoing communal tension in other parts of India has affected the province. Mr Nehru, during his visit in October last year, personally witnessed the disaffection with the Congress – he faced hostile demonstrations throughout his visit, including some stone throwing he barely escaped. The Pashtuns are Muslim warriors, and clearly do not want to go under the suzerainty of Hindus, which is how they view the

Congress. The Muslim League is a natural ally, and has in turn intensified its propaganda amongst the tribes.'

Dickie angled his chin as he thought over the matter. 'Appears like a drastic turn in events indeed. Where is Mr Khan in all of this, with his popularity amongst his people?'

Olaf Caroe exhaled deeply, as if in the midst of a tiresome instruction. 'Ghaffar Khan is viewed as a party politician – an approach which doesn't sit well with the independent Pathans. I would encourage His Excellency to fly down to Peshawar for a personal assessment. I believe you will find the NWFP is indeed on the point of crisis.'

On that ominous note, they broke for lunch.

An hour later, as the men made their way back to resume the Governors' Conference, Olaf Caroe was in animated conversation with Dickie, extolling the virtues of the Frontier landscape. 'To cross the bridge at Attock, where the Kabul river meets the Indus and where the Hindu Kush mountains loom large, is to come home.'

'Ah, an Eastern version of your Scottish Highlands,' Dickie mused.

The session resumed with Sir Evan Jenkins, Governor of Panjab. Regarded as a diligent, thorough administrator with a cool mind, he had taken over the state administration following the resignation of the premier of Panjab in early March.

'I am convinced that the situation is critical,' Jenkins began.

Thereafter, it was all downhill as Dickie further gleaned the complex mosaic that was Panjab.

'The Panjab province of 30 million people has been governed as one unit for ninety-eight years. Panjab and Bengal are huge provinces both, where Muslims and Hindus exist in roughly equal numbers. However, the Panjab situation is further complicated by a significant population of Sikhs, as you know.'

Jenkins mopped his brow. The thundering air conditioning was clearly not helping.

'Thousands of Sikhs fought in WWII. Demobilized thereafter, they still have their weapons. They will lose no time in assembling into a rough and ready army.' Jenkins cleared his throat. 'My years in the province have shown me that Panjab can only be ruled by consensus, not fiat.'

Dickie steepled his hands and glanced around.

'This is indeed a vexed situation,' he said. 'His Majesty's Government would like to transfer power to a united India. But the communal situation is grave, and escalating, and our departure date is fixed. Alternatives, gentlemen?'

Silence, heavy as a pall, hung over the oval table.

Until Jenkins decided to cleave it.

'In the eventuality that Panjab is to be partitioned, I'd assign a suitable name,' Jenkins paused, and from under his bushy eyebrows, gazed at the gathering. 'Operation Solomon.'

The biblical allusion was not lost upon any man in the room. Just as King Solomon had advised for the baby of squabbling mothers to be equally divided and shared between the two, the partition of Panjab would be wholly unnatural and extremely violent.

As the session concluded, men tumbled out into the Mughal Gardens for a group photo with Edwina and the wives who had accompanied the governors. With them, and yet apart, Dickie mulled over the conundrum he was facing. If India was to be partitioned, so would the two provinces at its eastern and western extremities. And yet, they benefitted greatly from their unity. Any attempt to divide them would only poison the communal fabric and destroy the centuries-old harmony of the provinces ...

In the group photograph, Dickie – seated in the middle of the front row, legs crossed at ankles, hands in lap, Edwina to his left and the governors' wives flanking them both, the governors standing behind two rows deep – managed a smooth brow and a modest smile. In his mind, though, was the tumult of dark forebodings on Bengal, Panjab, and the Frontier; even the quieter provinces seemed like they were sitting on the edge of a volcano. Indeed, a decision had to be reached quickly. What loomed ahead was the risk of a complete breakdown of administration. Which could mean one thing alone.

Civil war.

19
Laur (April 1947)

As Mehmood walked down the road, he rolled his shoulders to relieve the sore muscles. Another long day of hoisting trunks and tokris, bags and holdalls, up umpteen stairs and down unending platforms, had come to an end. Was it just his feeling or was all of Panjab packing up suitcases and heading elsewhere? He could swear some passengers were moving house piecemeal – their baggage included rolled-up bedding, moorahs, and dressers! Heavy unwieldy items were not a coolie's delight. Exhausted, he wanted to sink into his jute bed. Some days, Mehmood wondered what he would be doing if he had not followed his father in the profession? He twirled one tip of his moustache, a habit that facilitated his thinking. Or so he thought. Beli Ram scoffed that it was a trick to make Mehmood appear aloof, like he was some nawab. The recollection made Mehmood snort.

He could hear crickets chirping and the night air was cool despite the heat of the day. Whilst the railway station was bustling at midnight, the area leading to Mohalla Barkat lay quiet. Mehmood was at the crossroad when shadowy figures suddenly leapt out at him.

'Oye!' Mehmood started, stumbling backward.

The men, their faces half-covered with the loose ends of turbans or other cloth, had him surrounded. They studied him with unblinking eyes. Four of them. But this was not the scary part. In their hands were a scythe, a lance, a knife, and a lathi – enough to make minced mutton of him. Mehmood felt sweat sprout on his forehead.

'Padshaho,' he said in an even voice, addressing the men as 'kings' despite clear evidence that they were rogues. But that Lauri term of endearment was meant to disarm, to signal that no offense was meant or taken.

'Mehmood Bhatti,' a gruff voice said. 'Where are you coming from?'

They *knew* him?

'Laur Junction, padshaho.'

'Without your sidekick, we see,' another man laughed.

When Mehmood didn't join in the laughter, the man dipped his head and stared. 'The Hindu runt you keep by your side.'

Why were the men interested in Beli Ram? Mehmood twirled his moustache as he thought.

'Oye,' a man tapped Mehmood's shoulder with his lathi. 'Are you into laundebaazi? You like boys, hmm?'

Mehmood recoiled. 'Have the ladies of Laur been granted paradise, gentlemen? For why would I commit such a grievous error?'

A couple of the men burst out laughing. In the distance, a horn tooted.

The man with the lance lowered the cloth from his face, letting it hang around his neck. He had the beginning of a beard which did not hide his firm jaw. 'Listen, Mehmood,' he said, his voice low and authoritative, 'we are from Mozang. And we are here to guard our Muslim mohallas … like Barkat. So what business brings Hindu men like Beli Ram there?'

Beli Ram had been coming to Barkat since before these men were born, likely. What business was it of theirs? But Mehmood knew better than to voice his thoughts.

'You are well informed, so you would know how my father, Ghulam Bhatti – may Allah grant him peace – rescued the poor orphan child and took him under his wings. He used to beg on the station. Abba started him off as a tea boy, then trained him to be a coolie. Beli Ram and I practically grew up together.'

'Be it so, that doesn't make him a Mussalman, though.'

'That I agree. Makes him part-family though?'

'Why not convert the pehnchod then?' another man snarled. 'Do we need more Hindu infestation in Laur?'

Mehmood nodded slowly, as if pondering the suggestion. When Abba started to wean Beli Ram from his relative – one of the resident beggars of Laur Junction, who pocketed the orphan's alms – Beli lost the piece of tarp on which he spent his nights. Ghulam Bhatti had five mouths to feed already, to which he added a sixth, to his wife's consternation. Beli Ram made sure to turn in his daily earnings to Begum Bhatti, which ensured the boy had a roof over his head. Until he could rent a one-room dwelling.

'Listen, Mehmood!'

The man with the lance, clearly the leader, held up one hand. 'A battle's coming. It will be won by the side that's best prepared. Now you are Mussalman, like us – we know where your loyalty is. But this Hindu whose very name is after a Hindu god, the pehnchod can only be on the enemy side. Right? The line is very clear. And to reinforce it, we are putting up barricades at entrances to our mohallas and keeping watch. Like today.'

A truck approached, drowning the man's voice. They waited for it to pass. The leader surveyed the crossroads.

Released from the man's interrogation, Mehmood rolled his shoulders. Wasn't Data Ganj Baksh the patron saint of all Lauris? Be they Hindu or Mussalman, Sikh or Parsi, rich or poor ... Where were the barricades at the famed shrine?

'So,' the lance man raised his brows, 'make sure we never sight your Hindu friend in the mohalla again.'

Did they even know Beli Ram? That he fasted on Eid? Because how could he eat when Mehmood couldn't?

'In a time like this,' the man with the scythe spoke in a thick raspy voice, 'what need is there of kuffar friends?'

'Padshaho,' Mehmood offered a placatory smile, 'Beli Ram was brought up by my Abba, as I said. He's almost family.'

'In which case, it's time to *make* him family. Take him to a qazi and get him converted. Swell our numbers, we need more men.'

Bloody war-returned soldiers! So long had they been on the battlefield that they needed another war to keep them occupied now. Every Muhurram, Beli Ram gathered flowers to shower on the procession. Every Ramleela, Mehmood and he went to Minto Park to catch the action together. Holi, Diwali, Eid – all were occasions for sweets. What conversion were these idiots talking of?

Mehmood continued to smile and nod, his mind churning, one hand sharpening a moustache tip. Meanwhile, a couple of men walking in the direction of Mohalla Barkat were sighted. Before heading off to accost them, Lance-man slapped Mehmood on his back.

'Remember what we discussed. Otherwise, next time we encounter Beli Ram, we'll have to pull down his pyjama for verification!'

20
Delhi (April 1947)

The aerial survey revealed broken mosques, burning hamlets, corpses spread over a mile ... Jawahar's brow was furrowed as the plane flew over fields waterlogged because of the monsoon. Soon, a crowd came into view ... 15,000-strong, at least ... armed with axes, spears, torches. On a rampage.

Jawahar turned to Lt Gen. Roy Bucher to land.

'No way!' Boucher shouted. 'I cannot allow that.'

'I insist,' Jawahar half stood up.

A reluctant Bucher began to lower the plane.

Jawahar jumped out as cries of 'Jai Hind!' and 'Mahatma Gandhi ki Jai!' greeted him.

The useless chants made his blood boil as he faced them.

'Why are you massacring your Muslim neighbours?' he shouted. 'Where is the victory to Bapu if you become a bloody mob?'

The horde shifted uneasily around him as he looked into their eyes. What blood lust had converted these simple Hindu farmers into killing machines – their axes smeared like those of

111

butchers? He continued with his berating and threatening. He would bomb them by air if they did not cease the killing. They would have to murder him first, trample over his corpse, and satisfy their lust for blood. His breath came rapid, shallow, as he faced them down.

Behind him stood an uneasy Bucher, hand on his weapon.

Jawahar's chest heaved. The air was heavy with moisture, sticky with the smell of sweat and blood, as flies droned overhead.

'Go back then!'

A scruffy man hoisted a spear as he advanced towards Jawahar. 'Go back!'

Incensed, Jawahar was at the man's throat before either of them realized. He wrestled him to the ground, mud squelching as they pummelled, ringed by feet, bare, slippered, mud-caked, bruised, the spear limp on the ground. A shot cracked the air, the circle shifted and Jawahar was physically removed from his wrestling companion by Bucher.

'Steady,' the Lt Gen. growled, gun in his right hand as he watched the throng.

An indignant Jawahar glared at the sullen onlookers. Behind him, the plane whirred.

'We should leave,' Bucher said through gritted teeth.

The ringleader on the ground was stirring. Hands reached down to hoist him up.

Go back!

The cry came from somewhere deep within the mob. It was picked up by the sullen crowd and rang around them. Until, a new one joined the chorus.

'Jawaharlal murdabad!'

Death to Jawaharlal!

He screamed.

Jawahar was sitting up in his bed. The window curtain showed the barest hint of light outside. Pre-dawn. He had screamed in his sleep. Heart thudding, Jawahar breathed deeply, trying to calm down. Another nightmare. They had become frequent of late.

He swung his legs off the bed and walked around the room.

He felt a weight on his shoulders. In a brisk move, he removed his linen kurta, tossed it on the bed, bent double at his waist, placed his palms on the floor, tucked his toes, lifted his hips and, in one agile move, completed the headstand. He could count on it to calm his mind. The tiled floor was cool against his skin. Inhaling deeply, he sought repose.

The incident his mind had recalled was in the aftermath of Noakhali last November. When the Muslim League's henchmen had led death squads to an orgy of communal violence in Calcutta. In turn, the RSS cadres had joined the fray in neighbouring Bihar, where Hindu peasants had turned butchers to avenge Noakhali. He had seen it first-hand. And his body hadn't forgotten …

Was Bapu right then?

He said Mahabharata, the story of feuding brothers, was in the blood of Indians. He feared the demand for Pakistan would lead to that atavistic path of destruction.

And yet, above all, the Mahabharata was a story of dharma. When every individual followed his dharma, cosmic dharma was maintained. When he didn't, it was adharma. Pralaya.

Bapu was in Bihar, trying to act as a healing balm for stricken individuals … and failing. Noakhali had spurred Bengali Hindus towards partition, even as the killings in Bihar had convinced Bengali Muslims of the need to break from 'Hindu' India. The plague had spread through the rest of the country: Brother was drinking brother's blood.

21
Laur (April 1947)

L ahore was starting to burn.
It was not just the unseasonable heat, conflagrations were flaring up between communities, cohorts, comrades. Even as love was, at least in the patch of weeds beside the bank of the Ravi, where Tara and her sepoy rendezvoused.

'Tell me, O sepoy from the Great War,' Tara asked Malik one day, 'how do you best volley a soda bottle such that it makes its mark?'

Tara's father ran a store that sold soda water bottles in Anarkali, Lahore's fancy market with its prized stores of apparel, hosiery, shoes, and the eponymous pomegranate juice. Named after a legendary dancing girl, whose beauty rivalled that of a pomegranate blossom's, the bazaar cashed in on the association, its juice regarded as the most savoury, the defining taste attributed to secret ingredients that each shop claimed it uniquely added.

'Tch! Tara!' Sepoy Malik swatted a fly that came between them. He knew what she was alluding to.

Tara's father was canny enough to bottle fresh pomegranate juice and sell it, leveraging off the natural synergy of being in the glass bottle trade, and did healthy business with the royal fruit of the Mughals. But in early 1947, what had started to occupy the businessman was not growing revenues but exploring the lethal potential of thick glass soda bottles. One such bottle, lobbed from a height, could serve as an effective missile. Stockpiling empty soda bottles was not good for trade, but it was great for defence. Quietly, he had arranged for one truck to be delivered home at night. Under the cover of darkness, the family carted the bottles to the rooftop, arranging them such that they could be gathered and lobbed at top speed, without wasting precious time.

'We could be the next target,' Tara shrugged. Her father had insisted as much as they stood on the rooftop of their two-storey house – carefully stacking the soda bottles. With its aerial view for reconnaissance and a vantage point for defence, it was the appropriate lookout point. Of late, before nightfall, people bolted gates, barricaded doors, barred windows and then trooped to rooftops to scout for flames. Flames signalled rampaging hordes. Perhaps Father was right? Tara recalled the grenade, hidden under the many layers of her trousseau in her trunk. A shadow crossed her mind: What if she never got to wear the silks and satins …

'Your father's become paranoid,' Malik hissed. 'This is madness! Lauris seem to be preparing for war, but listen to me, a WWII returnee. We just have to wait for the British to quit India. That was the pact between them and the Congress. And once they leave, both communities will get hold of their—'

'Aim for the face,' Tara interrupted him.

'Whaaat?'

'It's most vulnerable to glass shards.' Then she elaborated how her father had wasted several bottles – a sin for a thrifty trader – in teaching the family how to aim for the face.

'Really, Tara,' Malik shook his head in exasperation. She could be so obstinate. He had attempted to get the grenade back, but she insisted upon keeping it as a token of his love. All he wanted was to link hands with his beloved and watch the tall mustard sway in the breeze, smell the rain-dappled moist earth, whisper sweet nothings to her and plan for the future because the past needed to be put behind. Even the sight of his poorly leg did not dampen his enthusiasm and optimistic planning for what awaited, because, bloody hell, he had already paid the price for his future!

'You should not encourage him, Tara – the war is over and we have a future to look forward to.'

Tara removed her hand from his and sat upright. Her eyes glinted as sunlight, dappled by the leaves of the mango tree beneath which they sat, lit up her tresses. Her nose was as sharp as a scimitar, upon which her nose pin shone; her skin the colour of golden wheat; her mouth, generous—

He was about to kiss her when she pushed him away.

'Just because you fought a war in foreign-land, don't forget that people at home also know violence.'

22
Delhi (May 1947)

'Until I went to Kahuta, I had not appreciated the magnitude of the horrors that are going on.'

Dickie's recent visit to NWFP and Panjab had been illustrative, at the least. Jenkins had driven Edwina and him to a little village 25 miles from Rawalpindi. It was representative of India's half-million villages, except, it was lain to complete waste. All 3500 residents dead. Burnt shells of homes left behind. Because Muslim miscreants had attacked the village.

Pug nodded. 'If we do not make up our minds on what we are going to do within the next two months or so, there will be pandemonium.'

His bulldog jaw, which had lent the nickname 'Pug' to General Hastings Lionel Ismay, made his manner appear lugubrious – or did he *truly* believe the situation was irretrievable? Dickie waited for his chief of staff to complete his thought.

'And if we do – make up our minds that is – there will be pandemonium,' Pug concluded.

Dickie tapped his desk and gazed at the Ashoka trees extending like sentries down the Mughal Gardens. Any other man could be accused of hyperbole, but this was Churchill's former chief of staff, the eyes and ears of the Prime Minister who oversaw World War II as a generalissimo. Dickie had arrived in India thinking that the deadline of June 1948 for Britain's exit was hurried; needlessly, as some in London had cautioned. But he was increasingly convinced he could not afford to wait that long. According to all accounts, in Panjab, all parties were seriously preparing for civil war, and, of these, by far the most business-like were the Sikhs. They were bent upon avenging the Muslim killings. Ismay evidently shared his misgivings.

Dickie turned his head to ask, 'Was there anything in particular that triggered that foreboding?'

'Reports are coming in daily of the communal violence. It is spreading, like some devouring flame.'

'But we have to balance our desire for speed against the framing of a workable solution.'

'Certainly.' Ismay's jaw was set.

'Yet?' Dickie prodded.

'I get the feeling that the mine may go off any moment. The situation everywhere is electric.'

Pug was not a man prone to panic. When Dickie had offered him the post of his chief of staff, Ismay had voiced that it was one of the most delicate, and perhaps distasteful, assignments imaginable for a Viceroy. However, he had added, 'If you are going out to play the last chukka twelve goals down, count me in on your team.' It was definitely the last chukka – that much Dickie had ensured from Whitehall with the agreement on a deadline for the transfer of power. And the use of that sporting metaphor was unsurprising considering polo was Churchill's favourite sport, and Ismay one of Churchill's favourite generals.

According to the ex-Prime Minister, no one ever came to grief through riding horses, unless of course they broke their necks – which, taken at a gallop, was a very good death to die. But Dickie Mountbatten had no intention of dying.

Ismay's chukka metaphor was apt though ... They were in the land that had birthed the term chukker, and Dickie was determined to leave India in good shape. The troubling question really was the assessment of how many goals down they were.

In the rocky foothills of the North-West Frontier Province, he had faced a surging sea of rifles and guns in the arms of excited Pathans shouting, 'Pakistan zindabad!' The previous evening, a shot was fired through a window of the Government House – the Pathan supporters of Muslim League voicing their opinion loud and clear. He had chosen not to dress in stars and orders, considering it was not a formal occasion. His green bush shirt was the colour of a Haji who had made the pilgrimage to holy Mecca. And then, it burst forth: 'Mountbatten zindabad!' Green, the colour of Islam, had saved his skin. But it had also become clear to Dickie that the situation in the province required immediate attention.

'We need a referendum in NWFP to assess the will of the people before the government of the province can adopt any stance over a partition.'

'Nehru doesn't want a referendum,' Pug shrugged.

'Because the Congress will lose the Frontier.'

In which case, another obstacle ahead would be Nehru ...

Dickie tapped the desk with his knuckles. 'To arrive at no decision at all might be the worst of all. At this early stage, I can see little common ground on which to build any agreed solution for the future of India. Jinnah is not willing to manoeuvre, and without his agreement, unity can only be imposed on India by force of arms.

'Truth is, I have not been able to crack Jinnah, and this has never happened to me before.' He sighed. 'But it is also clear, as this white-hot day, that we cannot cede the entire Panjab to him.'

Ismay inclined his head. 'We need an alternative to the Cabinet Mission's Plan.'

'Indeed. India divided into three units perhaps: Hindustan, Pakistan, and the princely states. And certain powers vested in a central authority. What do you think?'

Pug Ismay straightened and gave a crooked smile. 'That would satisfy nobody.'

'Precisely. Whatever option I look at, somebody is going to be distressed.'

When Dickie had accompanied his cousin, the Prince of Wales, on his visit to India in 1921, he had traversed the length and breadth of South Asia. The new vistas, experiences, games – he had gone dippy over polo! – had stimulated him immensely. He had speared his first pig in Jodhpur, hunted black buck from the Rolls-Royce of the Maharaja of Bharatpur, shot his first tiger in Nepal … Yet, the incident that was surfacing frequently since his Viceregal turn was that of the black panther he'd shot in Patiala. How his pride had nosedived when he had discovered the animal had been removed from a zoo and doped.

Dickie slapped the desk and stood up.

'Time to call the play-acting bluff. I am convinced that all the leaders, with the exception of Gandhi, have tacitly accepted the idea of partition. Pug, I depute you to work out the details of an alternative strategy.'

23
Laur (May 1947)

'Don't take me the wrong way, Kishan Singh-a! Unlike you, I'm not educated. So, I speak my mind plainly. And I speak what I see. Iqbal warned me that you are a big city gentleman. That you work in an office, unlike us village folks.'

Jujhar Singh smiled gamely as he coaxed his whiskers with his fingers. He was a bear of a man, with abundant facial hair that reached down to his chest. His eyes crinkled with merriment or perhaps it was his plump ruddy cheeks that gave that impression. In a white lungi–kurta, he sported a turquoise turban printed with yellow squares. He had arrived that Sunday afternoon from Lyallpur, bearing a sack of wheat from Iqbal Singh. Jujhar Singh was in the city to meet with other organizers who were trying to raise funds. Eighteen prominent Sikh leaders had issued an appeal to the Panth to contribute at least Re 1 per head for a 50-lakh fund to enable the Sikh community to fight Pakistan.

Kishan Singh shook his head. 'You embarrass me, Singh saab. Of course, I will contribute. I am just not sure if I can motivate others to do so …'

'And why is that?'

Kishan massaged his hands as he reflected on the older man's question. His mind had begun a poem at some point:

Of late, I fear the blush of dawn,
The day it yields is a rash—

'Hmm?' Jujhar Singh prodded.

Kishan returned to the enquiry. What was the reason for his reluctance? The request, after all, was to raise money for a right cause. At a time when each community was looking out for its own people, wasn't it only appropriate then that the Sikh quom did the same? Otherwise, between the Hindu–Muslim blades, the Sikh might get chopped …

'My worry is that … if every community is concerned only with its own … who will think of Panjab?'

'Your concern is valid, Kishan. But tell me, what is Panjab if not you and me and Iqbal and all of us Panjabis put together? Including your Muslim neighbour and your Hindu officewala. Our Panjab has Parsee and Isai too. Has had for a long, long time. Why, our ancestors even welcomed the angrej, despite the fact that they look like a monkey's bottom.' Jujhar let out a hearty laugh.

Kishan Singh grinned. He had read hilarious accounts of those first encounters. The Panjabi dressed in loose garments to survive the heat of the plains. The English in their tight-fitting trousers and flushed faces were an arresting anomaly.

'Only problem is that lately,' Jujhar Singh's smile faded, 'some Mussalmans have decided they want to make Panjab Pakistan. How can we allow that, tell me?'

Jujhar Singh stretched his legs, coaxed his feet out of his well-worn juttis and began to rub them against each other. 'What happened in Kahuta, huh? From where did the Muslim horde arrive? Like a pack of wolves, they descended upon the sleeping village. With buckets of petrol, too … Setting fire to Sikh and Hindu houses. Those who escaped from their burning homes were doused with petrol and became human torches. Such carnage!'

Kishan sighed. 'I read the fire swept to the Muslim quarter as well, and completely destroyed Kahuta.'

Jujhar Singh nodded. 'Why then, brother Kishan, do you hesitate? The Mussalman is not bad. But his leaders are. Jinnah and his ilk. They are demanding their precious Pakistan, and they want to build it over our lands, our homes, our corpses even.' On that ominous note, the older man slid his feet back into his juttis and stood up. 'Okay then, I'll be off.'

Kishan walked him to the makeshift barricade at the entrance to the colony. He stood there for some time, watching the tall figure of Jujhar Singh recede. Returning home, he sighted a truck being loaded several houses down from his own. Why, it was the residence of Nishtar Singh Arora! He walked up to enquire.

The wooden gate was wide open as men walked in and out, carrying furniture and bedding. Nishtar Singh's older son stood in the verandah overseeing the men.

'Son!' Kishan Singh hailed him. 'Where is your father?'

The young man wished him, dipped his head, instructed one of the passing men, then hurried towards Kishan. 'Sorry, Kishan Singh ji, these men have already broken a few items. I thought Father had told you. Though, it has been rather sudden.'

'Told me what?'

'That we are moving to Ambarsar.'

'M-moving? But why?'

The young man exhaled. 'Father is convinced that Pakistan is coming.'

Kishan shrugged. 'And he knows that Ambarsar will not be in Pakistan?'

'He hopes … Also, Laur is getting unsafe with each day. My sisters and mother were sent away much earlier—Oye! Watch that table's glass top. Sorry, Kishan ji, I have to—'

'But your shop …' They did a brisk trade in papar-variyan. 'This house?' Kishan Singh addressed the young man's back.

'We source our papar-vari from Ambarsar only – it's a family business, and we have relatives in the wholesale trade there. Father sold our Laur shop to buy another one in Ambarsar. The house – we're still looking for a buyer. Are *you* interested?'

∽

After he reached home, Kishan Singh was too agitated to sit or lie down. He paced the verandah, the garden outside ablaze in the afternoon sun. Inside, his daughters were studying for their respective exams. He could hear Narinder's recitation above the hum of the fan.

Nishtar Singh had upped and left so abruptly. Not even a word said. Admittedly, the two men were not the best of friends, mere neighbours, but they were the only two Sikh families in the colony … With Nishtar quitting, he was the lone one left. And the Sharmas across had moved out too; though, Dinanath had retired from his government job and returned to his ancestral home in Jammu.

Still.

'Bapuji,' Pammi popped her head through a living room window that overlooked the verandah. 'Isn't it too hot outside? Why don't you take some rest? Or read? I'll bring you a glass of sherbet?'

Kishan stopped his frenzied pacing and smiled at his daughter. Her radiant face would cheer him any day. He nodded, stepped inside and shut the netted door. As he walked to his bedroom, he recalled that Nishtar Singh's older daughter was with Surinder in Class X. The matriculation exams were just a few weeks away. Why then had Nishtar plucked his daughter out of school before she could sit for her exam and complete her matriculation? What had spooked him so? Besides, Nishtar was a pucca Arora businessman who would never relocate house and business without being certain that the new city was a better prospect than his old one.

As he took off his slippers and sat on the cool bed, Kishan Singh realized he needed to start thinking like other alert Panjabis, men like Jujhar and Nishtar, who were keenly observing which way the wind was blowing. Meanwhile, he, Kishan, had buried his head in newspapers and developed paralysis. So what should he do?

Whom could he turn to for information? In Laur … in Ambarsar … in Dilli …

He racked his brain. Instead, it completed the poem he had begun earlier.

Of late, I fear the blush of dawn,
The day it yields is a rash—
of wild stories,
For the fingers to gouge and scratch.
Dusk is bloody therefore.
Night gives no respite,
I toss and turn,
And awake to a rash that has grown.

Not half-bad, it would need more work. But, he forced himself to the dire matter at hand. Laur … Ambarsar … Dilli …

Dilli! Of course! Dilli. How had he been so thick?

Kishan leapt out of bed towards the narrow desk where he kept his books and pens. Cousin Shamsher worked in Dilli. Had so for long enough that they had not seen him in years, but ... His hands shaking, Kishan snatched a notepad and pen, and sat down to write a letter. Shamsher was employed in the Viceroy House. One in a staff of over 5000 or so. Shamsher had to know something about Pakistan – where, when, how ... Either way, he would know more than Kishan Singh, who, at the moment, was feeling like a lost cow.

On that hopeful note, he began to write a letter as Pammi entered with a glass of sherbet.

24
Delhi (May 1947)

Vallabh gazed out of the window of his study. A crow was perched atop the garden tap, angled such that its beak probed the mouth, seeking water. He made a mental note to ask Manibehn to keep an earthen vessel of water near the tap. It was not just the leaders who were feeling the heat.

The country was roiling. Caught in the cauldron, unable to see beyond its confines, people would realize too late that the fire had scorched them all. Reports of violence in Panjab and Bengal were arriving with alarming regularity. Just that day, there were fresh incidents of violence against Hindus and Sikhs in parts of the NWFP. When he met the Viceroy, who had recently returned from visiting the province, Vallabh had been blunt.

'There is a civil war on and you are doing nothing to stop it. You won't govern yourself and you won't let the central government govern either.'

The temperature in the Viceroy's room had risen to boiling, despite the frigid air conditioning—

A knock, and Vidya Shankar entered.

'Sardar, V.P. Menon is here. It's urgent, he insists.'

Vallabh frowned and inclined his head. Menon bounded in soon after.

With an extended hand, Vallabh indicated that the reforms commissioner take a seat. He himself stayed standing, his back to the window. Menon sat on a chair's edge and wiped his brow with a folded kerchief.

'Sardar, this couldn't wait. The Viceroy and his advisers have settled on a plan of transfer of power whereby ...' Menon swallowed hard, 'India, Panjab, and Bengal would be partitioned.'

Vallabh's frown deepened. 'The Congress is reconciled to that, as you know. With great reluctance ... But yes, reconciled.'

'Sardar ... it is a bit more dire than that. The plan calls for power to be demitted directly to provinces and the princely states, *who* would then decide whether or not they want to form an Indian Union.'

'That ... is a recipe for fragmentation.'

Except for the mild consternation in his voice, Vallabhbhai appeared calm to Menon. He recalled how a Congressman had described him as 'a volcano in ice'.

Menon wiped his face and neck again. 'Two principal aides, Ismay and Abell, have already left for London on 2 May with the draft of this Plan Balkan—'

'Plan *Bal*-kan, you said!'

Menon nodded wordlessly.

'The snake can shed its skin, but that doesn't make it new. The British have a genius for wrecking things. Some days, I find it hard to believe that is *not* their intention as they prepare to leave India ...'

In October 1946, he was a home member in Viceroy Wavell's interim government when the secretary of state decided to stop recruitment into the ICS and terminate connections with the services before the date of the constitutional changes. Foreseeing the problem, Vallabh had decided to win the loyalty of the Indian members in the ICS and also form a new service called the Indian Administrative Service. A week ago, he had addressed the first batch of IAS probationers. After which, he had invited the thirty–forty men to his residence to get to know them better and to galvanize them for what lay ahead.

'We are entrusting you with work of great national importance,' he had said. 'I have enjoyed working for the country … I invite you to share in the same pleasure.'

The transfer of power was some time away, but nation-building could not rely on the Raj's calendar. Having just heard of the Viceroy's Plan Balkan, Vallabh wasn't sure exactly *what* he could rely on the Raj for …

'Do we know what HMG thinks of the plan?'

Menon pursed his lips and shook his head.

Hands behind his back, Vallabh paced the study floor. Through the ajar window, the cawing of a crow sounded. For some reason, his mind was journeying back to the time before he went to England … After practicing law during the day, he would often relax at the Gujarat Club with Vithalbhai and some friends, playing bridge and sharing gossip. Once, Wadia challenged him to a game of bridge, and lost nearly twenty pounds against him. The next day, Wadia lost double that. His wife forbade him from visiting the club the next day!

'Do you play bridge, Menon?'

Lost in thought, V.P. Menon took a moment to reply. 'No.'

Vallabh nodded. 'It's a game that reveals a man's character more than his skill. Technique helps, for sure, but what helps more is whether you can read the situation based on the cards in your hand.'

He paused. 'So what cards do we have in our hand, hmm?'

Realizing it was not a question that required an answer, V.P. Menon watched attentively as the home minister paced his study.

'What do we have that the Viceroy – indeed HMG – wants? By granting which, we gain their goodwill?'

Now Menon could not stop smiling. He sat upright. 'Dominion status.'

'Even the Indian princes, who feel more closely aligned with the British monarch than the Congress, will be comforted if we stay within the fold of HMG. Which ... hmm ... gives us two birds with one stone.'

Menon grinned. 'Seems to me that the most essential attribute of a bridge player is figuring out what the opponent wants.'

Nearing the window, Vallabh laughed. Something fell out of the sky, startling the crow into flight. Hurrying, he flung open the glass pane and peered outside. A pigeon had collapsed. The cloudless sky was white-hot. Dehydration.

Turning to the reforms commissioner, Vallabh said briskly, 'Now that their exit is public, the British will hand over power come what may – even if it leads to complete chaos. Without a strong central government, a country so divided by community, language, and culture will end up in anarchy. In which case, Menon, we have to draft a plan that will ensure the centre holds.'

'Right away, Sardar! As we have discussed before—'

A glance outside the window – 'Give me a minute' – and Vallabh started to head out of his study towards the kitchen.

The water bowl couldn't wait.

25
Laur (May 1947)

Dusk, and yet there was no respite from the heat. Mehmood wiped his face with the end of the thin cotton headscarf. Not satisfied, he unravelled it and wiped down his arms and neck. Then he slung it over one shoulder. At least his work for the day was done.

'Oye, Mehmood!'

He turned to see Beli Ram waddling towards him, his red kurta hanging limp. 'Let's go,' he urged, grabbing his elbow and pivoting him forward.

'Where to?' The heat was making Mehmood querulous. A dip in the Ravi river was what he needed – cool water washing off the rivulets of sweat that laced him all over.

'Forgotten?' Beli Ram asked with an upturned palm. 'Didn't we say we would drop into Kishan Singh's at the end of the day?'

'Uh … okay,' Mehmood shrugged and fell into step. His eyes were darting around for the nearest water tap he could drink from. As they neared the platform exit, he sighted the tap: Muslim water. 'One minute.'

Beli Ram watched as Mehmood opened the tap, cupped his palm and drank greedily, his Adam's apple bobbing. With the last palmful, he washed his face, dabbing his hairy forearms with wet hands as he rejoined his friend.

Outside Lahore Junction, the sky was bloody with dusk, birds cawing as they flew homewards. The two friends walked down Railway Road. The clatter of horse hooves, trilling of bicycle bells, and cries of roadside vendors filled the air. Reaching the crossroad, they turned into Bazaar Road. Mehmood smoothed down his moistened whiskers as Beli Ram eyed a watermelon, slices of the fruit lined up invitingly on the vendor's cart. He was gravitating towards it when Mehmood's hand cuffed his wrist.

'Whaa—'

With his chin, Mehmood indicated a couple walking ahead. The woman was dressed in a pink salwar–kameez, her long plait threaded with silver parandi swaying with every step. In the fashion of young women of the day, her head was bare, the chunni draped over her shoulders. She seemed to be cradling some books in her arms. The man walking beside her was talking, right hand outlining things in the air.

A smile lit up Beli Ram's face. Pammi and her neighbour. Linking one arm into Mehmood's, he made to follow the couple. Mehmood gave him an indulgent nod and fell into step.

'These college students study a lot, eh?' Beli Ram marvelled.

'When they take a break from protest marches,' Mehmood snorted.

'True. If not for these students, there would be no one standing up to the League—'

'In the streets, you mean?'

'You think I might get to speak with Pammi ji?'

The prospect of which was making his friend blush. 'Chill, Beli,' Mehmood clamped a hand on his shoulder. 'She might mistake you for a carrot!'

'Oye!' Miffed, Beli Ram shrugged off the constraining hand. 'Let's see when Mehmood Bhatti fancies a girl. In love, will he be The Great Gama or Mian Majnu?'

Mehmood laughed. 'Beli, my friend, the thing with Panjabi men is that they can wrestle camels to the ground, but in matters of the heart, they are destined to be losers. So, take my advice: Quit before you begin.'

Beli was too distracted to even wave a dismissive hand. Ahead, the couple were branching off into Mohni Lane, a shortcut to Kishan Singh's house. The friends waited for a tonga to pass before crossing the road. The sky had darkened abruptly. Compared to Bazaar Road, Mohni Lane was not well-lit, and Mehmood was temporarily irked by the young man's decision.

Until shadows arose from the side of the road and his heart sank.

The Mozang gang.

Mehmood tugged Beli Ram back, who protested, before Mehmood clamped a hand over his mouth. With his eyes he indicated what he had sighted. After his encounter with the men from Mozang, Mehmood had updated Beli Ram and taken care not to be seen with him in his mohalla. Getting caught now would be dangerous. But things didn't look good for the two students either, another Muslim and infidel friendship – which Beli Ram had deduced as well.

'We have to stop them from entering Mohni,' Beli Ram said, panic lacing his voice.

'Too late. I'll engage with the Mozang men – that might give the couple enough time to clear the lane; it's short. Stay here.'

'But Mehmood—'

'Stay!' Mehmood hissed before jumping into the street and crossing quickly. Nearing the mouth of Mohni, he slowed down and strolled forward casually. Pammi and her neighbour were well into the lane now, which was deserted but for a couple of stray dogs and a cyclist. Children playing hopscotch or gulli-danda during daytime had all been called home for bath and dinner. The Mozang men were lurking in the shadows, but one was trailing the couple. In the man's hand was a scythe.

'Padshaho!' Mehmood hailed.

A man barrelled up to him, striking the ground with one end of his upright staff. 'Pehnchod, get out!'

Mehmood pretended not to have heard. He narrowed his eyes in confusion, dipped his head, and did another salaam with his right hand, making himself obsequious.

'Padshaho, my regards. I was passing by when I saw you and thought to pay my respects.'

'Meh-mood.'

The quiet voice came from the shadows. It was the leader, Bagga, Mehmood had learnt. A returnee from the wadi ladai where he had fought alongside the angrej. The tip of his lance was picking up stray light and glinting. If the rumours were true, a parcel had arrived from Ambarsar recently, addressed to Bagga and other Muslim goondas. It contained glass bangles and mehndi, gifts for their unmanly behaviour as the RSS blasted Laur with bombs. Stung by the jeering from their religious counterparts in a city where they were not even in the majority, the gangs were roaming the streets of Laur like Malaki Maut, stabbing and killing and dispatching non-Muslims from Pakistan-to-be.

Mehmood aimed a salaam in his direction.

'Have you sorted out your infidel?'

'I have spoken with the mullah at our mosque. He's agreed to do the conversion. A-any day now.'

'So what are you waiting for? A mahurut? An auspicious Hindu day?'

The mocking voice had an edge of danger. Mehmood gulped down his fear and clasped his hands together in supplication. From the corner of his eye he could see the scythe man closing onto the couple. A shriek. He saw Pammi cower as the goonda pounced upon them. Around Mehmood, men emerged from the shadows and, whether it was intended or not, he was encircled by them.

Ahead, the gangster waved his scythe at the couple. Pammi's male companion appeared to be reasoning with the scoundrel instead of begging for forgiveness, mercy, atonement – whatever would get them out of the dark alley and out of harm's way. Mehmood had a sinking feeling in the pit of his stomach.

'SIL-ence!'

The command sounded like a gunshot in the lane. The scythe man held Pammi's head by her braid, the blade of his scythe at her neck. Her companion had gone absolutely still. In the sudden hush that had descended upon the lane, a figure came hurtling down from the other end.

That duck's waddle could only mean Beli Ram. On a mission to rescue Pammi like he were the legendary Dulha Bhatti instead of the infidel coolie the men of Mozang were looking to lynch. Mehmood's hands rose to his head, his heart to his mouth, his body sought flight but his feet stayed rooted.

Beli, Beli, Beli! Why won't you stay out like you are told …

Mehmood's mind recalled a street fight from his boyhood, when a couple of older boys had turned on him. Beli had waddled in, flinging his legs in uncoordinated frenzy, landing a kick now and then, until the enemy, unable to get hold of him, had beaten retreat – with greasy hands. Beli Ram had oiled himself liberally before jumping into the fray.

As one man, the Mozang gang moved forward, their weapons aloft.

Mehmood thought of his options. None came. His mind as still as his feet.

A trilling sound cut through the air. A bicycle. The rider, finding his way obstructed, rang the bell again and again. He was a big Sikh, or the cycle was small. Even in the relative dark, Mehmood could make out his big arms, broad chest, flowing beard, and tall turban. Bagga swivelled. Sighting the cyclist, he roared 'Allah-u-Akbar!' and dashed forward. The Sikh was dismounting when Bagga's lance speared his right leg. An almighty cry as the Sikh tried to wrench his leg free and Bagga bore down.

'Ya Ali!'

His goons surrounded the cyclist, knifing him from behind, hitting him with the thick staff. The scythe man raced down to join the fray.

'No more Sikha shahi! Kill the infidel!'

Seizing the moment, Mehmood scampered down the lane to where Beli Ram and the shaken couple were fleeing. Pammi was crying, 'No-no-no', and looking back repeatedly.

'Go, go,' Beli Ram urged. Joining them, Mehmood caught the young man's arm and dragged him as he sprinted. In turn, Pammi was almost carried aloft by the man's other hand and Beli Ram. As they exited the lane, Mehmood took one hurried glance back.

The Mozang men were weighing down upon the burly Sikh, who was on his knees now like an ageing bull. Assorted cries ricocheted in the lane, accompanied by the sounds of hacking.

Not a single window or door opened, the residents of Mohni aware they were in a war zone.

～

Pammi was in shock. Her male companion, Asad, after helping them past the entry barricade, had shot to his home, trembling uncontrollably. Mehmood and Beli Ram deposited the shaking daughter with the railway clerk, updated him quickly, then fled.

As his younger daughters comforted their terror-stricken sister, it took a long time for an ashen Kishan Singh to grasp all that had transpired. When he pieced it together, the father was even more distraught than the daughter. The man slaughtered in front of Pammi was Jujhar Singh. A gentle giant. Who had visited them last Sunday. Who had misgivings over the future of Panjab. Who feared that Pakistan would be built over Sikh corpses. Like his.

26
Simla (May 1947)

'**B**ogus English baronial!'

As their open-top Buick wound its way up the narrow road, Edwina gazed at the house that appeared propped up by a thicket of pines, the snow-clad Himalayas looming behind.

'It will do,' Dickie shrugged. 'After averaging seventeen hours a week for six weeks, I am just about worn out. If it helps me recuperate … Before Pug returns and we start a fresh round of meetings.'

On 3 May, in London, Pug Ismay had presented to the Cabinet the Mountbatten Plan for the transfer of power. It provided for partition, with Bengal and Panjab having the option of being split between India and Pakistan, joining in entirety with either nation or going it alone. The princely states too were free to decide their own future.

'You poor darling,' Edwina said. 'You will admit it's a hideous house though.'

'I did suggest to Douglas that he put us up in a hotel. He wouldn't hear of it.'

'He takes his duties seriously,' Edwina nodded, 'responsible as he is for the movement of the household.'

Something about her voice made Dickie examine her closely.

'Well,' she shrugged, 'he did insist it would take at least a month of planning to get the Viceroy and his family up to the Viceregal Lodge in Simla. Three of us and our two guests!'

From the rear seat, Pammie – with Mizzen in her lap – perked up. 'Who are we expecting?'

'I have invited Pandit Nehru and Krishna Menon over. Some walking expeditions in this crisp air will reinvigorate all of us.' The Viceroy looked crisp enough in his suit, his patrician face angled to the hills dipping by as the car worked its way up the steep road.

'It *was* getting frightfully hot in Delhi,' Pamela agreed.

Dickie turned to Edwina. 'I think I put Douglas in a bit of a flap, but really, I told him we were not planning any dinner parties or elaborate luncheons.'

Edwina raised her brows. 'Colonel Douglas Currie, military secretary responsible for the movements of the Viceregal household, clearly felt that you had no *idea* of the work involved. In the end, he agreed to let us go with a skeletal staff.'

'Skeletal … hmm,' Pamela said. 'How many exactly is that?'

'One hundred and eighty,' Edwina said airily.

∽

At 7000 feet, after a bumpy flight from Ambala, and four hours on the road up, it felt good to stretch his legs. Edwina might complain about its looks, but the lawns of the Viceregal Lodge were quite lovely. And the rooms cosy enough. Dickie walked through the lawn, breathing in air by the lungful. Marvellously cool.

'The air *is* wonderful.'

Edwina was walking down the lawn, Mizzen in her arms.

'You should let that dog get a good run. He is seriously pudgy now.'

'All that delicious food the khidmatgars prepare. I have been tempted to steal it.'

'I wouldn't know anything about that now,' Dickie laughed.

Mizzen was released and the terrier went yapping around, exploring the bushes in one corner of the lawn. Winking, Edwina linked her arms with her husband as they resumed strolling, grinning at the memory. They had just arrived at the Viceroy's Mansion when a servant had appeared carrying a silver tray on which was displayed a dish of pure-white minced chicken breast. For the Vicereine's dog. Having left a Britain still in the grip of post-war austerity, they were used to rationed food, while the dogs were fed scraps. Far too good for the dog, Edwina decided. Dismissing the servant, she disappeared into the bathroom and worked her way through the chicken breast. Mizzen had to do with chicken bones.

'Everything is progressing well with the team back home?' she asked.

'I'd urged the plan be considered and approved within ten days at the most. They have taken only a week! The parliamentary draftsmen have clarified a few items they deemed obscure, but really, no fresh element was introduced. Except,' Dickie lifted his right index finger, 'the proposal that the North-West Frontier Province be allowed to opt for independence as well.'

'Hmm … That will distress both the Congress and the Muslim League.'

'Equally. But Miéville is keeping in touch with the emissaries in London, and he informs me that all our proposals have been generally accepted. The NWFP is the one thorn left.'

Edwina listened, one eye on the Sealyham terrier who was stalking some prey in the thicket of pine trees bordering the lawn.

'I have fixed a meeting with the leaders of both the Congress and Muslim League for 17 May. And will release the text of the plan only twenty-four hours in advance. I want to give them minimum amount of time to fuss and suggest amendments.'

'Even with Panditji and Krishna Menon as our house guests here?'

'Yes, I intend to spend three tranquil days walking, talking, and doing the minimum of business.' Dickie smiled broadly at the serene row of cypress trees. Before a troubling thought broke the placid surface he had just painted.

Edwina noticed his smile fade. 'What?'

His mind's eye had cast Edwina and Jawahar below a cypress tree, their heads dipping into each other in intimate conversation. Well … This was not the first time she was showing interest in another man. In their many years of marriage Edwina had taken lovers – as he had taken girlfriends – but, in the end, she was always his wife. He had never hankered after an exclusive relationship with her – their marriage was an alliance as well and Edwina, a magnificent partner in his work. Besides, Dickie had to admit, he greatly enjoyed the company of the Congress Party leader himself. On that cheery thought, he was about to reply to Edwina when a niggling thought broke through instead.

'I have a hunch that despite agreeing in principle, Nehru won't like the plan.'

27
Laur (May 1947)

Men had started taking interest in kitchen implements. So Sepoy Malik's mother recounted as he sat down to breakfast that morning. The neighbour's wife chopped mustard greens on her wood-mounted sickle; the next day, she couldn't find it anywhere. The neighbour across lost her meat knife, the one that could slice a goat clean. The prong used to pluck hot rotis out of the tandoor went missing at another home. Someone lost the iron hammer that she used to crack open asafoetida. Tongs, saws, cleavers – everything had started to go missing, as if kitchen implements had developed a sudden taste for the exertions of the outside world. Even the humble phookni had vanished and many a housewife was left scrambling to improvise another way to blow air to start their fires.

'Phittemunh!' Ammi tossed her head as she rolled out a thick roti. 'As if we women don't know whom to blame.'

'Menfolk!' the sepoy supplied helpfully.

Ammi paused her rolling to grab her chin. 'Such strange affectations these men are donning! Hamido's man has instructed her to reply any greeting only with "aslam aleikum". And he's taken to wearing a fez daily, even in this boiling heat. Pakistan is coming, he says … Well, he's dressing for it certainly!' She snorted and served Sikandar another roti, despite his protestation that he was full already. All part of the project to fatten him up.

But what Ammi said was correct. Some part of his brain was registering the change in Laur. Sikh men were starting to wear large unsheathed kirpans. A Muslim leader was determining the population of districts by religion, in a bid to claim Muslim-majority areas for Pakistan. Anxious folks were starting to cut their beards or grow them. More night watchmen were sprouting up as gates came up where none had existed before. Now that he chewed over it, wasn't the air of Laur resounding with stories – more sinister than any the sepoy had heard during the war? A cow was slaughtered in front of a Krishna temple. Only because slabs of pig meat were deposited on the steps of Khair Din mosque. Even his father muttered about stocking up on grains and oil. As if in preparation for some siege ahead.

Yet, he had returned from jang-e-azam, the war of the world, and hadn't he seen worse already? True, Germany had attacked its neighbours; but this was different. Muslims and Hindus and Sikhs were not separate nations – they were Panjabis who had lived for years on the land, enjoying each other's festivities or ignoring them, but co-existing nonetheless. Once independence came, the troubled household would settle down with the departure of the English Shakuni mama, that perennial schemer driving a wedge between brothers. Sepoy Malik's years in war had shown him the true colours of both the English and their esteemed European civilization. Panjabi, Madrasi, Bihari, Gurkha, French, Italian, English – all had fought together as Allies. But discrimination and division was natural to the British, who made Indian soldiers work harder for lesser pay and fewer rations. Plus, they had their own version of the truth: Germany was wrong in invading other countries, but the British were right in staying on in India. He had volunteered to fight in order to earn a livelihood. He had done his duty and helped the English win the war, and now, in their own language, it was time for good riddance!

⌀

Strolling down Mall Road, Sepoy Malik felt rather content with life. Tara loved him; his job in security at a flour mill paid well, the owner impressed with the sepoy's English-speaking skills; his leg had stopped troubling him altogether. Neem trees were ablaze with white blossoms, birds were trilling, a bright yellow butterfly darted ahead of him – 'Spring has arrived with such abandon that the sun and moon watch it with wonder' … Ghalib, the poet, burst forth from Sepoy Malik in a hum, the war a distant memory. He passed a garden where the sight of buxom roses reminded him of his beloved Tara and the rose attar she favoured—

He stumbled, sound suddenly retracted from the world, then nothingness.

When he came to, the sky was blue through the leaves of a tree. Inside his head was a buzzing. He was lying on his back on the brick-paved footpath. His ears were ringing, like a grenade had gone off nearby. But he was not inside a trench. He sat up.

On the road ahead, the remains of a tonga crackled and burnt, the shell of its awning spitting tongues of smoke. Items of clothing were strewn about as if a dust storm had ripped them off the hanging line. A mangled limb. A … head? Sitting on the road without a body? He moved his eyes slowly, taking measure of his surroundings. Strips of flesh hung from the tall Ashoka trees lining the road. A brown leather shoe, not his, lay by his feet. In his lap was what looked like a fresh hunk of mutton.

Sepoy Malik convulsed.

War had come to the lanes of Laur.

28
Simla (May 1947)

Jawahar stormed into the lawn, hands clenched, trembling with fury.

He rounded to the rear of the lodge where steps led down the manicured terraced gardens. The dense darkness of night on a hilltop was punctured by thin light from outdoor lamps, but as he ploughed on, the light receded. Jawahar plunged into the darkness, propelled by anger and a desire to get away from the lodge. Plan Balkan. *Balkan*. Seriously?

His breath puffed ahead of him as he marched on determinedly – the night air cooling his flushed face, the dew moistening his sandalled feet.

Plan Balkan. The Viceroy's plan under which the British would depart India. Breaking down the country in its constituent parts and then putting them back together again. As if it were child's play! India, Pakistan, Princestan – he had heard of this before. But this plan presented an entirely new level of divvying up, in which each of the eleven provinces of British India would be free to decide its own fate – join either of the two dominions of India or Pakistan. For the provinces of Bengal and Panjab, there was a special concession: They could be divided along religious lines, or, if they so chose, become independent nations entirely! The North-West Frontier Province, the land of the martial Pathans beloved of British governors such as Caroe, which provided a necessary bulwark against an expanding Russia – the plan reserved for it the option of independence too. The 565 princely states, as allies of the Raj, were rewarded with extra-special treatment: Choose to join either of the two dominions, or opt out – presumably as feudatories of the British?

Just recalling the damn plan made Jawahar livid all over again.

Exactly what was Dickie thinking when he called him into his study to show him the 'top-secret papers'? That Jawahar would be *pleased* at the privilege extended? That Jawahar would express *satisfaction* with the Plan? That it was *exactly* the picture of order and harmony the Congress wanted to be left with upon Britain's exit?

White-hot rage flew through him …

He sought to calm himself, to think. His eyes having got used to the darkness, he started to run backwards. The scent of pine filled his nostrils and he exhaled vigorously, seeking release.

ം

Was Dickie being facetious with the title: Plan Balkan? Or matter of fact?

India was nothing like the Austro-Hungarian empire which the victorious Brits had carved up in the aftermath of World War I. Now, they were wrongly applying that formula of self-determination to India's constituent parts. But the constituent parts were first and foremost a creation and legacy of the British! India had its own unity, a sense of her being that was beyond geography. From Cape Comorin in the south to Amarnath in the Himalayas, from Dwarka on the western coast to Puri on the eastern, the same ideas coursed through her. In the Mahabharata, a text from 2000 years ago, a very definite attempt was made to emphasize the fundamental unity of India, or Bharatvarsha – from Bharat, the legendary founder of the race. Indeed, Indian culture was so widespread that no part of the country could be called the heart of that culture – unlike, say, Rome for Italy. Though often broken up politically, her spirit always guarded a common heritage.

It was the British who had come as foreigners, who had stayed on as imperialists, and, refusing to Indianize, had instead treated India as the political and economic appendage of Britain. Having ruled for centuries from London, via unelected potentates of the Raj, they were now acting rather solicitous of serving the interests of multiple groups in India. They wanted to cater to the Muslims, the Pathans, the princes, the Sikhs ... Jawahar snorted.

Plan Balkan was dangerous and cruel and irresponsible. A picture of fragmentation, conflict and disorder.

He paused and stood facing the mountains that loomed in the distance. An indistinct shape in the dark, but he knew them intimately.

His jail term in Dehradun had provided him with a fine view of the mountains, when permitted out for exercise. During that long period of solitude, with no interviews, no visitors, even when he could not see the Himalayas from his cell, he was ever conscious of its nearness, and a secret intimacy seemed to grow between them. Its solidity and imperturbability looked down upon him with the wisdom of a million years, mocked his varying humours, and soothed his fevered mind.

The cool night air was like a balm. He felt himself relaxing. The Himalayas had endured. India had endured.

Jawahar glanced back towards the lodge. Inside, Dickie had retired after showing him his grand plan for an independent India. Perhaps he was tossing in his sleep? Certainly, he had not missed Jawahar's explosive reaction.

Above him the night sky was a star-spangled blanket of velvet. He started to walk again, treading firmly, deliberately, lining up his thoughts. Congress had fought long and hard to reach this point. Just a decade ago, the English were incensed that Gandhi, an Indian, had been allowed up the Mall Road of Simla – the prestigious summer capital of the Raj. The resultant brouhaha had led to an enquiry in the House of Commons in London. And now, finally, the British were leaving India.

Yet, great dangers lay ahead. In many an empire's wake lay ruined nations. What had to be negotiated was that the India the Raj left behind was not a mere shadow of its true self: mutilated, ravaged by a civil war, devoid of functioning army, police, and other services. India could not be a skeleton. Upon which dangled the flesh of the many small states the departing British had carved up. Which the world giants – Russia, USA, China – could feast upon.

India would endure.

Physical exercise in the clear, cold mountain air had always helped banish his doubts and anxieties. It was time to frame a plan the Viceroy could work with. He'd hand it to him at breakfast in a few hours. Jawahar shot back into the lodge to begin drafting a note which detailed his objections to the proposals in Plan Balkan. It was past midnight, but he was past caring.

29
Delhi (May 1947)

The morning call from Menon had not surprised Vallabh.

The British genius for names had backfired. Jawaharlal had blown his top at 'Plan Balkan'. 'Nehru bombshell,' an alarmed Viceroy had remarked, according to Menon. In turn, Jawaharlal had written a long note to Mountbatten, laying out in great detail his objections to the proposals. Subsequently, the Viceroy had a meeting with Jawaharlal which, V.P. Menon, as reforms commissioner, attended. At the end of the discussions, with both parties in agreement, Menon was deputed to prepare a fresh plan for the transfer of power. The principles of which Vallabh was already aware of and in agreement with.

In the new plan, the *provinces* had either of two choices: To stay with the existing Constituent Assembly or opt for a new one to be constituted of members from West Panjab, East Bengal, Sind, and Baluchistan. Transfer of power, in effect, would occur between India and Pakistan. The NWFP and Assam's Sylhet district – with a clear Muslim majority – would choose between either based on a referendum. The *princely states* would have the right to choose between India, Pakistan or stay out. India would get dominion status, which would have no effect on its status of absolute independence. It could leave the Commonwealth at any moment it so wished.

From his hotel room, where he was busy preparing the alternative plan, Menon had kept Vallabh updated, and informed him to expect a call from Jawaharlal in the afternoon.

Any time now. Vallabh walked to his study.

He had just seen off his lunch guests, the Jamsaheb of Nawanagar and his Rani. Years of aloofness and antipathy had stood between them – Vallabh suspected the Prince was behind the hostility that had threatened his life in Rakjot in 1939. But the Jamsaheb was esteemed in Kathiawar, with several younger princes addressing him as 'Uncle'. The departure of the British would create a vacuum in which 565 princely states could get sucked in myriad ways. Wooing them was a top priority for Vallabh, and if that entailed breaking rotla with the Jamsaheb, so be it.

Indeed, he had welcomed his guests at the steps of 1 Aurangzeb Road, wearing one of his rare smiles. It ended up an altogether pleasant interaction of an hour and a half in which a new bond of friendship was sealed. Vallabh apprised the Jamsaheb of the dangers India would face from Pakistan all along the border from Rajasthan to Kathiawar. The Jamsaheb, in turn, gave his word that he would help to bring the princes round.

The phone rang.

Vallabh listened as Jawaharlal spelled out the new plan.

'There is no alternative but to accept it. Under it, we lose only a fraction of India. Under the other plan, we risk losing all of it.'

Vallabh's nine months in office had completely disillusioned him regarding the supposed merits of the Cabinet Mission Plan.

Except for a few honourable exceptions, Muslim officials from the top down to the chaprassis were working for the League. The communal veto given to the League in the Mission Plan would block India's progress at every stage.

'Whether or not we like it, Jawaharlal,' Vallabh continued grimly, 'de facto Pakistan already exists in Panjab and Bengal. Under the circumstances, I would prefer a de jure Pakistan, which may make the League more responsible. Freedom is coming. We have 75 to 80 per cent of India, which we can make strong with our own genius. The League can develop the rest of the country.'

'I do have two concerns ...' Jawaharlal paused over the static. 'You think the WorCom will accept it? And what about ... Bapu?'

'The Working Committee will agree to what the two of us jointly support.'

The line hummed.

'Bapu?' Jawaharlal asked again. 'This is Plan Partition ... and Bapu will want to have nothing to do with it.'

'Y-es,' Vallabh conceded.

As static buzzed, the two lieutenants of Gandhi were acutely aware that they were letting down the man who had led the freedom movement to this final juncture.

'We'll add a pinch of soda, and all will be well.'

The levity of the remark did not hide Vallabh's remorse. It was Bapu's habit to ask for a pinch of soda to be added to every food item. Which Vallabh jokingly parlayed into a remedy for every difficulty. Now he returned to the call at hand.

'It will be my responsibility to make sure that Bapu sees our point of view.'

Vallabh sank back into a chair, his face grim. For over a quarter of a century, he had sat at Bapu's feet in the struggle for India's freedom. Within a month of Gandhi returning from South Africa, he was hailed as Mahatma. Which Vallabh had dismissed back then: 'We already have too many *Great Souls*!' He converted, of course, becoming such a trusted lieutenant that when Gandhi was sentenced to six years in 1922, Vallabh was entrusted as the mason to carry out the job in the architect's absence. When he was suspected of cancer, Gandhi took great care of him, preparing mud packs and hip baths. When they were jailed together, he would take early morning walks with Gandhi, crush twigs into toothbrushes for him, help Gandhi with his letters and take his dictation. When separated by jail, they wrote to each other, with updates on their health and the world, their jailers never far from their minds. In one missive, Vallabh had evoked Lord Krishna's Viraat Swaroop – the one which blazed with the radiance of a thousand suns to a hesitant Arjun – to comment on the destruction that the British and other European powers were heaping on the world under the guise of WWII ... Their association had started with Gandhi addressing him as Bhai, which had lately changed to Chiranjeevi – as if he were a recalcitrant son who needed to be brought back to the fold. Vallabh sighed and stood up, with some difficulty.

His stomach was cramping. Frequently, of late. Doctors advised rest, light reading, no stress. Maari naar tammare hathe ... My life is in your hands, lord, but I need time to complete my duty.

Vallabh walked slowly. In Sabarmati jail, the jowar roti supplied to him daily had to be soaked in water before it could be eaten. Was that when he gave up smoking? Jail meant no cigarettes either way. 'Life's a fleeting show' – the ashram bhajan came to him. Recollections from the past came to him often nowadays.

In his mind's eye, he saw the house in Karamsad where he grew up. One wall was painted over in botanical dye, with tigers, peacocks, mounted Indian soldiers facing Europeans, and a scene from the Mahabharata. A familiar scene: Bhishma lying on his bed of arrows which Arjuna had shot into the patriarch with such ferocity that when he toppled over, the pierced arrows separated him from the ground. But Bhishma, the Pitamah, the grandsire, did not die, instead watching the war between his battling grandchildren until the end.

Bapu could not bear the thought of India being partitioned, but the bitter truth was that in the hearts of Indians, lines were already drawn. Fresh stories of communal violence began each new day of the home minister.

Vallabh had often followed Bapu blindly – subjugating his practical self to Gandhi's idealism. Leading a Congressman to grudgingly comment: 'Sardar is in a class by himself as a blind follower. His eyes are clear and bright. He can see everything, but he deliberately allows his eyes to be blinkered and attempts to see only with Gandhiji's eyes.'

But times had changed.

Gandhi. Jinnah. Patel. Three men from Gujarat who had worked together as one team at one time for one goal. Now the British were leaving, goal achieved, but the team had fractured. A civil war was looming. Or partition. Partition was in their hands, civil war wasn't. Once it started, when and how would it end? How many would lose their lives? The Hindus were in a majority and might win, but at what price? Could they afford another Mahabharata?

With a deep breath, Vallabh straightened.

Bapu was Mahatma. He was not.

30
Laur (May 1947)

'Do you have to wear such bright clothes?'
The words rolled off the sepoy's tongue, which had become slippery of late. Even his brow was perennially furrowed, something that Tara noticed as she looked at him, unsure.

'Bright?'

'Okay, good ... Expensive good salwar–kameez, silk or ... whatever this fabric is.'

'Why?' A mutinous look set in her eyes.

'Because it draws attention, unnecessary attention. Why can't you wear simple cotton?'

'Dress like an old woman, you mean?' Tara cocked an eyebrow at him as she bit into the still-to-ripen guava he had lobbed off the tree with a volley of stones earlier.

'Tch, Tara!' Sepoy Malik breathed through his nostrils. He was irritable, he knew, but what harm would come if she stayed under the radar for some time? He had barely survived the grenade attack on Mall Road, his hometown had changed ...

Couldn't she see that? Disbanded soldiers were amongst the attackers, looting from their own people …

'We aren't even married, and already you act like my master!'

'Not master, Tara,' Sepoy Malik spoke softly. 'I'm just looking out for you. Laur is teeming with religious lunatics—'

'Mad men, you mean?'

As she bit into the guava, her teeth left their impression on the green skin and her lips were moist. The sepoy's loins were afire, his spleen fervid. Did she have to be unreasonable?

Chewing noisily, she asked, 'In this men's game of tit for tat, why should women have to suffer? Hmm?'

Exasperated, he threw up his hands. 'This is not our Mahbharat, you don't have to be Draupadi!'

Tara stopped eating and glared at him, looking exactly like the fiery beauty blamed and celebrated for her part in the Great War. She pursed her lips, took a deep breath, and with deliberate calm, flung the half-eaten guava in the shrubbery and stood up. She did not tell Malik the plans she had overheard the men in her family discussing in the eventuality they were attacked. 'Lock up the womenfolk in one room, burn them alive. Better that than the shame and dishonour of the abused, disfigured women they were seeing in Laur lately …' She smoothed her kameez and patted her chunni in place. Just as she had patted the green metal gourd when she had accidentally removed it from the trunk as she plucked another one of her new trousseau suits to wear. Her frustrated mother had slapped a palm to her forehead. 'Phittemunh! What's come over you, girl? Wearing wedding clothes before marriage!'

'Sepoy Malik,' Tara angled her chin at him. 'Daily, I am going to wear good clothes *only* – Mahbharat or not, we are all going to die anyway.'

31
Delhi (May 1947)

Jawahar looked up at the sky – cloudless, starry. Rain would be welcome, but like the infernal politics afoot, summer showed no respite. His khadi kurta clung to his back as he walked, though Maulana seemed to be at ease in his customary sherwani.

'I heard there's a demand from the Sikhs as well ...' Maulana enquired.

'Yes, they would like a separate state of their own, to be called Khalistan. And in the NWFP, they fancy the idea of a separate Pathan state. And the League's local bodies in Bombay and the United Provinces would like the right to self-determination in certain parts of those provinces.' Jawahar drew a long puff and blew smoke out.

'Jinnah's Pakistan will look like no other nation on earth.' Maulana smoothed his goatee. 'Like pieces of mutton in the curry of India!'

'Well, you know the myth the English have helped popularize ... "India is a religious country above everything else ... Hindu, Muslim, Sikh take pride in their faiths ... and testify to their truth by breaking heads".' Jawahar swatted away a mosquito and looked around. The two friends had come to a stop in the garden. The staccato cheeping of crickets invaded their stillness. In a speech a few days ago, Jawahar had declared that the Muslim League could have Pakistan if they wished, but on the condition that they did not take away other parts of India which did not wish to join. The din of crickets was not unlike the din of sundry interest groups that had abruptly risen as dusk was setting on the Raj.

'How have we reached here, Maulana?' Jawahar muttered.

It wasn't meant to be answered, and the two friends and colleagues resumed their walk, each carrying his own burden of unfulfilled expectations. A year apart, Maulana the older, the war for freedom had cost the men their adulthood as they inched to threescore years. Maulana had taken that pen name 'Azad', freedom, determined as he was to crusade against the British as a journalist, writer, and freedom fighter. As president of Congress during the war years, he had headed negotiations with both the Missions – Cripps and Cabinet – deputed from London to examine the demands of nationalists. Maulana embodied the Congress, a nationalist party unlike the Muslim League, whose credo was that only they could politically represent the interests of Muslims. A petulant Jinnah had called Maulana Congress's 'showboy'.

Maulana, his mouth set in a grim line, said, 'It is unfortunate how Patel has swallowed Jinnah's drivel that there are two nations in India. You know I don't subscribe to that view.'

'Neither do I. If religion was the basis of nationality, why, there would be multiple nations in India. These nations exist in most villages, in varying proportions, with no boundaries. A Bengali Hindu and a Bengali Muslim live together, speak the same language, share the same customs. In Panjab, it is not uncommon in Hindu homes for the eldest son to be brought up a Sikh. Would that therefore mean two nations in one home?'

Jawahar eyed the stub of his cigarette, before crushing it under his foot. He liked his father's approach to religion. A cheerful agnostic, Motilal had left religious matters to the women of the family, treating the question humorously. In his childhood, Jawahar had accompanied his mother or aunts for a dip in the Ganga or a visit to holy places – all of which left little impression on him.

He flicked his wrist. Time for his meeting with Vallabhbhai.

Maulana offered to walk with him. 'India's problem is economic, not communal.'

They stepped out of 17, York Road.

'Absolutely. And yet, the British have built the narrative that no Indian can speak for India ... Only for Bengal or Panjab, or for the Muslims or Hindus. The picture of a fragmented India has been essential to the Raj's story. A lie told repeatedly becomes truth. The Nazis said that but the British have practised it in India.'

'Divide and rule. Jinnah is faithfully playing the British game.' Maulana pointed at an elegant vine-covered boundary wall they were passing.

The plaque at the gate said: '10, Aurangzeb Road, Residence of M.A. Jinnah'.

'I am an essential element which has gone to build India. I can never ... *never* surrender this claim. And yet,' Maulana's voice cracked, 'it ... it feels like the end of a dream.'

Jawahar placed a reassuring hand on his friend's shoulder. A bat flew low through the air, darting into the thicket of trees beyond the wall. He knew Maulana's pain; he felt it acutely. Born in Mecca to a family of scholars of Persian heritage, Maulana was a prodigy, fluent in Urdu, Hindi, Persian, Arabic, Bengali, English; a formidable scholar; a rebel who took on both the British and communal politicians in his community; a fervent advocate of nationalism and unity. But, three decades later, that effort was being wrecked by the calculations of a man who was using religion for his political end. Would Jinnah's two-nation theory stand to scrutiny if he paused to recall that his origin was indeed Hindu?

A group walking down the footpath greeted them. The men nodded in acknowledgement. A half-moon had risen in the sky. Like a doodh peda freshly bitten into. The milk fudge of childhood festivities ...

Jawahar didn't have an appetite for sweets now, but as a child he had gobbled them fresh from the kitchen. Dussehra, Diwali, Navreh – in Anand Bhavan, his Allahabad home, the family celebrated the festivals of their community and of the Gangetic plain in which they had settled. Either way, Kashmiri Brahmins were a product of a mixed Hindu–Muslim culture.

'Remember Lahore, 1929?' Maulana smiled weakly. 'You rode to the Congress session on a white horse to proclaim Purna Swaraj?'

In an attempt at cheer, Maulana was recalling a happier time. But Jawahar remembered an incident from even earlier. 1924. When, straight from the Delhi Unity Conference, he had rushed to Allahabad where a Hindu–Muslim riot had broken out. Some problem about music played in front of mosques during Ram Leela celebrations. Thereafter, the procession was abandoned for a decade. It was a Hindu festival, but it drew crowds from all over the district and other towns – an open-air affair in which Muslims also swelled the crowds, an occasion of joy and good cheer. But the carnival had been killed due to religious disputes, denying children and adults of the festive bonhomie. Religious fanatics – what killjoys they continued to be!

Jawahar stole a look at Maulana – despondent – who did namaaz five times a day as prescribed in Islam. In that sense, Maulana and Bapu were similar, their politics grounded in their faith. Jinnah, who probably never did namaaz, was using his faith as a carving knife to create a home for Muslims, many of whom – peasants, artisans, khidmatgars – he had no empathy with. As member of Congress, hadn't Jinnah recommended that membership to the party be open only to matriculates?

Maulana sighed. 'We've come a long distance ... not *exactly* to the destination we planned ...'

'Now, time is on a horse that is threatening to overtake us.'

In the still summer air, both friends walked shoulder to shoulder until they reached 1, Aurangzeb Road. A shared nod, and, wordlessly, they took leave of each other. Somewhere a peacock was crying out. Its plaintive note hung in the air long after the men had parted.

32
Delhi (May 1947)

In Viceroy House, the light on at 2 a.m. in the night was not due to exertions of the Viceregal staff engaged in the upkeep of the South Asian Versailles. Indeed, the staff was sound asleep and the one person awake in the household was the Viceroy himself. Engaged in the task of poring over the tapestry of his family genealogy.

After an eighteen-hour workday, tracing his linkage to Charlemagne, who united western Europe in AD eighth century, was pleasantly relaxing. In that complex mosaic, the royal families of Europe – the Romanoffs, the Habsburgs, the Hohenzollerns, the Wittelsbachs – were all connected to Dickie. And to the royal family he represented.

Dickie sat back in his chair. He had first visited India in 1921 with his cousin, the Prince of Wales. A jollier time certainly – for he had proposed to Edwina whilst here – compared to the distinctly prickly climate now. Prime Minister Attlee had picked him for his 'extraordinary faculty for getting on with all kinds of people'. Jinnah, though, with evident disdain for each one of the Viceroy's ideas, was testing that faculty on a regular basis. The Muslim League leader had even faulted the deadline of June 1948.

'Is it your intention to turn this country over to chaos and bloodshed and civil war?'

For a frigid man, Jinnah could be quite melodramatic.

Dickie squared his shoulders. One of his conditions for accepting his new role had been to ensure the government announce a firm date for the transfer of power. How else would the Indians believe that he had indeed come to end the Viceregal system? With twelve months left to accomplish his mission, he had doubled down on his routine. His mandate was to keep India united, if possible, or to salvage something of value from the wreck – either way, it was to get the HMG out.

Dickie walked to the tall French windows and gazed upon the extensive Mughal Gardens that stretched outside – in the dark, all lay quiet.

The genealogy map was his way to unwind at the end of a hot day, when the soaring heat of an approaching Indian summer paled against the heated exhalations of the country's leaders. Nehru though, with his aristocratic air, smelling eternally of crushed rose and cigarettes, was a radical leader Dickie could work with. Indeed, Edwina and he had hit it off well with Gandhi's political heir. Edwina, even more so than him.

In his mind's eye, Dickie saw a young woman strolling in the green as her honorary grandfather sat across from him. Gandhi, mindful of propriety, had sought permission from the Viceroy for Manu to ramble.

'Certainly,' Dickie had replied. 'All this is yours. We are only trustees. We have come to make it over to you.'

That was his first meeting with Mr Gandhi. Thereafter, he had brought his breakfast along – goat curds. Which was all very well until the old man insisted he try it. Dickie had refused politely. But Gandhi had insisted again, a mischievous smile playing on his lips. With Edwina looking on, Dickie had taken a tentative spoon. Suffice to say it was the most disgusting green porridge he had ever had. A sourness surfaced on his tongue at the memory. He padded back to his desk where his mother, Princess Victoria of Hesse-Rhein, and his father, Prince Louis of Battenberg, traced their lineages back to Queen Victoria of England and Czar Nicholas of Russia. Comforted by the branches of his family tree weaving through Europe's great dynasties, Dickie turned his eyes to the wall-mounted clock. It was 3 a.m. Time to head to bed. The morning ride with Pamela was scheduled for 6.30 a.m. and he would not miss its solace. He switched off the table lamp, shut the study door behind him and walked down the carpeted corridor.

At Pamela's door, Dickie paused and popped his head in. The gentle rising and falling of her chest indicated she was fast asleep. Curled around her head was Neola, a baby mongoose the staff had found in the sprawling gardens and gifted to Pammie. Apparently, its mother was missing. Dickie smiled. Pamela was filling in that role well – Neola seldom left her side, riding on her shoulder or the back of her neck. The mongoose needed to be house-trained, of course, and had learnt to make puddles on newspapers. Unfortunately, Neola had also found some papers on his desk to pee on: death warrants awaiting his signature.

On that thought, Dickie shook his head and closed the door. That morning, he had encountered the chaprassi who had gifted Neola to Pammie. A Sikh with the dignified bearing of his people, he appeared distraught enough for Dickie to enquire about the cause. After some hesitation, the man divulged the contents of an urgent telegram he had received from a cousin in Lahore. His niece had witnessed at first-hand a man being slain in broad daylight in Lahore. So shook up was the young woman, she had lost her tongue!

What had Ismay said? '... India was a ship on fire with ammunition in her hold. Could they get the fire out before it reached the ammo?'

If power had to be transferred, speed was of essence. Could they wait another year? As things stood, June 1948 seemed distant ...

From the mounting hysteria and daily rising carnage, it appeared to Dickie that Hindus and Muslims had lost faith in each other. Irrational people did irrational acts. Like condemning a First Sea Lord of the Royal Navy because two German cruisers had eluded the British Navy during World War I. Subsequently, his beloved father, Prince Louis, had become a victim of the anti-German hysteria sweeping Britain in 1914 and been forced to resign.

As Dickie padded down the hallway, his father walked ahead. Dickie had made the youngest vice-admiral since Nelson, an accomplishment he was very proud of. It was another step up in the ladder to become the First Sea Lord. To avenge Father's humiliation.

33
Delhi (June 1947)

The second of June dawned, a scorching day with temperature reaching 44 degree Celsius. That morning, the Viceroy had summoned the future leaders of India and Pakistan for a briefing on Plan Partition, now duly approved by London.

The Congress Working Committee debated the plan for ratification. Mahatma Gandhi remained unconvinced as he concluded his brief speech.

'I find myself all alone. Even the Sardar and Jawaharlal think my reading of the situation is wrong and peace is sure to return if partition is agreed upon. But the future of independence gained at this price is going to be dark.'

That portent about partition hung over the WorCom's feverish discussions. Eventually, the Committee ratified the plan, duly noting that Gandhi had said, 'I disagree but will not stand in the way.' Thereafter, Congress President J.B. Kripalani, Baldev Singh as the Sikh representative, Jawaharlal, and Vallabhbhai headed in a car to Viceroy House. The Muslim

League would be represented by Jinnah, Liaquat, and Abdur Rab Nishtar.

'This could well be a historic day,' Jawaharlal mused.

'Yes, unless Jinnah comes up with another of his schemes to delay things,' Vallabhbhai replied darkly.

'Like his corridor idea,' Baldev Singh snorted.

'He was serious. An 800-mile corridor through India to link East and West Pakistan!' Jawaharlal still couldn't dislodge that idea and its silliness from his head. Bigotry was something he didn't comprehend. When visiting Germany in 1935, he had made sure to patronize Jewish shops. The sight of the swastika, a Hindu symbol of good fortune, appropriated by the Nazi bigots annoyed him greatly. And yet, he couldn't deny that, to an outside observer, most Indians would appear extremely bigoted as well – the way they were at each other's throats currently. But then, he had always felt he was too idealistic, unbending, and aloof … Unlike the average Indian, and unable to walk in step with the West – was he fated to fall between the two?

'He has the gift, you know,' Vallabhbhai added, 'of coming up with such fantastic nonsense that he expects to be taken entirely seriously.'

Baldev Singh swivelled around from the front seat. 'It died a quick death, though.'

'And hopefully that will be end of it!' Vallabhbhai looked out of the window at the Ashoka trees lining the broad avenue of Kingsway. 'Do you know, on the night of 30 May, the Viceroy sent me a missive upon his return from London?'

The other three men in the car listened attentively.

'Through V.P. Menon. Asking for my agreement to a proposal that Calcutta be jointly controlled by the Congress and the Muslim League for a period of six months.'

'What!'

Jawaharlal had shot up from the other end of the seat, squeezing Kripalani in the middle, who looked equally concerned.

'Jinnah's been demanding that for some time now, as you know. Perhaps he added that as a caveat for his continuing support?'

'What did you reply?' Jawaharlal demanded.

Vallabhbhai raised his brows, a hint of a smile on his lips. 'Not even for six hours!'

34
Delhi (June 1947)

The next day, all the leaders returned to the Viceroy's study, having already turned in their signed acceptances of the Plan. It had been the worst twenty-four hours of his life, Dickie was convinced.

Right after the previous day's briefing, Gandhi had walked into his study, finger to his lips, indicating it was his day of silence. Despite which it took the Viceroy forty-five minutes to explain why the Cabinet Mission Plan could not be enforced if any party was opposed to it even as Gandhi scribbled his replies on the backs of old envelopes. Dickie could see why the Congress Working Committee was thoroughly annoyed with the old man. At midnight, the other Great Leader had turned up.

Jinnah expressed his inability to accept the Plan without the authority of the Council of the Muslim League, which would take another week to assemble.

By which point, Dickie had lost it. 'Mr Jinnah! I do not intend to let you wreck all the work that has gone into the settlement. Since you will not accept for the Muslim League, I will speak for them myself.'

It being midnight, the coolest part – if at all – of the day, the air conditioning in his study was arctic. And yet, enough heat was generated to melt ice. Jinnah, after all, would lose his Pakistan for good, and Dickie would have to resign and go home. Right, Dickie had breathed deeply – he could not let on how very worried he was. Finally, he found a solution.

'I will take the risk of saying that I am satisfied with the assurances you have given me, and, if your Council fails to ratify the agreement, you can place the blame on me. I have only one condition, and that is when I say at the meeting in the morning, "Mr Jinnah has given me assurances which I have accepted and which satisfy me", you will in no circumstances contradict that, and when I look towards you, you will nod your head in acquiescence.'

After which, Mr Jinnah had trotted off into the night.

Now, they were all seated around the oval table, Nehru to his right, Jinnah to his left and Baldev Singh and Kripalani across.

'Gentlemen,' Dickie began, 'I am grateful that the three parties have aired their objections to different specific parts in the Plan.' He was aware, however, that not one of the suggestions would be accepted by either of the other parties. 'I do not propose to raise them at this meeting. Would you signify your consent to this course?'

The representatives nodded.

'Well, gentlemen, the Plan seems to represent as near to a 100 per cent agreement as it is possible to get.'

Kripalani and Baldev Singh, as representatives of Congress and the Sikhs, consented, adding that they considered that the Viceroy had correctly interpreted and recorded their views.

Jinnah, of the Muslim League, gave a barely perceptible nod of his head.

Sweat broke out on Dickie's brow. For the first time in history, no party had raised any objection to a plan for independence, Dickie noted with relief. 'The Plan will now be announced officially,' he declared.

A pause.

None of the leaders raised any objection.

His confidence buoyed, Dickie continued. 'I would appeal for restraint on the part of subordinate leaders and the burial of the past in order to open up the prospect of building a fine future.'

Liaquat Ali, deputy leader of the League, shifted in his seat to the left of Jinnah. 'Your Excellency, restraint is needed not so much from subordinate as from super leaders ... For example, Mr Gandhi at his prayer meetings.'

Kripalani shook his head, 'Your Excellency, none needs to be informed that all Mr Gandhi's actions are devoted to non-violence.'

Jinnah coughed into his white kerchief, then stuffed it into the sleeve of his jacket. 'Liaquat is saying that Mr Gandhi is inciting the people to do as they like and look to authorities other than the leaders at this conference.'

Jawahar, exasperated, removed his reading glasses and flung them on the table.

A few months before he died, Iqbal, the poet and the inspiration behind the idea of Pakistan, had summoned him. Iqbal was in a reminiscent mood that day, wandering from one subject to another. At one point he said: 'What is there in common between Jinnah and you? He is a politician; you are a patriot.' Jawahar did not know if he was a patriot. But Iqbal was

certainly right in holding that he was not much of a politician
– and Jinnah bloody well was!

Perhaps he had exhaled too soon, Dickie thought, as he
watched the grown men squabbling at the table. Until, Mr Patel,
serene as a Roman senator viewing gladiators, spoke up.

'Your Excellency, Mr Gandhi will loyally abide by any
decision taken here by the representatives of Congress.'

'Gentlemen,' Dickie seized the chance to close the deal, 'I
think this matter has been ventilated sufficiently. It is time we
turn our attention to other pressing concerns.'

With a flourish, the Viceroy hoisted a bound document
above his head and banged it down on the table. The startled
men looked down. *The Administrative Consequences of Partition.*
Thirty-four closely typed pages of foolscap, a masterpiece of
compression, that Dickie had got prepared in advance to bring
the leaders right up against the hard executive realities of their
political decision.

The first paragraph stated that power would be transferred
on 15 August 1947, ten months in advance of the June 1948
deadline, ten weeks from that very meeting!

Their stunned faces, Dickie noted, were indication enough
that the men, intent thus far on securing independent nations,
had given no thought at all to the administrative consequences
of their demands.

∽

Outside, the Delhi heat was stifling, the day starkly bright, as
the Viceroy bundled the men to the All India Radio station for
a broadcast to the nation.

Freedom was coming.

35
Laur (June 1947)

A crowd had gathered in Kishan Singh's garden.

The radio on a wooden table in the centre was the reason why. Around it sat Kishan Singh and several other men on moorahs, stools, and chairs; many had simply hunkered down on the ground while a host of people stood around. The radio was playing some bhajan, its melodious recital failing to soothe the feverish speculation of those gathered. Sarkar was going to make some big announcement – that was all they knew.

Kishan Singh probed his beard, his mind clouded by the murder of Jujhar Singh still. Pammi stayed fearful, trembling at the rustle of a window curtain even. Afraid of stepping outside, she had missed classes. She sat with an open book, but didn't turn the pages. When Kishan Singh tried to talk about that tragic evening, Pammi would burst into tears. Work in the kitchen might take her mind off things, he had thought, but she went in to make tea for the family, and let the water boil on and on until the pan started to burn. He saw the curtain of the living room window part momentarily. Narinder, likely. She was on double duty now, to keep an eye on her elder sister and help him in the kitchen. Much like Laur city, the equilibrium in their house was upset. The routine of school and study, railway and writing had broken. He thought he would write about Jujhar Singh's death to make sense of it, but his hand got sweaty and no words came forth. The miscreants hadn't just slain the old man who was on a mission to save Panjab, they had rent the fabric of Laur and Kishan Singh wasn't sure he had the words to stitch it back. Daily, a new horror erupted in some part of the city – stabbing in Shamli, arson in Anarkali, a bomb going off inside Bhatti Gate ... Mata di maar. Smallpox was punishment from Mata Sheetla, so people believed. Which mother had Laur so upset that its body was oozing violent pustules—

Shh ... Shhh ...

The bhajan had died, yielding to static. Beside him, Hakam Singh had held up his large hand for silence.

A clipped voice started speaking in English.

'Viceroy,' Hakam provided.

Few men around were comprehending the language. Yet, everybody was held in thrall to the radio. Kishan Singh sighted Beli Ram and Mehmood in one corner. Beli Ram had a hand clasped to his back, head inclined, as if he was trying to read between the lines of the Viceroy's speech floating in the still summer air. Mehmood caught his eye and dipped his head. Kishan Singh acknowledged it with a grateful smile. If not for these two men ... He shuddered at the thought.

'... have faith in the future of India and I am proud to be with you all at this momentous time. May your decisions be wisely guided and may they be carried out in the peaceful and friendly spirit of the Gandhi–Jinnah appeal.'

The Viceroy had concluded. But instead of evoking Gandhi–Jinnah, a warning about the wrath of Sheetla Mata might have made all Lauris consider their current recklessness ...

Meanwhile, Mehmood was finding it all rather tedious.

This new voice belonged to Nehru, Panditji, leader of Congress and India. At least he spoke a language Mehmood understood. '... the great destiny of India ... travail and suffering ...' He elbowed Beli Ram in the chest. Who advised patience with shuttered eyes as he leaned in and whispered, 'Treat you to pulao after this, okay?'

'Jai Hind!' the radio crackled.

The evening was hot, not a leaf stirred. Besides which, the crowd of men were raising the temperature. Even the lane outside had filled with people drawn by the loud radio. Static again. A voice from the crowd in the lane asked Kishan Singh to repeat loudly what had been relayed.

'Jawaharlal Nehru said azadi is coming. AZADI! Coming! NO violence ... must make a fresh start.'

The onlookers were not too enthused, some nodded weakly, a few shouted Jai Hind. Next, the high-pitched voice of Jinnah started, again gitter-mitter, gitter-mitter. 'Pakistan ... Hindustan ... Mussalman ...' interspersed, here and there, were words Mehmood understood.

'Pakistan zindabad!'

'Pakistan zindabad! Quaid-i-Azam zindabad!' The cries rang out in the garden.

'Yes,' Kishan Singh assented, 'Jinnah has spoken of Pakistan. Let's hear Baldev Singh now.'

The man seated on Kishan Singh's right leaned in and started whispering something. Hakam Singh. To whom Mehmood had recounted the killing of the Sikh in Mohni Lane because Kishan Singh had so requested. Mehmood did not let on that he knew the killers. A steel insignia on Hakam's blue turban gleamed in the dull light of the porch. A fearsome sword was strapped to his waist. Mehmood had heard that he led a roving Sikh death squad, which was targeting Muslim villages. What exactly was Hakam doing here, in Kishan Singh's house?

'But where will this Pakistan be?' someone asked.

'Here, where else?' rang back.

'Where here? Laur?'

'Aaho, Laur! Laur is part of Panjab. Panjab is part of Pakistan.'

'Teri pehn di!'

'Panjab is part of Sikhistan.'

'Sikhistan is part of Hindustan.'

'So, where will Pakistan be, pehnchod?'

'Pakistan will be wherever Muslims are!' a voice thundered. 'Just as the Great Leader of Pakistan, Quaid-i-Azam Jinnah, has declared. Anyone who doubts this is an infidel and a traitor.'

Heads turned to identify the speaker, but it was dark and crowded and—

Hakam Singh leapt out of his chair.

'Who dare speak thus?' Hakam spun in a slow circle, addressing the men that ringed outwards from the centre where the host sat. 'You think we will let our holy shrines fall in your filthy hands? The lands we have cultivated with our sweat and blood, we will offer on a plate to you to lord over now? The angrej took Panjab from our boy Prince. Now we will take it back!' His right hand rested on the hilt of the sword that swayed as he moved. 'Come forward and show your face, braveheart! Why bother respected Nehru–Jinnah? Let's settle the matter here and now.' With that, he brandished the sword high and a hush fell over the entire gathering as all held their breath. In the quiet, the radio sputtered on, and Kishan Singh had leant in so close to hear that he seemed to be roosting atop it.

'Shh ...' Kishan Singh urged. Baldev Singh was speaking. He had represented the Sikhs to the Viceroy, but Kishan wasn't sure if Baldev understood the terror that the possible partition of Panjab had unleashed on the people. Now the leaders had confirmed it, condemning Panjab to pox …

Mehmood twirled a moustache tip. The radio kept spitting up the word 'Sikh'.

Since none took up his challenge, Hakam Singh returned to his chair, the unsheathed sword resting in one hand.

At last, it ended. Mehmood exhaled, nodded at Beli Ram, and spun away from the gathering. He was feeling warmer than when he had arrived, despite the fact that the evening had lengthened. He examined the night sky where bright stars had begun to twinkle. No clouds. No sign of rain. And the infernal heat—

Beli Ram clapped him on the back as the two friends made their way back up the alley. On the other side of the railway station was Mian Mir, where pulao was so good that passengers specifically got some packed before entering the station to embark on their journey. 'First, lassi, then pulao, hain,' Beli Ram chirped.

Mehmood shook his head. '*What* are we celebrating?'

'Azadi! Coming soon, didn't you hear? No more angrej, no more Angreji!' Beli cackled. 'Pigeon–kabootar, udan fly … now angrej is flying!' he pumped his folded arms.

'If we survive. The angreji sarkar is granting Jinnah Pakistan. And Nehru, Hindustan.'

'No Sikhistan,' Beli Ram added.

'Where will we be?' Mehmood asked.

'Where? Here! Where else?' Beli Ram pretended to recoil at his friend's foolishness.

'And Jinnah? Where will he be? And Nehru?'

'Oye, what do you care where Jinnah and Nehru will be? Are you their munshi?'

'But Jinnah wants Pakistan and Jinnah will live in Pakistan. And Sikhs, like Kishan's friend, want all of Panjab because their gurus lived and preached here.'

'So what of it to us?' Beli Ram countered. 'We are small fry. We will sit quiet and bide our time. When the storm is over, everything will be back to usual. People have to earn a livelihood or not?'

They had reached Mian Mir's, which was bustling as always. Finding a spot at the end of a long bench, they sat down facing each other. Mehmood rolled up his sleeves, inching them up to his armpit almost.

'Oye, Beli, do you walk around with eyes shut? Haven't you seen the Muslim Leaguers parade through Laur, Quran in hand? Didn't you see that Sikh being hacked with your own eyes? Muslims want to drink the blood of infidels—'

'Really? When they won't even drink their water.'

Tch! Beli Ram had spoken the truth, which made Mehmood madder. Now was not the time for truth – the truth was not making sense any more. He tried again.

'Jinnah will establish a Muslim state. If Jinnah wants to live in Laur, then Laur becomes Pakistan, see. Then you and I become Pakistani.'

Beli Ram gulped. 'Say Mehmood, of which mosque did Jinnah use to be the mullah?'

'*Muu*-llah?'

'Un-hunh. All these dreams of a mosque as big as entire Panjab.'

'Donkey!' Mehmood glared at his friend. 'Jinnah is a crafty lawyer and the League leader. Much like Nehru – of Congress. Every man wants to have his own kingdom. Ranjit Singh did. Akbar did. The angrej did. Now Jinnah and Nehru do. Only

Jinnah wants Pakistan for Mussalmans. Which means no place in Laur for your kind.'

A plate of stemming pulao arrived. Two glasses of lassi were plonked next to it. They dived in with their fingers, chewing the tender liver, blowing into the bone for marrow, ploughing the field of golden rice with their fingers. Absorbed in the pleasures of pulao, they let earthly questions of land and freedom linger.

'Know what,' Beli Ram said, as he licked his sticky yellow fingers, 'I know what Jinnah is going to do.'

Mehmood eyed him from above the rim of the lassi glass.

'Muslim Pakistan, Hindu Pakistan. Like Muslim water, Hindu water at the station. Different, yet same-same.'

Mehmood snorted. 'Muslim pulao, Hindu pulao.'

Beli Ram belched. 'No eating from the same plate.'

The two friends turned their gaze to the wooden table. The brass plate – licked clean, no rice grain clinging to the upturned edge even – sat between them.

'Okay, pay up!'

They looked up to see the serving boy ready to clear the table. He barked the bill amount, gathered the plate and glasses in one hand, and proceeded to wipe the table with a rag. 'Others are waiting to take your place.'

36
Delhi (June 1947)

'I will see you at lunch,' Edwina said as she reached her study, right next to that of the Viceroy's. 'I have more meetings than I can manage until then.' She grinned ruefully. 'I want to celebrate the King's birthday, but it's so god-awfully hot that I'm positive we will all be very sweaty and very bored.'

Pamela nodded. The heat was certainly getting to Mummy – she was yelling at Daddy more than usual. 'Right-o. I'm off to the school.'

'Ta-da, Pammie!'

Giving her mother a cheery wave, Pamela started down the corridor. She enjoyed her visits to the estate school where the children of the domestic staff studied. The sight of Neola nestled around her neck amused the children mightily! As part of her official duties, she was the chief visitor for the school and had also begun volunteering at the tented clinic, which treated poor people who could not afford proper medical treatment or could not be persuaded to go near a proper hospital.

A chaprassi in scarlet-and-white uniform paused to allow her to pass.

'Shamsher Singh!' Pamela recognized him as the staff member who had gifted her the baby mongoose.

'Miss Sahib,' he inclined his head.

'As you can see,' she petted the mongoose riding her shoulder, 'Neola is doing very well.'

He gave her a smile that didn't reach his eyes.

'What's wrong?'

Shamsher Singh shook his head.

'You look sad. Perhaps I can help?'

'No, no, all good, all good.'

Pamela frowned and instinctively copied her mother. 'I insist you tell me.'

'Miss Sahib,' Shamsher Singh sighed and patted his shirt pocket, 'it's a letter I received from Lahore, from my cousin … It … it has some disturbing news.'

'What news?'

'Disturbances in the city are growing daily and the … the latest announcement hasn't helped.' When Pamela frowned, he explained, 'The Viceroy's announcement that India will be free on 15 August.'

'Really! Why would that be the case?'

Shamsher Singh scrunched his mouth, unsure. When Pamela continued to wait for an answer, he spat out, 'Soon. Too soon.'

'But I thought Indians couldn't wait to get rid of us.'

The chaprassi examined his feet.

'Isn't that true, Shamsher Singh?'

'Be as it may, Miss Sahib. Still … the announcement has made people nervous in Lahore. No one knows where Pakistan will be … Will Lahore be in Hindustan or Pakistan? Which has made the miscreants in the city quite bold. I am going to write to my cousin to come visit me here until the situation cools down.'

'Well, that sounds wonderful!' Pammie exclaimed, as Neola chirruped and slid down her arm to go exploring in the bordering lawn.

'Ye-es.'

He looked up. 'My eldest niece is Parminder, we call her Pammi. Which is similar to how Lady Sahib calls Miss Sahib.'

'What a coincidence! I would love to meet Pam-mi when she's here.'

The door to the Viceroy's study opened, and the sound of a telephone ringing and the clacking of typewriter keys poured out. The chaprassi looked towards the study. Alan Campbell-Johnson stepped out. Sighting Pamela, he enquired if she was waiting to meet the Viceroy. When she declined, he asked the chaprassi to wait, checked his wristwatch, scanned the corridor, before ducking back in.

Pamela smiled. 'I'm sure it will all be okay.' She made a clicking sound with her tongue for the mongoose and scanned the grass. 'Daddy says we are giving India back to her people. The sooner we are out of here, the better.'

The mongoose scurried across the corridor, scampered up her leg and arm to perch on her shoulder. From her pocket, Pamela pulled out a snack which she offered Neola.

Shamsher Singh was wagging his head in that peculiar Indian way which Pamela didn't know to read. 'You don't agree?'

'Miss Sahib, have you heard the story of the Pandit's mongoose?'

'Panditji too has a mongoose?'

'Pan-dit ji? Oh! No, not Pandit Nehru! This is a story about a Brahmin who lived with his wife, baby boy, and a baby mongoose.'

'All right then. Let's hear it.'

Shamsher Singh nodded. 'So the mongoose's mother had died, and the Brahmin's wife took the animal in and started to raise it as her child. However, as the son and the mongoose grew, the Brahmin's wife started to worry. The mongoose was, after all, a wild animal ... How safe was her son with him? What if he hurt him? These thoughts weighed on her mind. So she kept a watchful eye on the mongoose. One day, she had to step out to fetch water. She asked her husband to keep an eye on their son. The Brahmin forgot and went out to beg for alms. When the woman returned, she saw the mongoose on the doorstep, his mouth bloodied. Screaming, she assumed the worst and flung the pitcher at the mongoose. Hurrying inside, she found her son playing on the cot. And on the floor lay a snake that had been mauled to death. The Brahmin's wife realized the mongoose had saved her son from the snake. She rushed outside. But the mongoose had been crushed to death by her pitcher. Overcome with grief she started wailing. In her haste, she had killed the mongoose who was like another son to her.' The chaprassi stopped, his eyes on the distance. 'Haste makes waste, Miss Sahib—'

The Viceroy's study door swung open and his press attaché stepped out.

'I see you are still here, Pamela,' Alan Campbell-Johnson said with an air of mild surprise. With his fingers, he beckoned Shamsher Singh. 'Hurry in now, jaldi jaldi.'

37
Delhi (June 1947)

On their civilizing mission in India, the British had accumulated 565 princely states in their imperial kitty through a protection racket. The British would deploy troops to protect the princes from external and internal aggression – pot calling the kettle black? – and collect monies for the same via the presence of a British resident housed in the state capital. This arrangement satisfied both parties: The British could concentrate on the provinces directly under their control, the princes could rule untrammelled. United by their indifference to proper governance, both parties prospered. Until the party pooper arrived: WWII.

Now the Viceroy, on a self-annihilating mission, was also tasked with severing the umbilical cord between the British Crown and native princes. With the transfer of power, paramountcy – the sovereignty of the overseas King over India's princes – would end. Overnight. At the stroke of midnight, 565 princely states would be set loose into the world. Scary.

The princes were, in the words of an erstwhile Viceroy, Lord Curzon, 'frivolous ... vicious spendthrift ... idlers'. Considering that the Crown was their mentor, the Lord was being either forthright or fraudulent. Either way, what could not be denied was that the Crown had cosseted the princes and muzzled the people. Time to own up: 'I have sinned.' The Latin word General Charles Napier used to broadcast his conquest of Sind – peccavi – was due for another outing. Instead, Conrad Corfield, the political adviser responsible for the princely states, was urging the princes to go rogue and declare independence.

'It's no part of my job to make things easier for India,' Corfield had offered, nose in the air.

Any wonder then that on 11 June, Sir C.P. Ramaswami Aiyar, Dewan of Travancore, announced that the state would be sovereign and independent with the Raj ending. A similar announcement followed the next day from the Nizam of Hyderabad. A dangerous trend. The 565 princely states – some large, some small – accounted for almost half of India's landmass. Kashmir and Hyderabad each were roughly the size of Great Britain.

Any wonder then that Jawaharlal Nehru blew a fuse.

'Corfield claims the princely states have a right to declare independence once the British leave. This, despite the fact that too many states are too small to be viable as independent states. The political department is acting in a way that's highly damaging to Indian interests,' Jawahar complained to Vallabh as he recounted his meeting with the Viceroy. 'I demanded the Viceroy make a judicial enquiry into Corfield's malfeasance.'

Vallabh paced his study, hands behind his back.

'Jinnah was there as well,' Jawahar continued. 'Only too happy to aid the princes who want to seek independence. In his opinion, nothing limits the states from exercising any choice.'

'And why not?' Vallabh stopped pacing for a moment. 'The Dewan of Travancore has announced his intention to appoint a trade agent in Pakistan. The recent discovery of thorium in the state has got many parties excited, foreign nations included.'

A knock at the door.

'I asked Menon to join us.'

V.P. Menon walked in with a folder in one hand, the other clutching a kerchief with which he wiped his forehead. 'It's the heat wave,' he said as he greeted the two leaders. After an exchange of pleasantries, Vallabh indicated Menon take a seat.

Propped on the sofa, Menon placed the thick folder on the centre table and opened it. 'Now that the 3 June plan has been accepted, the Viceroy is keen to resolve the thorny issue of the princely states. Whilst the Congress view has always been that paramountcy should devolve to the governing power in Delhi once the Raj ends ... *legally*, there is no Indian Union yet.' Menon paused and wiped the back of his neck. 'We're inheriting six complete provinces – Bihar, Bombay, Madras, Orissa, United Provinces, Central Provinces – and truncated portions of three – Panjab, Bengal, Assam—'

'And unless we find a way to integrate the 565 princely states,' Vallabh interjected, 'the Mother India we know will be riddled with gaping holes. Or cancerous sores.'

'Kashmir and Hyderabad will be more than sores ...' Jawahar's eyes flashed.

'There are times when I think,' Vallabh's broad nostrils flared, 'now that the British are leaving, I should give them a return gift. No matter that they have overstayed their visit by 350 years ... atithi devo bhava ... A return gift is due nevertheless; a suitable one ... So how about referendums in Scotland, Ireland, Wales? To allow their people to choose whether they want to stay united with England, and, if not, to simply part ways. A partition of Great Britain. Appropriate, no?'

Since no answer was needed, each man nursed his thoughts as the ceiling fan busily spun hot air. The wide-open window brought no breeze in, except for the incessant calling of the brainfever bird. It was crying out for rains, but the monsoon was delayed and the heat showed no signs of abating.

With a sigh, Jawahar turned from the window. 'We have two months to rope in the princes. Near impossible, it would appear.'

'Panditji,' Menon scooted forward on the sofa, 'I heard from my sources that Corfield was advising the Nawab of Bhopal, and other princes, to band together and bargain collectively with the Government of India after 15 August. I updated the Viceroy right away that Corfield is sabotaging his attempt to create an integrated India ...' Menon paused, the two leaders listening. 'I believe the Viceroy is on our side.'

'About time!' Jawahar flung out a hand. 'Wavell could hardly see beyond Jinnah and his League.'

Menon nodded before continuing, 'The Viceroy has affection for the princes, many of whom are his friends. But he also believes that accession to India will benefit the princes, and if they miss their chance now, Britain will not be in a position to assist them.'

'I'm willing to believe that,' Jawahar said. 'I have convinced the Viceroy to set up a States' Department to take over from Corfield's Political Department. Vallabhbhai,' he turned to his pacing colleague, 'I would like to put you in charge. You know, I have no truck with princes.'

'The princes also run from socialists, Jawaharlal,' Vallabh grinned.

'Don't get me started. The behaviour of these maharajas appalled even the illiberal Lord Curzon, who called them philandering fools, drunkards ... even half-mad. Holkar harnessed the bankers of Indore to a state coach and whipped them as he drove them around the city! The Raja of Kapurthala is only to be found in Paris, the Rana of Dholpur is always sozzled ... The ... the Nawab of Junagadh lavishes money – not on his subjects, but on opulent weddings of his dogs. *Dogs!*'

'They are rotten fruit, I agree with you. Incompetent, worthless human beings; deprived of the power of independent thinking. Their manners and morals are those of the depraved. Yet,' Vallabh squared his jaw, 'we have to think of the people in these states – ranging from Udaipur to Tripura.'

'Sardar, Panditji,' Menon requested their attention with an upturned hand. 'May I suggest we treat them, say, like a "collection of rare birds", who were hand-fed by the Crown. In which case, we use the services of the Viceroy to coax them into India.'

Vallabh sat down on the chair across Menon. 'And what is the Viceroy offering to these rare birds?'

Menon cleared his throat. 'The same benevolence that the Crown offered. If the princes sign treaties of accession with the Government of India, we will be responsible for their foreign affairs and defence, and they retain their autonomy and privy purses.'

Vallabh massaged his jaw. Jawahar shook his head.

'Rare birds ... We cannot simply throw them into the wild,' Menon reasoned.

The fan spun laboriously, its exertions filling the room. The brainfever bird was sounding demented now.

Jawahar exhaled loudly. 'In which case, make 15 August the deadline for accession.'

'Absolutely! Sardar?'

'Five-hundred-and-sixty-five states in the bag within two months. It's a tall order, Menon.'

'The Viceroy's help will be most essential to our task. I have seen him interact with the princes. They value his relationship to the Royal Family, and Lord Mountbatten has a great gift of persuasion.'

Jawahar snorted. 'The princelings will bow to a foreign sovereign, but not join hands with other Indians.'

'O-kay. Let's set up a joint business with Lord Mountbatten to buy and sell princely states.' Vallabh squared his shoulders. 'It's a tall order, almost as tall as the distance from Kashmir to Kanyakumari. But,' he looked from Menon to Jawahar, 'if we succeed, we will add back to India more territory than that we lose to Pakistan through partition. And one day, Menon, *after* we have secured India, you must write about it. You must write about it so that our grandchildren learn how we wrested India back from the nation of shopkeepers, province by province, state by state, inch by inch … Generations to come must not look at the map of independent India and say: "Look, the British gave India back to us and we gave Pakistan away."

'No. No. No. We took back our India and, piece by piece, put it together again.'

38
Laur (June 1947)

It was the middle of June, past midnight, and yet it felt like he was walking in an oven. Mehmood's safa was limp with the sweat it had mopped off his face and arms since the morning. Even the city seemed to have dropped dead from the heat. Not a soul was about. Where were the people who took their cots out to the rooftops or the lanes to sleep under the starry sky in the summer? Hoodlums had put enough fear in Lauris that they preferred to roast indoors rather than get dispatched to heaven in one instant. Mehmood sighed. When would this nonsense end? Would it end—

He stumbled as his foot hit something large. He flailed about, before losing his balance and crashing to the ground. Whatever was on the floor cushioned him partly. The alley was dark. With his hands, he felt the earthen ground to get his bearings. They came away wet. Sauri de! Mehmood brought his fingers to his nose. The sticky-sweet smell made him gag. As his stomach heaved upwards, Mehmood recoiled, shuffled backwards on his bottom and, gasping, grasped the nearest thing he could hold onto to stand up. Shaking, he flattened himself against the wall, his eyes narrowed. The memory of Jujhar Singh's murder flooded him. He wiped his hands roughly on his coolie kurta. He had been hearing about this …

Ordinary Lauris, slain, stabbed, slashed in the narrow alleys of the Walled City as they went about their business, unaware that the hour was late, that in the shadows of the cramped bylanes lay men who would slice your neck before you could blink, that nobody was safe, Hindu, Muslim, or Sikh … Kishan Singh had said that, from reading the daily reports of casualties in the city, it appeared as if a game of tit for tat was on.

His eyes had got used to the dark. Mehmood could discern the crumpled figure of a man in a tang pyjama and shirt lying in his own blood. He was glad he had insisted Beli Ram stop work at five in the evening like some office clerk and go straight home while it was still daylight outside. Beli had protested. But Mehmood had asked Beli to swear on his life. A sulking Beli complained he was being treated worse than a helpless woman. But he was adhering to 'Magistrate Mehmood's curfew', as he snarkily labelled it.

Now that he had stopped trembling like a leaf in a storm, Mehmood started to scurry out of the lane.

But a tremendous rustling sounded as light glimmered from the other end. A group of men entered the lane, a flaming torch held aloft in some hand at the front. *Adiya,* Mehmood berated himself, *why would you walk through Mohalla Sareen, a non-Muslim locality?*

The group broke into jaunty chants as it moved forward. Their shouts echoed off the walls of the narrow lane, which lit up as more glowing torches in the hands of the mob came into view. Momentarily, Mehmood was reminded of some Lohri festivity – folks singing lustily around a bonfire.

Pakistan ka naara kya?
La illaha illa Allah!

Mehmood's nose pricked. A stinky smell accompanied all such rioters – their torches were rags, dipped in kerosene, tied around the ends of sticks. Around two dozen men, armed with flaming torches, scythes, gandasas, and one rifle, at least! The reality of his situation hit him. He gulped down his fear. So close, the gang had become one body with multiple limbs, shadowy faces, and crowning torches.

Pumping a fist, Mehmood joined in the chanting.

His bloodied clothes and hands must have qualified him instantly. One of the men beckoned him over and he slid into the group, chanting mindlessly. The body on the floor was crushed under their feet. Mehmood could swear he heard the bones crunch, the flesh tear as they sallied forth. Until they came to a halt in front of a shop. 'Gupta Medicals'. Some men broke down the wooden door and all of them poured inside.

'Take all you can!' a voice thundered.

The men started sweeping stuff off the shelves and into the jute sacks they carried.

'What?' A hand smacked Mehmood's shoulder. 'Are you a new bride waiting for permission?'

Mehmood bounded to the nearest cabinet, flung open the glass doors and stared at the bottles lined in front.

'Grab those!' The man beside him had a metal canister with a yawning mouth. 'Careful, they are glass.'

Mehmood grabbed the bottles, lined them in the can, then grabbed more, stacking them with care as he went.

'Gupta pehnchod!'

'Let us see him set off more bombs in our mohalla now!'

'Saala RSS henchman!'

'Good job, good job!' the man beside Mehmood approved, his voice delighted. 'Know what these are?' He cackled. 'Ammonia bottles. Smash them to the ground and they will emit fumes which make people tear up! Now those,' his eyes indicated the cartons on the top shelf. 'Get those! Bromine ampoules.'

Mehmood followed dutifully. Was this hoodlum a doctor? A compounder, perhaps? As he turned to place the cartons in the can, he realized there was no space left. The man instructed him to remove a couple of ammonia bottles and replace them with the carton.

'Hold on to the rest,' his hoodlum instructed on a wink. 'As good as ammonia, if not better.'

The thuggery was over as abruptly as it had begun. Once outside, some men hurled flaming torches in the shop. Its wooden front caught fire immediately – dry like tinder from the lack of rain. Tongues of flames wrapped the interior. The men were hurrying away when they heard a loud combustion. Mehmood glanced back and was horrified to see how quickly the fire had spread to the surrounding houses. Screams were beginning to pour forth as people awakened to the flames and smoke invading their homes.

From Mohalla Sareen, the gang was quietly heading to Shahi Mohalla when the shrill cry of sirens sounded.

The goondas knew what to do. As Mehmood too made motions of running, the group broke into smaller units and melted away into the maze-like alleys of the Walled City. Soon, Mehmood was alone, cradling his stash of bottles and cartons.

At home, he deposited the chemicals in the storeroom behind piled-up quilts and blankets. He did not want his mother to accidentally locate them as she pottered about the house. Mehmood washed his bloodied hands, threw off the grimy kurta, wrapped a lungi around himself and lay down bare-chested on his cot. Resting his head atop one folded arm, he studied the starry sky. Lauris were stockpiling ammunition for the war ahead, the battles had already begun, the kanjars had just dragged him into one!

What lay ahead … Mehmood searched the sky.

In the inky dark, no answer descended from above.

39
Delhi (June 1947)

The Mountbattens were at breakfast. The heat was omnipresent. Having left the coldest English winter on record, they were now experiencing the hottest Indian summer in seventy-five years. The khidmatgar served a fried egg to Dickie, who was just picking up his fork and knife when there was a dash of grey fur, and the egg simply vanished.

'Not again!' Dickie exclaimed. 'This is plain getting out of hand.'

Edwina and Pamela laughed, as the khidmatgar suppressed a smile. 'Your Excellency, I will fetch another,' he said and made to turn.

'Wait!'

The khidmatgar halted and Dickie said, 'When you return, do not serve the egg until I tell you to.'

'What exactly do you have in mind, Daddy?'

'Save my breakfast from your Neola, for one. After which, I shall teach him to eat his own breakfast – like any self-respecting mongoose ought to.'

'Ah, darling! You have expertise in training a mongoose now?' Edwina picked an apple slice.

Dickie helped himself to a cup of tea. 'Hopefully, the mongoose will not delay me for my first meeting. The Nawab of Bhopal is a tricky customer, but I do feel an obligation to help settle the question of the princes.'

'Tell us more, Daddy.'

'Well, the way I see it, I have three courses open to me. I could ignore the problem and leave the princely states to their future. That's one. Or I could adopt the Napoleonic route and create new nations out of the existing states. Something Mr Gandhi is vehemently opposed to. You do recall what he told me, Edwina? That the princes were essentially a British creation; small chieftains built up as allies to weaken Indian resistance to the Empire. Not to consider that Nehru would be absolutely livid. He has already declared that he will encourage rebellion in all states that choose not to go with India.'

Dickie sighed as the Simla memory of their postprandial discussion of Plan Balkan. He did not fancy another encounter with an incandescent Ja-wa-har. Really, his prison terms had made Jawa-har quite nervy.

'The third, of course, is to actively assist with their accession to either India or Pakistan,' Edwina concluded.

'I have to admit, the first is tempting. But that would mean jilting the princes whom Queen Victoria put on a par with *our* princes way back in 1858. And it would lead to the Balkanization of India, which Nehru has already accused me of aiding. The second is a pipe dream for sure. If we were to make a go of it, we should have initiated it ten years ago. Which really leaves me with the third option.' His brow dipped.

'Except?' Edwina queried.

'Well, for that I have to extract reasonable terms from India. And the Congress leaders are not in a pliant mood. Sardar Patel thinks the problem is unimportant. Indeed, he's told me that after the transfer of power, he expects that the people would rise, overthrow their rulers, and rally to independent India! Mr Jinnah, of course, is happy to go with anything that makes things difficult for the Congress.'

'The fact that not too many princes would accede to Pakistan plays directly in favour of the Muslim League,' Edwina concluded shrewdly.

'Precisely.'

'Daddy, do you think 15 August is too soon? That we are being hasty?'

'If we tarry, Pammie, we won't have anything left to give away. The Indians are at each other's throats on an hourly basis.'

The khidmatgar had returned and was waiting patiently by the side.

'Hold on,' Dickie instructed. He grabbed his fork and knife, and with hands positioned above his empty plate in dive position, ordered, 'Now!'

With one deft move the khidmatgar ladled the fried egg onto the plate. Dickie's hands descended upon the silky yellow yolk shimmering in a cloud of white. He would have taken a jab, but the grey, furry creature proved swifter and cannier than the Viceroy, and once again his breakfast was dismantled before his disbelieving eyes and salivating mouth.

'This has to *absolutely* stop!'

The implements clanked back into his empty plate. Scraping his chair back, Dickie stood up. 'Pamela, I request your assistance in training your mongoose to be self-sufficient.'

Pamela rose, Neola on her shoulder as the Viceroy took the floor. Edwina's eyes gleamed as she leaned forward.

'The mongoose loves his eggs; the mongoose must learn to eat his own eggs. I have instructions from "Rikki-Tikki-Tavi" on what exactly a mongoose is to do.' Dickie dropped to the floor, lifted his arms, his feet planted squarely behind him. 'Neola takes the egg in his front paws, takes it to the nearest rock or wall or any hard thing, hurls it, the egg cracks, and there, ready to eat.'

As Pamela looked disbelieving, Dickie reassured her with a wave of his hand. 'It's only because Neola came to us too young and had no mother to train it.'

'And now you will be the mother?' Edwina snorted.

'Kipling, really. I learnt this from reading him.'

Dickie and Pamela, with Neola on her shoulder, returned to the table. The khidmatgar was despatched to fetch some hard-boiled eggs.

'The way I see it,' Edwina picked up the thread of their earlier conversation, 'you need a formula that offers a chance of reconciliation.'

Birdsong floated in the air. In the lush gardens that stretched as far as they could see, a man waved a large flag to keep pigeons and crows at bay. The murmur of the swimming pool and its heavenly blue was a relief even at that early hour; Edwina and Pamela had their hats on as a shield from the blazing sun. Dickie was considerably redder than he was three months back.

'Yes, something to keep both sides happy. Don't forget, I will have to launch a charm offensive on the princes even if the Sardar were to provide me reasonable terms for accession.'

The khidmatgar returned.

Dickie took a boiled egg and returned to his crouching position on the ground; Pamela joined him with Neola in attendance. He tossed the egg, it cracked. Neola scrambled to it, sniffed, then returned to his perch on Pamela's shoulder.

The Viceroy was most unimpressed, as the women burst into laughter.

'Dickie! He has no reason to learn. The kitchen provides him with eggs regularly.'

'Well, then he should learn to let others eat their share,' Dickie complained.

Pamela retrieved the egg from the floor and started to shell it. This gave the khidmatgar and the Viceroy a chance to breakfast. When the egg was half shelled, Pamela offered it to the mongoose. He clambered down from her shoulder to the ground where she kept it and started to gobble it down. Pamela rejoined her parents at the breakfast table.

Having partaken the fried egg, Dickie wiped his mouth with a linen napkin. 'I have to admit, as cousin of the King-Emperor and a Viceroy, I feel a particular responsibility towards the princes who attach a great deal of significance to their historic ties with the Crown of England.'

'Look at you!' Edwina gazed at her husband. 'In this lounge suit, you look as handsome as any cousin of the British King could. You will seduce them.'

Dickie nodded, unsure. Why did he feel that his wife much preferred the sartorial style of the rose-in-achkan-lapel Jawa? Pecking her on the cheek, he strode away. In his mind, the meeting ahead loomed large. Nawab Hamidullah, Prince of Bhopal, had resigned his chancellorship of the Chamber of Princes in protest at the planned transfer of power. The Raj had betrayed his state, which would assume independent status now. A position that was bound to incense both Nehru and Sardar Patel. Besides, the Prince had considerable influence over other princely states … With the transfer of power, the Crown's special relationship with Indian princes would end. But Dickie would remain cousin to the King – which the princes valued.

And the fact that he was still the Viceroy would be handy in dealing with the prickly princes …

Hearing peals of laughter, Dickie turned to look behind.

Neola was running around bumping into things, the half shell of the egg sitting on his head like a helmet. The mongoose was a complex creature; it wanted companionship like a dog, but refused discipline like a cat. As complicated as the country he was a native of.

40
Laur (June 1947)

The fire started at Shahalmi Gate.

That sticky Saturday night, two men snuck past the sentries guarding entry to the infidel mohalla. Between them, the men carried barrels of a solution they then flung on the doors of the ancient houses crimping into each other. Quietly, they proceeded down the lane. Buckets and barrels of water that the mohalla had stocked up on to fight fires got a sloshing as well. Then the men lit their torches.

The fire fed hungrily on the wooden doors of the houses and shops, roaring to rooftops, circling the chabutaras, leapfrogging homes. Like some crazed conqueror of yore, it ravaged the maze of dwellings within the Walled City. The flaming torch of Shahalmi was seen from several kos away. The air smelt of burnt flesh and made people sneeze as the spice shops of Shahalmi crackled. Fumes darkened the sky.

Where was the fire brigade, the police, the ambulance … fire brigade, police, ambulance … fire brigade police ambulance …

The screams of people trapped inside the warren of Shahalmi gladdened the hearts of the Muslim goons – they had won the war for Laur! Hindus and Muslims in nearby localities donned tin helmets, gathered bricks, surveilled from rooftops as they readied for assault.

An attacking horde led by demobilized soldiers arrived at Tara's colony. The men on the rooftop alerted the womenfolk and waited to mount the planned defence. Below, Tara and her sisters proceeded to wear several kameezes, one atop the other. Her mother made them do that, in preparation for fleeing: 'Carry on your body as many clothes as you can, jewellery hidden within. *Quick, quick, hurry, hurry!*' Tara wore her entire trousseau almost, layering one kameez upon another, silk over satin, flowing over fitted – she could have embedded an entire arsenal in those folds.

Above, men lobbed thick glass bottles at the mob. Several found their mark, but the trader in soda and juice, fizzy flavourful drinks that hydrate throats in the time of heat, had severely underestimated the power of glass bottles to quench the raging heat of communal violence.

It was glass versus guns, and the shards couldn't douse gunfire.

Tara was hauled from her home by her long hair. She resisted. They grabbed her arms. She dug her feet in. They dragged her along like a rag doll. She cried out. She reminded her attacker that he was a comrade of her sepoy, a brother to him therefore, her brother-in-law in effect …

He laughed. He had better uses for her, he said. His comrades joined him in his demonic laughter. It took them a while as they stripped her of those layers.

Tara flailed on the floor. Around her, Pitaji and her bothers watched with vacant eyes. She felt the Mills bomb nestled against her bosom. She closed her eyes and remembered her sepoy.

The bashful boy with brown eyes and long eyelashes, who looked away when she locked eyes with him in school. The teenager who loped around her like a happy puppy. The young man who signed up for war to earn enough money to be able to ask for her hand.

Adiya, did you never stop to think you might never return?

No. Sikandar Malik wore her love like a shield and came back to her. Bashful again because of his limp. More handsome though. Could anyone dangle a cigarette with his careless grace? The night of their smokey lovemaking in a boat – *really, Tara?* – by the Ravi coursed through her.

Oh, Sikandar, I would take you with one leg even!

Except, she was the one caught in a khasma-nu-khani war now. And she couldn't let her sepoy down.

In a field of tall mustard where the smell of young mango blossoms wafted, Tara swayed on a rope swing that floated back to where Sikandar stood to push her. She laughed as he indulged her. Back and forth she went, between her beloved and the sky, higher and higher.

I will meet you yet again, Sikandar.

Tara pulled the pin of the grenade.

41
Delhi (July 1947)

The car had barely pulled onto York Road and Papu was dozing, sitting upright.

He was sleeping three or four hours every night – a sleep punctuated by nightmares, she knew. Sanjay woke up often and as she nursed him or changed his nappy, she was aware of when Papu thrashed about in his bed or paced his room. The distressing news from Panjab weighed on him. As did the separatist demands erupting from unlikely places. The Naga tribes in Assam wanted Nagastan and Tamil separatists had cabled Prime Minister Atlee from Madras with a request for Dravidanadu. Then there were the countless committee meetings, endless memos, economic plans, foreign delegates to be entertained—

Indu cast a quick look out. They were approaching Connaught Place. She wanted to pick up dried fish paste to cook fish curry for the Burmese delegation the interim Prime Minister was hosting for dinner. As the driver slowed, Indu tried to catch his attention in the rear-view mirror.

Khaliq noticed her flailing hand. With the barest tilt of his chin, he questioned her wordlessly.

'Viceroy House.' Indu mouthed the words and, with a slow sweep of her hand, indicated he continue driving. Khaliq had driven her grandfather, and her, in pigtails, and had now moved to driving Papu. That lengthy association had attuned one to the other. The car purred on. She would buy the paste upon return. They passed the handsome colonnaded Imperial Hotel, then down Queensway. Using her sari pallu, she fanned herself. The monsoon was long overdue.

Despite which, the Mughal Gardens in the Viceroy House's elaborate estate looked resplendent. Papu awoke with a start as the car came to a stop.

'Good morning, sleeping beauty!' Indu teased him.

He rubbed his eyes in an endearing manner that reminded her of Rajiv. Then tapped his cheeks and blew air out of his mouth. 'I could sleep for a hundred years,' he yawned. 'I worry though that what will wake me up will not be the kiss of a princess but the exhalations of Mr Jinnah.'

Both father and daughter burst out laughing.

༄

Alan Campbell-Johnson escorted Jawahar into the Viceroy's study. Here, the frigid air reminded him of his native Kashmir – so removed from the fires burning in Lahore, his maternal home. As the two men shook hands, Jawahar reminded himself to keep a check on his emotions, and took a seat.

'Your Excellency, the situation in Lahore demands our immediate attention. As you are aware, fires continue to burn, there is daytime robbery and arson, even as the police watch!'

'Mr Nehru, I am in constant contact with Governor Jenkins, and he is doing everything possible to contain the violence. However, the police simply cannot stop every single act of arson or stabbing. The people have to stop acting out. Now that the Panjab Legislative Assembly has voted for the partition of the state, one expects tempers will cool down.'

Jawahar shook his head repeatedly. 'The League is behind this. Our intelligence shows that a local Muslim magistrate, in cahoots with a Lahore goonda … a … a Billa Jat, is behind the attack on Shahalmi Gate. When the fire crew showed up, the magistrate ordered the crew to turn their hoses around. Instead of water spraying on the burning homes, it was flowing back into the canal!' Jawahar shot upright. 'Preposterous!'

With his right index finger, Dickie tucked back the collar of his shirt. It was the ungodly heat which was fraying tempers. Besides which, Nehru was clearly over-working himself – the man looked a wreck.

'… over 250 homes burned to the ground. At this rate the city of Lahore will be just a heap of ashes in a few days' time. Are we to be passive spectators?' Jawahar's eyes implored the Viceroy.

Wild stories were circulating in Lahore, Jenkins had informed him. Of how Hindus rushing out of burning homes were gunned down by the police, who were predominantly Muslim.

'The administration of Governor Jenkins is doing its best to quell the mayhem. But, as you know, intel gathering is disrupted because informants are switching their loyalties to their own communal militias—'

'Your Excellency,' Jawahar rested his palms on the Viceroy's desk and leaned into him. 'Forgive me, but the fate of Lahore affects me more intimately than it might other people not connected to that city. My mother came from Lahore, and part of my childhood was spent there. We cannot sit on our hands and let the city burn.'

'So what would you have me do, Mr Nehru?' At Dickie's raised voice, Alan popped his head through the door.

'Declare martial law!'

'The Governor believes it will make things worse.'

Jawahar threw up both hands. He then walked over to the tall windows to stare at the Mughal Gardens. Outside the Shahalmi Gate was a small Hindu temple he would visit during his Lahore trips. Many years earlier, his father had had it built. A cheerful agnostic, he did it for his wife. To Jawahar, that temple was a beacon of his cosmopolitan Lahore: A city of believers of many faiths, and non-believers who humoured them—

'Though I must say,' Dickie's voice had perked up, 'for once you and Mr Jinnah are in complete agreement.'

As Jawahar turned, a khidmatgar walked in with a tray of chilled water. Behind him, Alan closed the door.

'Mr Jinnah wants me to issue shoot-at-sight orders in Lahore.'

Jawahar helped himself to a glass of water.

'I am not convinced that is the right course of action.' Dickie shrugged. 'The police and army are not immune to the poison of communalism. What would really help is direct and private pressure on the militias in Lahore, from both the Congress and the League. And we need to choke off their funding. Also,' Dickie brought his hands together as if concluding the matter, 'I propose we set up a multi-faith security committee here in Delhi.'

The Viceroy's suggestion to set up another committee, which would yet again issue petitions to people, to stop killing each other yet again, was a dud. In the past week, Bapu and he had visited a camp in Hardwar where thousands of Panjabi Hindus and Sikhs had sought refuge after the Rawalpindi riots. Stricken faces, pleading hands, matted hair – Jawahar did not need to close his eyes to see them. In Lahore, the League was emptying the city of Hindus and Sikhs. In Delhi, men like Liaquat were blocking the interim government from functioning.

The water had been refreshing. Jawahar placed the glass back on the tray.

'Your Excellency, you must allow the Congress Party a free hand in its own territory.'

Dickie frowned.

'We refuse to be dictated by Mr Jinnah any longer.'

'What do you propose?'

'Since we don't need the obstructionist League members in the interim government of India, we propose you kick them out.'

Dickie started. 'If not?'

'You must accept my resignation then.'

42
Laur (July 1947)

Sepoy Malik never saw Tara again.

Other people discovered the bodies of other women from that mohalla, their breasts chopped, bodies tattooed, necks slashed. But Sikandar never found Tara's body. The house of his father-in-law-to-be, armed to the rooftop with soda bottles for defence, was a death trap. The goondas had set fire to the house, the soda bottles exploding like bombs, carrying the fire to other houses. So severe was the inferno, it smouldered for days.

He tried to get inside Tara's house, search the rubble for her bones, but he ended up with a burnt hand. And a grenade pin. She did to herself what the men of her family had been threatening to do. Sepoy Malik made a sound like a strangled laugh. At some point Tara had mentioned to him what she'd overheard – he had rubbished her concerns, resistant as he was to any cloud on the horizon of his rosy plans. Should he be grateful she had exploded like some firework?

He could not recall Tara's face, but he caught her in glimpses. A front tooth that was chipped in a childhood fight with her brother. Glass bangles sliding down her wrist as she steadied her chunni. Her brows jogging – *So, sepoy?* – her nose pin – was it on the left or right? Left or right? Left-right, left-right leftright … In delirium, he stumbled about the smouldering ruins of his beloved's house, and the days of war returned with renewed clarity.

In the field he had discovered, even as he carried the bazooka on his shoulder, its range lay beyond what his eye could see. A lesson he forgot when he returned to Laur and began planning a union, the ground below cracking.

Tara was Hindu. He was Muslim. Correction. He *used* to be Muslim. With her gone, he was nothing. He was on no one's side.

Correction.

He was on the side of death.

Correction.

He *was* Death.

A broken leg, a burnt hand. An impaired soldier was no good on the front line. But he had seen Major Drew, his commanding officer, drag a useless leg across his tiny office, his right arm strapped to his chest in a sling, as he organized the movement of men and arms. Sepoy Malik's disbanded comrades were strewn over Panjab, fighting lone sorties or leading small groups of attackers. Organize them, combine their leftover guns and grenades, and he would get a militia and an arsenal.

Sepoy Malik had fought a war for the angrej. Now he would fuel one for himself.

43
Delhi (July 1947)

In a stucco bungalow on the Viceregal Estate, with the green shuttered windows closed, Cyril Radcliffe sweated like a horse.

The heat had walloped him as soon as he descended the aircraft on 8 July. London, too, was witnessing what the press liked to describe as an 'Indian summer'. Fools! They had to be on the ground to feel the infernal heat – there was no comprehending it; his brain was fried.

For which he held the Viceroy responsible.

Thirty-eight days to 15 August. To the independence of the subcontinent, and its concomitant partition – the latter task assigned to him.

Cyril tiptoed around the shaded living room, the ceiling fan stirring hot air. Which rustled the edges of ordnance maps and census tables littered over all available space. This was his first visit to India, a country of legendary mystique, and he did not know its B (for Bengal) from its P (for Panjab). And yet, the Bengal Boundary Commission and the Panjab

Boundary Commission were formed on 30 June, both under the chairmanship of Cyril Radcliffe.

He wiped his brow and exhaled loudly.

Incredible as it sounded, the Inner Temple lawyer was in the subcontinent to create a new country. To carve out a separate home for Muslims. Except, the census was six years out of date, and its authenticity was questionable to begin with.

He looked at the briefing sheets his young ICS aide had provided: districts of Panjab and Bengal, each listed with a statistical proportion of Hindus, Muslims, and Sikhs. The Sikhs were really an element to be considered in the Panjab equation. A fly buzzed over the sheets, riding the heat waves generated by the overhead fan. His mission was 'to demarcate the boundaries of the two parts of the Panjab on the basis of ascertaining the contiguous majority areas of Muslim and non-Muslims. In doing so, it will also take into account other factors'. The 'other' factors to be accommodated when deciding if a district was to go to Pakistan or stay in India were cultural, historical, geographical …

He recalled the arguments various parties were making.

Lahore had 600 gurdwaras, and the Sikhs, in a slight minority to the majority Muslims, lay claim to the historic city. Besides, it had once been a seat of the Sikh kingdom. But the Muslims were in majority, by sheer numbers.

Geography was another complication. Panjab was the land of five rivers. Now those rivers needed a nationality, a truncation into Muslim Pakistan and Hindu India. There were 3800 miles to be brokered. And 400 million lives at stake.

His forearms, the sleeves rolled up, had rivulets of sweat coursing down. He was leaving his damp stamp on the districts. How does an English judge, unskilled in map-reading, accomplish this task? Well, his ignorance could mean one thing:

impartiality. Besides, he had a first-class English brain, he felt the need to remind himself. He removed his glasses, slick with perspiration, and wiped them. His poor eyesight blurred the contours of his surroundings. The dizzying bright daylight, the engulfing heat, the incessantly sprouting sweat – surely he was at the mouth of hell? Clamping the spectacles back on, he poured himself a glass of iced water and drank greedily.

Sitting in the Viceroy's chilly study, he had informed him that the time given was too short. But the Viceroy and the leaders, Nehru and Jinnah, were intent on the deadline of 15 August. Since the carving of the subcontinent was a race against time, he took a Dakota ride over the rice and wheat fields, trees and orchards, dotted with homes – sloping-roofed in Bengal, flat-roofed in Panjab. And he came to the realization that the land through which he was to run his red line was far removed from the aqua-themed study of the Viceroy.

The clock struck the hour. He faced it grimly, a bead of sweat dangling from his chin. It would be a thankless task, at the end of which they would shoot him out of hand, both sides.

But they wanted a line.

He bent over the ordnance map spread out on one of the tables, both elbows on the paper as he peered – the Ferozepur salient to the east of Sutlej river in Panjab darkened with his dripping sweat.

So he would draw them a line.

44
Laur (July 1947)

Kishan Singh clutched the telephone like it was a lifeline. He had never before felt the need to make a trunk call, that too to Viceroy House. But Shamsher's last letter included an invitation to visit him in Delhi, to get away from Laur until things settled down. Sure enough, the city was getting hotter by the day: bomb blasts and fires as frequent as the rains, had those arrived. He had practically barred the girls from leaving home. Uncertainty seized him like high fever—

The buzzing on the line had changed to a shrill ringing. 'Hello!'

'Shamsher!' Kishan squealed in relief. 'Brother, how are you?'

'Kishan?' The voice said, unsure.

'Aaho, yes-yes, me only. All well with you and family?'

'All well here, Kishan pahji. This trunk call is costing you a fortune, I know. So let me tell you straight. Book your tickets and come to us in Dilli. Your parjai worries about the girls. Laur is burning, but we live in the staff quarters of Viceroy House – what can be safer? Hmm?'

Kishan nodded. 'True, very true. But, brother, do you have any information on whether your Viceroy is giving Laur to Pakistan or will it stay in India? This one question is driving the entire city mad.'

It was certainly the only topic occupying his colleagues. Hari Kumar had confided in him that the communists believed the British were determined to leave India in chaos so the world could see how, without them, the Hindus and Muslims would fight forever. Ahmed, of course, crowed daily about Hindus fleeing the city they called home. Mangat, who knew some top Congresswalla, said the party was confident Laur would remain in India. Which was why Hindus and Sikhs needed to hold down the fort until then. But Kishan had only one small home with three unmarried daughters to secure, and since he didn't know to fight, was flight an option? Iqbal virji was insisting he move to Lyallpur, where people weren't riled up as in Laur.

'... only thing we know for sure is partition. The country is getting divided, Panjab is getting divided, perhaps even Laur will. But the vand is happening. Daily, officers are sitting down to split items between two countries – soldiers, police, railways, records ... everything.'

Shamsher went quiet. Static sounded. Kishan Singh jammed the black telephone closer into his ear. 'Hello?' he said meekly. 'Hello? Hell-oo?'

'... the other day I heard them fighting over printing presses. They are splitting tables and chairs even ... I tell you, it is worse than a quarrel between derani–jethani!'

Kishan gulped, even more confused than when he started. A quarrel between sisters-in-law was a facet of daily life: tempers erupted, they exchanged sharp words, then returned to living in the same house. Except ... on occasions when a house got divided, a wall came up, splitting people, property, possessions ... But angrej ICS officers squabbling like women? Kishan Singh had only ever seen these suited-booted men giving orders, which the natives carried out promptly. *Exactly* what is happening now, the voice within him sneered: The Viceroy has ordered partition, Nehru–Jinnah have begun dividing assets ...

Rabba, Kishan sighed, show me some light.

'My lunch hour is ending. Kishan pahji, don't think too much. Just book your tickets. Okay?'

'O-kay.'

'Rab rakha!'

A click and the line started buzzing again. Kishan Singh paid a princely sum to the post office clerk and headed out into the searing noon.

∽

In the evening, as he took a rickshaw ride back home, Kishan Singh's mind churned with scraps of conversation he had tried to ignore while working. 'Hindu homes were selling for one-third their market price.' 'Half of Laur's Hindu population had abandoned the city.' 'The baniyas were taking their banks with them – who would loan money to the Mussalmans now?' 'The League wasn't waiting on the Viceroy's Partition Plan; they were getting Laur by expelling all kuffar, simple.' One fantastic rumour had riled up all of Lahore Junction, from the coolies up to the managers: 'Trains to India's capital were going with bags filled with gold bricks, jewellery and cash of wealthy Hindus.' Which added to the woes of the railway police, their hands already full with overcrowded trains pulling out of Laur. Which reminded him that he should book his Delhi tickets to avoid being waitlisted.

As he unlatched the gate, the complete stillness of his home arrested him. Usually, Pammi was in the shade of the verandah, studying. The voice of Narinder reciting some English poem or memorizing maths tables floated forth. He let the latch clang back loudly. No one opened the front door to greet him – not even Surinder who prepared his evening beverage of tea or sherbet. Kishan Singh hurried to ring the doorbell.

A teary Narinder opened the door. Kishan kept a soothing hand on her head. 'Wh-what happened? Where are your sisters?'

'Oh, Bapuji,' Surinder cried as she ran to him.

With an arm around each, Kishan comforted his daughters, even as he tore up inside imagining the calamities that had befallen his beloved Pammi. When the threesome reached Pammi's room, he saw her curled up like a foetus on her bed. His daughter was safe – the relief that flooded his veins made him weak in his knees as he wobbled to the edge of the bed and sat down.

'Pammi, puttar,' he said in his softest voice. 'What has happened?'

At his voice, the prone Pammi sat up – her eyes swollen, face flushed. Then, with a howl, she buried her head in his lap.

It took Kishan Singh some time before he pieced together what his daughters were mourning. Asad, their neighbour, had visited in the afternoon with some terrible news. Tara and her entire family were dead, their home set afire by goondas a few days back. 'No-no,' Pammi cried. Tara and she had plans to meet, they were to start work on Tara's bagh for her trousseau, Tara liked Pammi's embroidery, her stitches were so neat – and Tara would cook Pammi's favourite kadhi–chawal, the pakoras with fenugreek and coriander seeds, just the way she liked them ... and in sufficient quantity, so they would have some left over to go with evening tea ... no no no Tara couldn't just go no no no ...

Sitting on the edge of the bed, Kishan Singh cradled the hillock of his daughters, his arms holding the precious bundle together, his heart horrified yet unable to grapple with the enormity of the story. Kanwal Malik and Tara were not like the faceless people dying daily in Laur. Malik was an established businessman of Anarkali, the shop having been started by his grandfather. Tara and Pammi were thick enough for Surinder to complain about feeling left out. And though Tara failed matric repeatedly, which Kishan Singh disapproved of, it made no dent to their friendship or to Pammi's studies. Tara continued to laugh and banter – he had to shut his bedroom door to muffle her loud voice – as Pammi continued to ace her exams, even whilst sporting the nail polish that Tara painted on Pammi's fingers.

The images of what those goons might have done, would have done, had done, to Tara fried Kishan Singh's brain. Danger was at their door—

'I have to see Tara,' Pammi wailed. 'I h-have to see Tara's home ... See where they killed her ... I have to see Tara d-d-dead ... oh no, Taaa-raaa ...'

Narinder fetched a towel to wipe her elder sister's nose and dab her face as Pammi slumped over like a rag doll. Surinder, who, in her serious fashion, had a solution for most things, sat still with clenched hands. Crickets had started their raucous roll call. Around them, dusk was swiftly deepening into night. And Kishan Singh realized he didn't know the first thing about defending his house from attack. In his mind flashed an image of Lahore Junction: eerily empty, all tracks vacant, no engines, no compartments, no bogies, no coolies, no passengers ... Except for one train.

Single engine, three compartments.

And out of the deathly quiet, a matter-of-fact announcement.

'Your train is delayed.'

45
Delhi (July 1947)

In his office, Mountbatten looked as fresh as the laburnum blooming in the Mughal Gardens outside his study. The tear-off calendar, with a page to be ripped off daily in the countdown to independent India, hung on the wall behind him. The day of the month was at the top and, underneath it in bold, the words: 'X days left to prepare for the Transfer of Power'. He had issued one to each of his staff to keep them focussed on the mammoth task on hand, an independent India in less than a month.

Now, Dickie's gaze settled on the photograph on his desk. The framed picture of his father had travelled with him to all his postings. He must have got lost in thought for he registered some urgent enquiry in the air. 'S-ir?'

'Ah, Miéville.' Dickie turned to his secretary.

Miéville paused to look at the photograph of Prince Louis. 'Sir, if I may … He was a greatly wronged man.'

Dickie nodded his head. 'I have only one ambition – to go back to sea and then to become the First Sea Lord.' He knocked on his desk. 'But first, I must settle the business of India.'

He started dictating to Miéville.

'I am trying my very best to create an integrated India, which, while securing stability, will ensure friendship with Great Britain. If I am allowed to play my own hand without interference I have no doubt I will succeed.'

'Conrad Corfield is not going to be happy,' Miéville stated.

'Considering he spent his time at the Home Office in London trying his best to make my job difficult, I do not owe him any consideration of happiness.'

Hadn't Corfield worked systematically to obstruct his policy? It did not help that London was still debating the exact manner of implementation of its policy towards the native princes. However, Dickie had managed, for once, to get both the Congress and the Muslim League to agree on something: A States' Department to take over from Corfield's Political Department. He was relieved as well that the Congress had not put Nehru in charge, his socialist leanings at odds with the princes.

With a shiver, Dickie recalled Nehru's threat to resign. He had tried to reason, roping in the even-keeled Patel, to no avail. With Parliament approving the Independence Bill, Dickie had given Congress charge of all central government ministries – the League could only interfere in Pakistan-related matters.

Thankfully, Patel was a realist. On 5 July, he had come out with his policy statement, the gist of which was a formula created by the very capable V.P. Menon. It offered a chance of reconciliation for all parties concerned. Which Patel had conveyed in his usual forthright manner. Dickie skimmed over the communique again.

'We ask no more of the states than accession on these three subjects in which the common interest of the country is involved. In other matters, we would scrupulously respect their autonomous existence. This country ... is the proud heritage of the people who inhabit it. It is an accident that some live in the states and some in British India ... None can segregate us into sentiments ... better therefore for all to make laws sitting together as friends than to make treaties as aliens.'

A khidmatgar entered discreetly and removed the silver platter with tea and biscuits from the elevenses. VP had impressed upon Patel that the Viceroy's office, as well as his relationship to the Royal Family, would influence the princely rulers. They were a team now, the royal and the revolutionary, responsible for leading the princely rulers on the path to accession.

A knock, and Patel entered. In his khadi dhoti, he looked like a Roman senator in toga. Miéville excused himself.

'Your Excellency, I believe you had another interesting meeting with Mr Monckton.'

'Mr Patel,' Dickie said as they shook hands and sat across from each other at his desk, 'it had its dramatic moments.'

'I can't wait to hear all about it.'

Sir Walter Monckton, an English lawyer with a distinguished record in public life, was the Nizam of Hyderabad's constitutional adviser. Vallabh had heard from his sources that when Monckton heard of the former's appointment as head of the States' Department, he had commented that the Sardar would inherit the rights, but not the obligations of the paramount power. Since then, the lawyer had been blowing hot and cold, flying into Delhi to conduct negotiations with the Viceroy and V.P. Menon, consenting to nothing, while the Nizam refused to meet the Viceroy. A fanatical Muslim movement was growing daily in Hyderabad, encouraged by Jinnah, and the Nizam seemed to be astride a tiger he wouldn't know to control.

'I stressed, as I have done repeatedly, that the only safe option for the Nizam is to accede. After all, he is the ruler of a largely Hindu state. I informed Sir Walter that by adhering to his advice, the Nizam was bound to lose his throne. He was none too thrilled,' Dickie said wryly. 'He accused me of blackmail and threatened that if Hyderabad were pushed too far, it would go down fighting and kindle a civil war all over India.'

Blackmail, hmm ... Vallabh's mouth set. The Congress had requested the Viceroy to stay on as the Governor General of independent India and he had agreed. The fact that Jinnah had announced his own appointment as Pakistan's first Governor General might be another factor propelling the Viceroy's energetic work on the princes. Which might make men like Monckton question his impartiality, but how long would they continue to play bluff? Had it escaped the Nizam that his state was landlocked in the heart of Hindustan? With a population of almost 16 million, Hyderabad was India's largest state ruled by a Muslim dynasty.

'Mr Jinnah has been openly backing the Nizam, as you well know.'

'Indeed!' the Viceroy said sharply. 'He has already warned me that if the Congress tries to pressure Hyderabad to accede, every Muslim throughout India would rise as one man in defence.'

Vallabh would not let Hyderabad be a cancer in the belly of India.

'Your Excellency, when I reached England to study, I made sure to visit all the tourist sites in London in the first week itself. This ensured I would not be distracted by my unsatisfied curiosity during my education.' He smiled. 'We will stay focussed. It helps that we have a few weeks until the transfer of power.'

Miéville stepped in to remind them that Her Excellency with Pamela was awaiting them poolside for lunch.

The two men detoured through Mughal Gardens towards lunch, discussing ways to end the Maharaja of Kashmir's procrastination towards signing the Instrument of Accession. For which purpose Dickie had earlier flown to Kashmir.

'I advised the Maharaja that he must establish the will of the people and then, depending on the outcome, accede to India or Pakistan.'

The hardy canna's bright red flowers caught Vallabh's eye as he walked past. A true plant of the tropics, blooming in the blazing heat. But the plant occupying Vallabh's mind was another.

Kashmir and Hyderabad were the two apples of princely India that were the rosiest, and on the thorniest branch too. Each state was the inverse of the other – Kashmir, a largely Muslim state with a Hindu ruler; Hyderabad, a Hindu state with a Muslim Nizam. The Viceroy had made it clear that just as Hyderabad should concede to India, Kashmir should go to Pakistan. The only other possibility was to partition the state such that the smaller Hindu section of Jammu came to India. Which made sense to Vallabh, but not to Jawaharlal, a Kashmiri Brahmin.

'However, we never had a chance to discuss the situation in any meaningful way.' Dickie rubbed his chin.

In his mind, Dickie was seeing the elaborate state banquet laid out for his benefit when he flew down to meet Maharaja Hari Singh. At some point, when chicken curry was being served, a bell went off and, out of the blue, the band struck '*God save the King*'! Which meant of course that the guests, midway through spooning their curry, scrambled to stand up. All quite enchanting, but not what the Maharaja had planned. He got so miffed that it set off a colic attack, which made him cancel his appointment with Dickie.

'The Maharaja is indecisive, at the least … and seems evasive,' Dickie concluded.

'Hmm,' Vallabh nodded. If Hyderabad was India's stomach, Kashmir was the head. But it was decidedly Muslim. And coveted by Jawaharlal. Whom Maharaja Hari Singh had put in one of his jails the last time he had tried to visit the state … The fact was that Jawaharlal was emotional about Kashmir and, as a socialist, contemptuous of the Maharaja.

As they continued through the Mughal Gardens, each man occupied in his thoughts, Vallabh's mind took him back to 1936, when he had his nose operated and let go of his drooping moustache. After the operation, he was asked why he had shaved off his whiskers. 'I am a socialist now,' Vallabh had remarked. Those who were in the know understood his winking reference to Jawaharlal and his ilk of socialist radicals, who were going on about socialism when the need of the hour was for the Congress to focus on freeing India first – all else could follow thereon. From the corner of his eye, Vallabh glanced at the Viceroy. In January, when he had first heard of Lord Louis Mountbatten, he had assumed that with his new-fangled ideas, he would simply be a toy for Jawaharlal to play with. But Vallabh had to admit: After a few initial run-ins, the Viceroy and he had settled into an effective working relationship.

A bird chaser's yodel sounded in the distance. Vallabh watched pigeons swirl up.

Menon's 'rare birds' included a miserly, paranoid Nizam and a weak, vacillating Maharaja. Each had a sizeable army and was crowing about sovereignty. The duo would require all at the disposal of M/s Mountbatten & Patel to be drawn in – bullying, cajoling, seduction, charm … the iron well hidden in the gloved fist.

46
Laur (July 1947)

As he went about his ablutions, Beli Ram recited the Kalma, then the Gayatri Mantra, followed by the Mool Mantar.

The god of all of Laur used to be Rab. Now, Lauris had divided him too. Trying to appease all the gods, Beli Ram had learnt the Kalma from Mehmood and the Mool Mantar from Kishan Singh. The Kalma could prove a lifesaver even, if caught by marauders intent on orally verifying his religion. If they stripped him, he would be dead. Faith had become a matter of foreskin. The cries of 'Allah-u-Akbar' were drowning out 'Har Har Mahadev' in Laur and Beli was ready to convert. Except, the mullah at Mehmood's mosque said there were to be no more conversions – kuffar were to be expelled.

Beli gulped at the memory as he rinsed his mouth, which made him choke. Coughing, he was rising from his squat when a scream shattered the stillness of Sunday morning. He rushed to the door and stuck his neck out. Sure enough, a crowd had gathered near the giant banyan. Folks from the mohalla, he was reassured to see, not Muslim goons. But what were they—

Another scream, then a series of shrieks, and the crowd shifted slightly.

Beli Ram bolted his door shut and hurried towards the commotion. He wiped his wet face on the sleeves of his kurta. Ahead, Shammi Joseph stood on a chabutara, palms behind his back. At Beli Ram's approach, he turned and tossed his chin at him in acknowledgement.

'What's going on?' Beli hurried to Shammi's vantage point. Together, the two men observed the central spectacle which had drawn the crowd.

Billo, hair astray, in a shabby salwar–kameez, no chunni, spun with her arms stretched out. A man with matted hair, in saffron lungi–kurta, multiple long chains cascading from his neck, waved a broom in the air. In his left hand, he held a brass pot from which smoke wafted. He smashed the broom hard on Billo. She yelped and clutched her head. After which, the sadhu thrust the brass pot in Billo's face, the smoke enveloping her such that it appeared she was on fire. Billo screamed and tore away, rubbing her eyes, as she dashed about in the circle of onlookers. The sadhu lifted his chin imperiously and a male relative stepped forward, grabbed Billo by one arm, and dragged her back to the centre of the circle. The sadhu started whacking Billo with the broom – on her head, her chest, her legs, hitting her with mounting ferocity. Billo screamed and tried to protect herself with her hands, but the broom wouldn't stop raining down upon her. She fell to the floor and thrashed about. The sadhu's matted hair flew as his arms pumped and the broom thinned. Twigs broke loose upon Billo.

'Sauri de,' Beli Ram muttered.

'Stop cussing! Save the woman if you can.'

Lata Lily Joseph had joined them, a hand resting atop her pregnant belly. Shammi jumped to her side and wrapped an arm around her shoulder. 'Let's go home ... This is not good for you,' he urged.

Lata shrugged him off, her gaze fixed on Billo, who was moaning and whimpering on the packed-mud floor. Reed twigs adorned her hair, clothes, her bruised face and hands. The sadhu had discarded what was left of the broom. Now he was chanting, waving the smoke from the brass pot at Moolchand first, then the rest of Billo's family. Mai Peeto hurried forward, hands pressed together, to receive the smokey benediction. Others followed. The sadhu's voice rose. He glanced up at the sky and started to speak rapidly, his face contorting.

'What the *hell* is happening?' Beli Ram glanced from the crowd to Shammi–Lata.

'Exorcism,' Shammi answered.

'That I can see! But why?'

'Because Billo is possessed – so her family says.'

'Because she mutters all day?' Beli was still confused.

Lata swung her head at Beli Ram, who quivered under her withering look. 'She's been mumbling about unusual rain, haven't you heard? Red rain ... of blood and bodies and vultures ... Her mutterings are bad omens, apparently.'

'Which are causing the current problems in Laur,' Shammi added sorrowfully.

'Mad or what?' Beli scowled at him. 'Why not exorcise the Mozang men, haan?'

The sadhu, meanwhile, had wound down and the crowd started to disperse. Billo lay on the ground like yesterday's newspaper. Her clothes were tattered, a rent in her kameez exposed her flesh, there was blood on her face. Beli's eyes welled up.

As Billo's family members headed back to their house, he shouted. 'That's it! Walk away now, will you?'

'Shhh ...' Shammi tapped Beli Ram. 'It's a family matter.'

'*They* made it a tamasha,' Beli hissed.

Moolchand and family paid no attention to him, except to bang their door shut. The sun had risen high in the sky and the rooftops were barren. Billo would roast in the heat ... unless she sought shelter under the banyan tree ... Beli Ram wiped the sweat that kept sprouting on his face, feeling hot and helpless.

Lata spat on the ground. 'Pulping a woman to expel demons! What about that walking–talking demon?'

The sadhu was heading out of the mohalla, swinging his brass lota like a man who had finished delivering his dump.

A frantic Shammi patted the air in front of his wife. 'Calm down, Lata, my love, this is not our business.'

'*Not our business!*' Lata jeered. 'You men need to expel your own demons, which make you kill each other for land, ladies ... now Laur!' Swivelling on her toes, she started to walk back home.

Shammi shook his head and sighed. 'Okay, brother Beli. Got to get ready for church.' He started to follow his wife.

Beli Ram needed to get this off his chest. Ordinarily, he would head to Mohalla Barkat to meet Mehmood. But the damn Mozang men had made that impossible. He would have to sit at home and stew. As he passed the mouth of the alley into which Shammi had turned, something arrested him. Narrowing his eyes, Beli Ram scanned the whitewashed walls of Shammi's house. Two large crosses were painted in bright blue, one on each side of the door. The side wall carried large Urdu calligraphy: 'Isai da Makaan'.

With Muslims and Hindus torching each other's houses, Shammi's Christ might just save his. In the fight between elephants, didn't ants get crushed? Beli puttar, he reprimanded himself, why bother with Kalma when there's the Lord's Prayer?

47
Delhi (July 1947)

At lunch with Edwina and Pamela, as the khidmatgar served the first course, the discussion was politely non-political, the weather an integral part of it.

'Beastly, really,' Edwina said. 'Who would have thought we would arrive from the coldest winter in London to the hottest summer in Delhi!'

'Looks like this summer will set a record in more ways than one,' Patel drawled, his eyes twinkling.

Edwina grinned. 'I take the question of the princely states is settled?'

Dickie nodded. 'The monsoons are delayed, I am informed – but our plans are progressing, slowly and surely, you would agree, Mr Patel?'

'I have informed the princes that the government's terms would be stiffer after 15 August. After all,' Patel said, 'they have to understand that there is a limit to my capacity to restrain foes of the princely order.'

'Rightly so,' Edwina added, as she tucked into roast chicken.

Again, she grinned. A smile that was reciprocated, Dickie noticed, by Patel. Hmm ... What was he missing? The stern Sardar of the Congress had a jovial side that Dickie had just begun to discover, and this lunch was clearly an occasion where his wife was discovering it too.

'I believe Your Excellency has been rather forceful in his approach to some rulers. Menon informs me that the Maharaja-Rana of Dholpur asked you what you thought India would do if he did not accede. To which you replied, "Nothing."'

'Precisely,' Dickie spooned the brown gravy on a piece of bread, and looked up. 'I categorically informed him that was where his problem lay. His state would remain in complete isolation in the centre of an indifferent India.'

Edwina chuckled heartily.

That had been no laughing matter – Dickie tried to catch her eye, but she was busy concentrating on her food. Pamela, meanwhile, with her brows, indicated something beneath the table.

'The Maharaja of Jodhpur has had several meetings with Mr Jinnah. At the last one, I hear from my sources, he gave the Maharaja a blank sheet of paper, handed him his fountain pen and said, "You can fill in all your conditions." Highly irresponsible, you will agree?' Patel's penetrating eyes sought affirmation.

'Mr Jinnah has objected to our policy of accession, as you well know. And he has publicly announced to guarantee the independence of the princely states in Pakistan. That's some carrot to dangle.' Dickie registered the trail of sweat on his back. These poolside lunches were Edwina's fancy – he would much rather be enjoying this chicken in his temperature-controlled study. 'However, what cannot be denied is that the majority of states are irretrievably linked geographically with the Dominion of India.'

'As I said, Your Excellency,' Patel smiled serenely over his plate of rice and lentils, 'I am prepared to accept your offer, but you have to give me a full basket of apples.'

'Apples?' Edwina exclaimed.

'I will buy a basket with 565 apples, but if there are even two or three missing, the deal is off. The Viceroy and the home minister have struck a horticultural bargain.' Patel chuckled now.

Dickie, meanwhile, had sat back in his chair, his eyes intent on the action beneath the table. One of Edwina's high-heeled shoes, which she was in the habit of knocking off at mealtime, was dangling from a thick male foot. One of his wife's feet was bare, but the other was ensconced in thick sandals. Her Excellency and the home minister were trying on each other's shoes to mutual merriment.

'That's a rather precise number for apples,' Pamela said as she offered a piece from her plate to Mizzen, who was on his hind legs, begging.

The khidmatgar quietly cleared the plates.

Patel turned to Pamela. 'A history lesson, if I may, to help you understand? As British India expanded its boundaries, it entered into treaty arrangements with an increasing number of native princes. Under this treaty, the Raj would place a British resident in the princely state's capital to whom the state would then be subordinated. This would ensure they were not absorbed into the colonial bloc, giving the princes a degree of autonomy. To date, we have 565 individual states.'

Pamela's jaw hung loose. 'Well, you have your work cut out for you!'

Patel squinted at the sun. 'Some like Hyderabad and Kashmir are really large, like any European country you would know. While many, over 300, situated in Kathiawar and Gujarat, are petty principalities.' He paused. 'Some poor, some rich, some corrupt, some able – but all undeniably Indian. And that is why each one of them counts. The Congress has been clear for a long time now that the Indian states cannot be converted into an Indian Ulster.'

'*Ind*-ian Ulster – how?' Pamela glanced from the home minister to the Viceroy in confusion.

'You see, Pammie,' Dickie waded in, 'Mr Patel is referring to the 1921 partition of Ireland, where six counties of the province of Ulster chose to stay with UK as Northern Ireland. The rest joined the Free State of Ireland.'

'How interesting,' Pamela said.

Beneath the table, Patel was attempting to put weight on the high heels, trying to figure out what it felt like to walk in those shoes. Edwina, meanwhile, had both her feet encased in the black leather sandals of the home minister and was sitting cross-legged, at ease.

'Mr Patel,' Dickie said, 'If I give you a basket with,' he furrowed his brow, 'say 560 apples, will you buy it?'

Vallabh was aware of the recalcitrants. The Nawab of Bhopal, the Muslim ruler of a Hindu state, was an old friend of the Viceroy and a polo buddy. He knew that the Nawab had rejoiced at the news of his friend, Lord Mountbatten, coming to India as Viceroy, believing it was a signal that all would go well with the princely states. Vallabh had heard that the Nawab was now feeling betrayed. Facing the full force of viceregal charm, he was withering. The last Vallabh had heard, the Nawab was threatening to abdicate in favour of his twenty-three-year-old daughter. It helped that the royal leading the native royals to their pen was a cousin of King George VI, close enough to call the King-Emperor 'Bertie'.

'Well,' Patel shrugged, 'I might. But ...'

Dickie leaned forward and steepled his hands. 'Let's persist with the courtship then.'

48
Laur (August 1947)

Pammi stepped out of home, patting her chunni over her head. The afternoon sun smote her; besides, she was trying to stay hidden.

Bapuji was firm: No going outside, the city had gone mad. With strict instructions to them to double bolt the door from inside, and to *not* open it for *any* one – Asad, even – and to do their work quietly so as not to draw attention, he left for work on time and returned by 5.15 p.m. daily. But Pammi wanted to see Tara's home. It seemed such a betrayal to be safe while Tara ... vivacious, beauteous Tara ... Tara of the laugh and wink and lipsticks and boyfriend ... whom she had known since they played with dolls together ... had gone away forever ... a-a-and Pammi hadn't even said goo-goodbye. But Bapuji didn't understand.

'Puttar, there's nothing left but smouldering rubble.'

When she kept insisting, he promised that he would take her there himself *after* things settled down. Meanwhile, there was a trip to Dilli coming up, for which they had to pack and prepare gifts, hmmm?

'But who is Shamsher chachaji?' Pammi had sulked. 'I don't remember ever meeting him.'

Bapuji patted her head. 'That's okay. He's been working in Dilli for long. Hmmm ... I don't think he has ever seen Narinder, for that matter ...'

Pammi felt deflated. 'Bapuji, please, let's not travel. I don't want to go to a strange place—'

'We could go to Lyallpur?'

Iqbal Tayaji's abundant fields were welcoming, but Pammi didn't fancy being relegated to the kitchen, cooking mounds of rotis as she endured advice on marriage and suitable grooms ... Na! Nobody in the extended family understood her love for books and studies. She was so thankful for her Bapuji. On that thought, Pammi cheered up and suggested Bapuji send a picture of all of them to Shamsher chachaji, lest they be expecting three little girls and get young women at their doorstep instead! Which Bapuji had promptly actioned. They were leaving in a few days, their bags were packed and ready, and this was one last thing Pammi had to do. Quietly. She would be back before Surinder and Narinder awoke from their siesta, and Bapuji wouldn't have a clue.

Sticking to Railway Road, minding her own business, Pammi walked on briskly.

∽

'You know Nayyar saab? Who retired from the freight department last year? Yes, yes, that Mr Nayyar who always dressed in suit-boot like some English afsar. Well, he was walking through Anarkali when someone slit his stomach open;

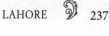

clean strike. One minute, our man is upright. The next, he's holding his intestines in his hands!'

Mangat clucked his tongue and crossed his arms to touch his ear lobes. 'Tauba, tauba! Such devilry in our city. It's as if Abdali has come visiting us again.'

Kishan Singh made a sighing sound, nodded in sympathy, and returned to his work. It helped that there was a large pile of papers on his desk. Behind which he hid daily as he tried to stick to his business. Too many people were riled up all over Laur. On the streets, the RSS and the Muslim League were playing Holi with kerosene-soaked rags. In the office, Ahmed and Mangat traded tales of atrocities, even as they kept count of which side had notched more killings. *The Tribune* was advising non-Muslims not to 'desert Lahore like cowards … but to fight like soldiers'. The *Dawn*, Jinnah's mouthpiece, was blaming Sardar Patel for everything. And Master Tara Singh was chanting daily, 'Remember Rawalpindi!' like the Mool Mantar. It would be good to get to Dilli—

'Oye, Mangat!' Ahmed waded in. 'Your Hindu Mahasabha men are making bombs in chemist shops. Why do you think there is no milk in Laur? Because Hindu goons set fire to the milkmen's colony. Why? Because Muslims lived there, hain! Oye, you worship cows, but will burn live buffalos—'

A loud throat-clearing sounded and Balwant Rai stepped in. The clerks bent their heads and pretended to work. Except for Hari Kumar, who had returned to work from his month-long imprisonment – for disturbing public peace – and was trying not to get terminated. Kishan Singh glanced at the wall clock. Two more hours to go. Mangat's gory story had rattled him. He couldn't wait to get home, secure the door, and listen to his daughters' plans for Dilli.

'The Viceroy's House? Reee-ally? We will be guests of the Viceroy himself?'

'No, silly! The staff compound of the Viceroy's House.'

'Still. What if we bump into the Viceroy's wife? Mrs Viceroy? Lady Viceroy? Pammi, how is she called?'

'Vicereine.'

'Vice-reen? Rhymes with ice cream!'

❧

Pammi was approaching Banni Hata, her heart thudding.

All through her walk, she had kept her head low, her gaze averted, but she had, nonetheless, drawn attention. A cyclist had trilled at her repeatedly. A rickshaw had slowed down and offered her a ride. When she declined, the man puckered his mouth and made horrible sucking sounds. There weren't any unaccompanied women walking about. She should just turn back. But she was so close—

A truck roared by, its draft flinging the chunni from her head. As she grappled with the wayward scarf, the truck slowed down, then started to reverse. Pammi skittered to the farthest edge of the footpath, wrapped her chunni snug around her head, shoulders, chest, and was about to continue forward when a man jumped out of the truck and started running towards her. Pammi squealed, swivelled, and started to run back the way she had come.

Her feet thundered in her ears, her heart was in her mouth, her braid whipped about like a snake, her chunni slipped, her feet tangled, and she hurtled to the ground. A burly hand grabbed her forearm, hoisted her, heaped her over a shoulder, and Pammi watched the road below blur as the man bounded with her. She rained blows down his back. She thrashed her legs to kick him. Tears filled her eyes. Panic seized her. She screamed. Her body hit a seat. The driver with thick whiskers leered at her as his companion climbed aboard, slammed the door shut, and the truck roared to life.

'No, no, no,' Pammi flung her arms as she tried to get upright, but the man with stinky breath was bearing down upon her.

A slap made her ears ring before her head crashed into the iron headrest.

⁑

No, no, no, Pammi puttar, why would you do this?

Kishan Singh sobbed and ran, up and down, up and down, the routes Pammi could have taken from home to Tara's. Nearing Banni Hata, he sighted the pink mulmul chunni with white lace that she had sewn for herself as she embroidered pillowcases for Shamsher's wife. His knees gave way; he collapsed to the ground and buried his face in the chunni.

At some point, he made his way to the police station. The constable on duty pooh-poohed his claim.

'What abduction?' He rapped the table with his staff. 'How do you know your daughter didn't run away?'

Kishan Singh begged with folded hands.

Constable Akram Majid grabbed the chunni, smelled it, and smiled. But he refused to record a statement. 'Wait, old man,' he counselled, 'she will return after a few days of debauchery.'

Kishan's ears burned with the calumny being hurled at his beloved Pammi. But he was at the mercy of the police, most of whom, he was now realizing, were Muslim.

'Please, sir, motia aleo, please, padshaho, please … Please help before it gets too late …'

'Too late?' Constable Akram leaned back in his chair, stacked his feet on the desk and twirled his moustache. 'Wait some more, Singh sahib, and you can ask Chief Minister Master Tara Singh to find your daughter.'

Hearing which, his colleagues thumped their desks and laughed. One stood up and farted loudly.

'Failing which, you can always petition Chacha Nehru, no?'

49
Delhi (August 1947)

'My estimate is that Sikh militants number over 20,000 now.'

Evan Jenkins sat upright, only his left hand, the thumb picking repeatedly at the index finger, betrayed the heat the Panjab Governor was feeling.

'They are battle-ready,' Pug added, 'having fought in the deserts of North Africa and the jungles of Burma during the war.'

'Also well equipped, having retained their weapons.'

They waited for the Viceroy to respond, but he appeared preoccupied. His Excellency was beginning to look worn out, Pug Ismay noted. Even Edwina looked dead tired nowadays and the couple were at each other's throats so frequently that Pug was increasingly acting the peacemaker.

Dickie was at the French windows of his study. In the Mughal Gardens, a host of gardeners tended to the geometric flower beds, the water fountains, the endless stretch of green grass. When the Sikh leaders had met Dickie to plead their case for the separate state of Khalistan, their solution was simple: Redraw the borders of Panjab, grant Jinnah a crescent on the western edge, grant Congress a slice from the east that edged the United Provinces, and the balance would be home to 80 per cent of the Sikh community. This would include their holiest shrines and the fertile canal lands that the Sikh farmers had developed over the years. On paper, a neat solution indeed.

'What happens to the 20 per cent Sikhs that are outside?' Dickie had asked.

Giani Kartar Singh, a Sikh leader who had accompanied Baldev Singh, had stroked his long white beard. 'If the remaining Sikhs in Pakistan, less than a million, were exchanged with Muslims in Khalistan, the problem is solved.'

'In case the Sikh solution is not accepted?'

The Giani had stroked his Santa Claus beard – the other hand cradling a sheathed long sword – and continued to lock gaze with Dickie. 'We have made Mr Jenkins aware of the alternative. The Muslims have already rid Rawalpindi Division of Sikhs, and appropriated our substantial land and property. The Sikhs will similarly get rid of Muslims from East Panjab and invite Sikhs from the west to take their place.'

Dickie heard his chief of staff clear his throat loudly.

'... it doesn't help, of course,' Jenkins was saying, 'that Sikh maharajas are bankrolling them. I hear the Maharaja of Faridkot has converted a distillery on his land into an explosives factory.'

Dickie started to pace the study floor. 'The Sikh plan for an exchange of population might have been a workable solution. But the Congress and Mr Jinnah won't hear of it.'

'The Quaid is eyeing the Sikhs who end up in Pakistan as useful hostages to ensure the well-being of Muslims left behind in India. His attitude,' Jenkins shook his head, 'is perilously unsound.'

'Neither will Mr Nehru consider the demand for Khalistan,' Pug pointed out. 'He has advised Baldev Singh and other Sikh leaders to await the result of the Boundary Commission.'

Jenkins probed his bushy moustache. 'The location of Sikh shrines and Sikh landholding will play a significant role in the Radcliffe award, I presume?'

The mention of Nehru reminded Dickie that he still had to discuss with the Prime-Minister-to-be the dates up to which the Union Jack might continue to be flown in India after independence. Edwina thought it a silly issue when compared with the plight of refugees pouring into Delhi. Apparently, she had lobbied hard for the Nursing Council Bill to be passed before partition, and finally sought Jawa-har's ... Jawa's help. Dickie had stopped tussling with the polysyllabic Ja-wa-har, shortening it to the handy Jawa. The bill was approved within two days – which was when Dickie had first heard of it. She really was working herself into a frenzy over her healthcare initiatives—

'When do we get to see it?'

'Hmm?' Dickie turned to Jenkins.

'The Boundary Commission award?'

'I am keeping Cyril at arm's length – if only for all to see that the Viceroy has no say in the dismemberment of the two states. I do hear that his digestion has taken a bit of a knock in the awful heat.'

'Well ... there is going to be continuing trouble with the Sikhs.' A grim Jenkins reiterated. 'When, and how bad, we cannot yet say.'

'How about arresting the Sikh leaders?'

'There seems little point in that. If we jail them in Indian East Panjab, they will no doubt be freed after independence. If caught in the West, they will likely be killed. And their followers are running on their own steam now, unlikely to be deterred by their absence. What I need is more troops and reconnaissance planes to hunt down the jathas. The fact is that rural communities in Panjab are inextricably mixed and the only way to deter the marauders is through the display and use of force on a massive scale.'

'Well, you have the Panjab Boundary Force for precisely that purpose.'

Dickie firmly believed that the Boundary Force would adequately meet any contingency arising from partition. A show of force by neutral units under British officers would ease fears in the border areas. In his meetings with Sikh leaders, he had used it as a threat to warn against future violence. The Boundary Force would meet any violent uprising with tanks, airplanes and artillery – in essence, the full force of the British Indian Army.

'With a promised strength of 50,000 soldiers,' Jenkins reminded him. 'At present, I have only 7500 rifles to cover twelve border districts that house 12.5 million people. Amritsar district, currently the most disturbed, is being patrolled by just *one* weak brigade.'

Dickie breathed heavily through his nose. For nearly a century, the British-led army, with its mix of Hindu, Muslim, Sikh battalions within the same regiment, had held India together. But the Congress and the Muslim League wanted their own armed forces under their control before 15 August. Now, dismantling of the Indian Army was underway with Muslim units transferring to Pakistan and non-Muslims to India. The partitioning of the army was intensifying the communal feelings within. Would a Sikh soldier fire upon a Sikh jatha? A Baluchi on Muslims? A Madrasi on a rioting Hindu? The fragmenting land had infected the army as well.

Dickie shook his head to clear it. 'Gentlemen, this partition business is sheer madness, and I have always maintained so … Any wonder we are sitting on a barrel of gunpowder now!'

'Good lord, no,' a solemn Jenkins objected. 'We got off that a long time ago. Now, we are sitting on a complete magazine which is going to blow up any time.'

50
Laur (August 1947)

Beli Ram poured steaming hot tea into two brass tumblers.
Mehmood had come to his house late at night to give his curfewed friend company. Now, pre-dawn, he planned to slink out before the mohalla woke up and started to crow like a rooster at the Mussalman in their midst. The news of Pammi's abduction had rattled poor Beli. At Lahore Junction, his eyes spun in their sockets as he scanned crowds and stared at every woman for sign of his beloved— What? Kishan Singh had lost a daughter – one could commiserate with him. What had Beli lost? He was in the legion of Majnus, their agony a source of bewildered marvel to poets and singers.

'I have a name.' Beli Ram handed a tumbler to Mehmood. 'Sepoy Malik.'

Mehmood blew on the proffered tea; the smell of fennel wafted up. He cradled the hot tumbler in his headscarf. Since Pammi's abduction, Beli Ram had been hunting for suitable ideas for defence.

'Apparently, he returned from fighting the war in France tully with asla, ammunition, and bravery medals. For a suitable price, the sepoy will part with a weapon.'

Mehmood distrusted the description instantly. Soldiers were running armed militias in the countryside and he wanted Beli to have nothing to do with them. '*Who* is this Malik?'

'Sepoy, I told you, no?' Beli looked querulous.

'Yes, but which community? How do you know he will help you?'

'Right. This "Malik" can be Hindu or Mussalman. But, from what I hear, his only interest is in making a sale.' Beli Ram slurped his tea, closing his eyes as he delighted in the brew.

Mehmood was amazed at his friend's ability to consume scalding tea.

'I have heard he has a trunkful of military-grade grenades. One of those can lop off the heads of an entire roomful of people.'

'Oye, Beli. What are we to do with grenades? We just need to be able to defend ourselves … not go killing others.'

'Aaho. We need two guns – one for you, one for me – and that will do to scare any ruffian.'

Mehmood scratched his chin where a tuft of hair served for a beard he had lately begun to grow. He was keeping his whiskers, which could be shaved off, if the need arose to fulfil the requirement of a visibly Mussalman look. He sipped on his tea and searched for a way to distract his friend.

'Let us go together. Once we are in the sepoy's neighbourhood, the right person can approach him,' Beli said.

'Okay,' Mehmood nodded. 'Together.' He glanced up at the sky; he should be leaving soon.

'Did you hear? Old man Kishan has left for Ambarsar.' Beli Ram drained the tumbler, placed it on the packed-mud floor, and cradled an imaginary weight in his palms. 'This big padlock I saw on his front door.'

Mehmood though had heard something entirely different. Old man Kishan was locking his two younger daughters at home while he walked the streets of Laur in search of his eldest one. He had stopped coming to work altogether. Mehmood had seen him on Railway Road, mumbling 'Waheguru … Waheguru', turban askew, eyes glazed. That wretched sight so wrung Mehmood's heart that he knew what the hen felt when the butcher squeezed its neck.

Best to let Beli believe otherwise. Mehmood stood up. Beli had begun his morning ablutions.

'He must have family there.'

Beli Ram was squatting in the corner – a twig of neem under his teeth. 'You know, Mehmood,' his voice came out thick and he spat, then cupped water from a bucket and swished it around his mouth. His face had turned dark.

'What?' Mehmood asked.

Standing up, Beli Ram wiped his palms on his kurta.

'Beli, were you prying around Kishan's house?'

'Oh-ho,' Beli Ram said as he returned to the jute cots, and started to fold the thin mattresses and bed sheets.

'I passed by his home just … just to see if Pammi had come back.'

'O yaara!'

Beli leaned forward, casting a look around even though there was nobody except for the two friends. 'Some nights before, as I passed by the house, I heard quarrelling inside. It came from the garden, and you know the boundary wall is along the lane. I stopped to listen … I heard a voice urging old man Kishan to join a jatha. They had arms and ammunition, and needed all able-bodied Sikh men of the neighbourhood to join them.'

Mehmood frowned. There was more light outside now, and he had to leave soon.

'When Kishan Singh stayed silent, the man reminded him he had lost one daughter already! Kishan cried. He said that he was old, he didn't know how to use a gun ... The stranger's voice got rough. "Look, Kishan, you have to make up your mind. The Mussalmans have burnt down our gurdwaras in Mozang. This is a return of the old Mussalman tyranny ... Have you forgotten what the Guru said? When all else has failed, it is right to take arms. Do you want to sit around, watch your other daughters be dishonoured?"'

Mehmood twirled his moustache.

'I barely had time to sneak behind a bush when a tall figure strode out angrily, his leather jutti crunching the gravel, the curved end of a sheathed sword peeping out with each stride. I recognized him as the blue-turbaned man from the day of the radio broadcast ... The leader of the Sikh jatha?'

'Hakam Singh.' From what Mehmood had heard, the man's death squad had acquired quite a reputation. 'Good that old man Kishan has left Laur. Now, stay away from his house and lane.'

Beli Ram stirred with some agitation. 'That's why I say we track down Sepoy Malik, and get a couple of weapons to begin with. Can't sit around like womenfolk, can we?'

Mehmood snorted. 'Beli, you are in no danger from the likes of Hakam Singh ... Unless he decides to recruit you.'

'And if Hakam is interested in you, he will have to talk to *me* first.'

With his puffed-up chest, Beli looked ridiculous. Mehmood had to laugh.

Beli scowled.

Mehmood clamped a hand on his friend's shoulder. 'Mobs with guns and torches and spears are attacking homes ... You think you will face them with your one gun?'

'But there is fire all around, and we need to find a way to save our skins until Nehru and Jinnah send the angrej packing.'

'Again that same idiocy!'

Mehmood shook out his headscarf and began to tie it around his head. 'You are so naive. Nehru and Jinnah were sitting in the two pockets of the very fine suit of the angrej. Now the angrej is leaving and giving two kingdoms to each of the two loyal boys. Jinnah gets his Muslim Pakistan. Nehru his Hindustan. Question is: What do *we* get? Do we get to keep our Laur? You and I?'

Beli Ram sank down on the cot. 'So what do we *do*?'

Despite being the same age, Beli had always looked to him for answers. And to Mehmood's credit, he usually had some. Not now, though.

Mehmood twirled his moustache – a gesture behind which he hid often.

51
Delhi (August 1947)

V.P. Menon had stopped mopping his brow. He would treat
perspiration like a true Malayali and simply live with it.
Until he reached the Viceroy's study, at least.

Independence was four days away; the basket of apples
Sardar wanted was short, and the chubby-cheeked Maharaja of
Jodhpur, seated beside him, was still seeking the highest bidder
for his apple. Sardar had already matched Jinnah's offer to the
Maharaja: He would be allowed to import arms, India would
supply grains if needed, a rail link to Kathiawar port would be
set up.

Yet, Maharaja Hanwant Singh continued to vacillate.

The car purred to Viceroy House where Menon was hoping
Lord Mountbatten might succeed in pinning down the Maharaja.
Hanwant Singh was the Hindu ruler of a Hindu-majority state.
Based on the principle of partition, Jodhpur should abide
by India. The Maharaja's own jagirdars were opposed to any
alliance with Pakistan. Critically, it was a border state, and
Sardar worried that the Karachi–Jodhpur–Bhopal pact that

Jinnah was instigating would be a dagger thrust straight into India's heart.

Menon's morning call with Sardar – they spoke twice daily – had been brief; he was losing his voice in the pursuit of the princes anyway. Sardar had reliably learnt that Maharaja Hanwant Singh had spent three days in Jodhpur thinking and was ready to accede to Pakistan. Despite the fact that Bikaner and Jaisalmer, the other two states geographically contiguous to Pakistan, had decided otherwise. Which was why Menon had scooted to Imperial Hotel, plucked the Maharaja and was ferrying him swiftly to the Viceroy.

Menon parked the Maharaja in the visitors' room and went to look for the Viceroy. Who had a delegation from Hyderabad awaiting.

'Here's what I suggest, VP,' the Viceroy said. 'I will speak to the delegation in Edwina's study – she is at a refugee camp directing the Red Cross's relief work. And you bring the Maharaja to my study and jolly him along until I can surface.'

'Yes, Your Excellency.'

'Very well,' Lord Mountbatten slapped his hands together. 'Oh, and before I forget.' He waved an envelope in the air. 'The Maharaja of Indore's Instrument of Accession arrived today … by ordinary post.'

∽

The Maharaja of Jodhpur was petulant at being kept waiting in the Viceroy's study. He sat for a bit, then paced the study, then looked out the windows to the Mughal Gardens, before retreating to a chair. Then he started to complain about being held hostage while he was perfectly within his rights to accede to Pakistan.

'From a purely legal standpoint, yes,' Menon concurred, his voice hoarse. 'But don't you want to consider the fact that your state is predominantly Hindu, as are the states neighbouring you? As are you! Imagine the communal tension once you accede to Pakistan.'

The Maharaja, emanating the aroma of sandalwood, fingered the pearl chains dangling from his neck and refused to engage with Menon. He was miffed, either because the Viceroy was not there to hold his hand or because he was contemplating the stirred-up residents of Jodhpur.

Menon put the Instrument of Accession on the table and cleared his throat. 'Perhaps it's—'

Hanwant Singh started to speak abruptly. 'The Sardar, the Viceroy ... you ... all of you have to agree to my demands ... the ... the ... the concessions I want before I sign anything.'

Menon laid his palms flat on the table and faced the Maharaja – an immature young man of twenty-four who had been crowned barely two months ago. 'Your Highness, if you want to sign on false hopes, I will agree to your demands.'

'Jinnah gave me a blank sheet of paper to write all my demands on!'

'Then I urge you not to be swayed by false promises.'

The Maharaja sank his chin into his achkan, and sulked into his pearls and brocade. Menon was wondering what to attempt next when Hanwant Singh shot upright suddenly, knocking his chair over. In his hand was a fountain pen, a very large pen ... No, it was a pistol concealed in the pen! And it was pointed directly at Menon.

'I refuse to accept your dictation,' the Maharaja shrieked.

The air conditioner roared and a strong blast of chilly air swept over Menon. Calmly, he said, 'If you think by killing me you will avoid the accession, you are mistaken.'

'I will shoot you down like a dog if you betray the starving people of Jodhpur!'

'Don't indulge in juvenile theatricals.'

Seconds ticked. The Maharaja's arm slackened. With a muffled moan, he slumped back into his chair.

Menon slid the Instrument of Accession forward.

∞

Later, V.P. Menon presented the fountain pen–pistol to Lord Mountbatten with a recount of his eventful meeting with the Maharaja of Jodhpur. Sardar Patel retired to bed that night with the knowledge that Jinnah's dagger had been blunted.

52
Delhi (August 1947)

Evening of 13 August, Cyril Radcliffe sat down at his table, a glass of scotch by his side. He had accomplished his task. The partitions of Bengal, Panjab, and Sylhet in Assam were done and delivered to the Viceroy.

Meanwhile, there was a stack of papers on the table – all relevant to the line he had drawn. They would go back with him to England. There, he would burn them, and never speak a word about the Radcliffe award. No good would come out of it.

He took a sip of scotch, the pedestal fan riffling his wispy hair, and, for the last time, reflected on his mission in India.

Daily, commissioners in Lahore and Calcutta had sent him transcripts of their hearings. As chairman of the Boundary Commission for both Bengal and Panjab, he had the casting vote to be used in case of dissent between representatives of the Congress and the League. The fact that his Hindu and Muslim colleagues disagreed on almost every controversial issue meant that he was really the only one taking the decisions.

Cyril sighed. His only hope had been to deliver a result that would dismay both sides equally; pleasing either or both was altogether impossible.

Outside his window, he sighted the men guarding his bungalow against assassins. 'Squit' had accomplished a not-so-insignificant task – what would his classmates, who had nicknamed him thus, say now? But, to be honest, like the rest of the country, he couldn't wait for 15 August to be free.

He took a long grateful sip of his scotch and started to write to his stepson in England.

... I thought you would like to get a letter from India with a crown on the envelope. After tomorrow evening, nobody will ever again be allowed to use such stationery and, after 150 years, British rule will be over in India – Down comes the Union Jack on Friday morning and up goes – for the moment I rather forget what, but it has a spinning wheel or a spider's web in the middle. I am going to see Mountbatten sworn in as the first Governor General of the Indian Union at the Viceroy's House in the morning, and then I station myself firmly at the Delhi airport until an aeroplane from England comes along. Nobody in India will love me for the award about Panjab and Bengal, and there will be roughly 80 million people with a grievance who will begin looking for me. I do not want them to find me. I have worked and travelled and sweated – oh, I have sweated the whole time.

53
Delhi (August 1947)

In the Viceregal mansion on the evening of 14 August, Dickie and Edwina Mountbatten were watching the latest Bob Hope movie, *My Favourite Brunette*. Mizzen lay sprawled by Edwina's side, his ears perking up every now and then.

Dickie stretched his legs. A little romantic comedy on the night when he had helped end the Raj – undoubtedly the jewel in the British Crown – would not be unwonted. Jinnah was getting his Pakistan; the Congress was getting an independent India, albeit truncated; Patel had his apples, mostly; and, as Gandhi himself had stated at a prayer meeting, 'the British Government is not responsible for partition'. The deed was done.

In a few hours, at the stroke of midnight, India would be free. The astrologers had been rather tiresome about the date of 15 August – something about the inauspicious alignment of the stars for so significant an event – but midnight on 14 August had saved all parties concerned from embarrassment. The Constituent Assembly would be meeting soon.

Plans had come to his notice of one or two local ceremonies in Bombay that seemed to suggest there may be a ceremonial lowering of the Union Jack and its replacement by the national flag. He had communicated to Governor Colville that the Union Jack should not be in evidence on that day to avoid all possible risk of insult to it. Jawa was entirely in agreement with him on that count. It had been exhausting; the strain of not showing any strain killing on some days, but it was done.

On screen, as Dorothy Lamour walked into his office, Bob Hope skedaddled across on some crisis of his own. Which reminded Dickie of the Radcliffe award ...

Details had begun to leak, and there had been flare-ups of communal bias from both parties. Should he make the awards public upon receipt or hold off until independence celebrations? Thankfully, Cyril had handed the complete package on 13 August when Dickie was leaving for the Independence Day celebrations in Karachi. So he had locked away the award until after the celebrations were over in both Pakistan and India.

It always looked so easy in those Tarzan pictures!

Dickie chuckled. It must have been loud enough for Edwina turned briefly from the screen. He smiled at her.

It might appear easy to onlookers, but Dickie had to admit, during the five months that he was engaged in jollying the princes along, he had not allowed himself the congratulations he would have offered another on achieving such a momentous task. Everything he had touched had turned out well. Nothing like blowing his own trumpet! Hadn't the King-Emperor himself acknowledged in his letter: 'I am sure that there is no one else who would have accomplished this feat in the short time at your disposal except yourself.'

Everything you touch turns to rigor mortis.

Though, the protracted negotiation with Hamidullah Khan over Bhopal's accession to India had cost him his polo buddy and second-best friend in India. A friendship of twenty-five years sacrificed in the call of duty, small price to pay. Dickie inhaled deeply and shifted his weight on the armchair.

As Supreme Commander of Southeast Asia he had stopped the Japanese offensive into India and reconquered Burma, but this had been the more exacting task with multiple battlefronts.

The Dewan of Travancore had amassed a thick file of press cuttings that illustrated the wickedness of the Congress Party and therefore the improbability of acceding to such an entity. 'You have to stop reading the newspapers if you are going to allow yourself to get upset in such a manner,' Dickie had counselled him.

He snickered at the memory.

Edwina was studying him, instead of the screen.

'Enjoying the film, darling?' Dickie asked.

'As would you ... if you watched it,' she answered serenely.

'What makes you think I am not?'

'You are laughing at all the wrong moments.'

Dickie turned his attention to the screen.

Knives were following Bob Hope, flying in the air after him as he ran and dodged, a few barely missing his head.

Edwina stroked Mizzen. She hoped the refugee situation would resolve soon with independence, as everyone assumed, but ... since her first visit to a refugee camp in Multan in May, things had only worsened. More refugees, more camps, and the same appalling health conditions. She had insisted that a health clinic be set up in every refugee centre. But the officials she communicated with were reluctant to implement her suggestions. So she left notes for Dickie. In the end, there was always Jawa, who, despite the hundred and one things on his mind, found time for her.

Edwina sighed. From the corner of her eye she could see Dickie's eyes had glazed over again. In his mind he was likely going over the past six months and gloating over his achievements. But her mind was straying to London – the war, volunteering for the St John Ambulance Brigade. A wealthy heiress, people had sniffed at her. But she noticed the lightbulb that was missing, the absent bathrooms, the filthy shelters. Then she lobbied officials with every little detail. What was minor for the ministers could save lives on the ground. So she had deployed all in her arsenal: pulling rank, fluttering eyelashes, cajoling, bullying.

She had a depressing feeling it would all be handy in the days ahead.

Outside the window, a tree blazed with bright yellow flowers. Amal-tas. Native name for laburnum. Way past its peak flowering period, a gardener had pointed out quizzically as he studied the cloudless sky for the much-awaited monsoon. The blazing colour should cheer her up. But it didn't, conjuring an old memory instead.

After the blitz in London, Edwina had seen many flowering trees in the areas that were badly hit. It was quite astonishing really – unseasonal blossoms amidst the devastation. Until a friend, who was an avid gardener, revealed that when a tree was about to die, it may bloom and set fruit in a last-ditch effort to have progeny.

Edwina shivered. The amaltas should let go of its blossoms, secure that another flowering season would arrive.

54
Delhi (August 1947)

The appointed day.

And thus it had arrived. After long years of struggle, India had awakened to freedom. At one minute to midnight, in the packed hall – the ceiling fans churning the hot air – Jawahar had stood up before the newly created Constituent Assembly of India, and announced to Indians and the world that the time had come for the country to redeem her tryst with destiny.

He had woken at his usual time. As he did his asanas, birdsong floated from the open window. And a packed day awaited. Swearing-in of Governor General Mountbatten, Viceroy no more, and ministers at Government House. A hoisting of the national flag at the Constituent Assembly. And, later in the evening, a flag ceremony at India Gate.

Joy had flooded his heart, taking him by surprise. He did not recall when he had felt this unadulterated happiness last. Perhaps as a child, in the kitchen of Anand Bhavan, snuggling into his mother's sari folds … He had known a diluted version of it, moments, even extended periods, of contentment, which came from being fully absorbed. In jail in 1944, tending to the little garden they had created out of the rocky soil. In watching Dando the cat's mysterious coming and going. Writing *The Discovery of India*, during which he had discovered that the Western-educated man who carried within him the burden of an anglicized past had indeed become Indian ... with Bapu. Who had trained them like soldiers, with great discipline and strictness, after which prison almost felt like a rest ... Weaving in jail, on Bapu's advice, and spinning the yarn which became Indu's pale-pink wedding sari ... There had been moments of intense pleasure even. With Kamla, the only woman who had shared something of his lonely personal life, whom he had loved despite proving himself the worst possible husband because of his public commitments ... In the mountains, where India was always in her youthful glory. During exercise, when he felt supple and productive. Re-reading Tennyson. Occasional cheekiness at somebody's expense ...

From where he stood, upside down, in his customary headstand position, a laugh had escaped him as he recalled an old incident.

In Lucknow prison, the English superintendent, irked at Jawahar's stack of books, remarked that he had himself finished his general reading at the age of twelve. 'Clearly,' Jawahar agreed, 'that had saved the superintendent from troublesome ideas and helped his rise to the inspector general of United Provinces!'

There was joy in learning from the prison gardener in Dehradun, who helped him with planting a variety of English garden flowers – the altitude and cool winters enabling it – and amusing him with his rendering of English names of plants: Ali Haq for hollyhock! In his travels abroad, when he connected with like-minded people. In his travels through India, touring every province, covering 50,000 miles by car, rail, bullock cart, foot. Interacting with some 10 million Indians, who taught him that India had emerged over time with a richness rooted in layer upon layer of cultural influences and changes, which would in turn give it the strength to continue adapting to the challenges of a modern world.

The world that day appeared perfect. Like a great wrong had been righted. India had shrugged off her shackles and had stood upright, ready to claim her rightful position on the world stage.

Jawahar inhaled deeply, filling his lungs with the fresh morning air, his toes stretching. His five-foot-four frame felt immeasurably tall.

∽

It was raining babies. They were in the air, like balloons without threads, descending, descending, onto a churning human ocean. Arms deftly plucked them out of the air, or caught them mid-flight. While other flailing arms clutched the air, the nearest limb, someone's shawl to get a grip as the gathering surged and heaved and shifted like a giant beast.

The city had erupted into festivities which rivalled multiple Diwalis in a day. Everywhere Jawahar looked, there were people, half a million or so. The flag hoisting at Princes' Park at 6 p.m. was planned meticulously with ceremonial grandstands and military parades for 30,000 people. But the parade was impossible now, with not a spot on which to rest one's foot. Bicycles and babies were being passed around overhead, there being no space to park the bicycle or hold the baby without crushing it. The crowds had taken complete possession of all the chairs, standing on the backs, arms, and seats. Even the grandstands were submerged with people celebrating a free India. From the tiny platform that surrounded the flagstaff, Jawahar watched the crowd exulting. In the distance, he sighted Manibehn and Pamela Mountbatten in the crush of people – they needed rescuing. He plunged into the sea of gaiety. Reaching them, he grabbed their hands.

'I cannot come, I am afraid. Where do I put my feet? I cannot walk on people!' Pamela said bemused.

'Of course, you can! Today, nobody will mind. Take off your shoes though.'

With that they sailed on, Jawahar leading the two women over the bodies of people who cheerfully passed them on. 'Raja Jawaharlal!' someone hailed. When an obstruction surfaced, he grabbed the topi off the head of the man and smacked it to get him moving out of the way. At the tiny platform, he made Pamela and Manibehn stand with their backs to the flagstaff, afraid they might get knocked over by the excitable crowd.

The lance pennants of the Governor General's bodyguard fluttered in the distance as the Mountbattens' car crawled into view and stalled at twenty-five yards from the flagstaff. It looked unlikely that the occupants would be able to navigate their way forward. Dickie and Edwina were waving to the crowds, who cheered and waved back. Jawahar tried to call for order, but couldn't hear himself above the din. Once again, he sallied forth to get them. But the churning sea of people was proving difficult to manoeuvre.

As the tricolour was unfurled against the sky, a light rain began to fall and a resounding cheer broke through. He stood in the sea of his countrymen and women, unable or unwilling to return to the flagstaff. The Governor General, standing upright in the car, saluted the flag. A bright rainbow appeared emblazoning saffron, white, green – the colours of independent India – in the blue sky. Jawahar felt curiously light. As if Indra himself had unfurled the tricolour from his indradhanush!

∽

Unable to reach his car, Jawahar hitched a ride with the Mountbattens, sitting cross-legged on the folded hood of their car. People clung to the sides of the car flinging their hands forward for a shake, showering them with flowers and flags. Assorted cries of jubilation rent the air. As they wended their way through, they gathered passengers who looked like they were about to get crushed under. A woman thrust her baby in Edwina's arms for safekeeping. Jawahar caught Edwina's eye and the two exchanged a smile.

'Jai Hind! Long live India!'

'Pandit Nehru ki jai!'

'Mountbatten ki jai!'

'Pandit Mountbatten ki jai!'

All barriers of caste, creed, colour, sex, nationality had been broken in that joyous gathering. Bapu would have liked that. But Bapu was in Calcutta, despite Jawahar urging him to stay in Delhi. 'What is there to celebrate?' Bapu had asked, anguished over partition, 'the vivisection of the Mother'. In Calcutta, he was immersed in prayers and soul searching and keeping peace. Jawahar cupped his face in his hands, trying to still his mind.

One step enough for me.

Words from his favourite Christian hymn floated in his mind. He had learnt from Bapu the importance of the immediate moment and the possible action.

Closing his eyes, he savoured the moment.

India was free … broken in parts … bruised, but free. There was an essential unity to India that no partition could destroy. To that much-loved motherland, the ancient, the eternal, the ever-new, it was time to redeem their pledge. It was time to bind himself to her service. It was time to build a new nation.

55
Laur (August 1947)

'Let's go see the border!'

Beli Ram stood in the narrow lane, his hair standing on end, hands akimbo. In his rumpled kurta–pyjama he looked like a chicken which had escaped halfway through plucking. Mehmood gripped his friend's shoulders.

'What?' Beli Ram protested.

'Stop it, Beli! I showed you the newspaper, didn't I?'

Beli Ram hunched forward, boring his eyes into Mehmood's face. 'You think you know everything. Do you know whether this land,' he dragged a hand through the air, indicating the stretch of the lane, '*this* land that we are standing upon – and that you are acting like a nawab upon – *this* land belongs where? Pakistan? India? Where are we? Which country? Where?'

Mehmood tightened his grip on his friend's thin shoulders. 'We are in Laur.'

'So?'

'Laur is in Pakistan.'

'Says who?'

'Says Jinnah.'

'Ainvayi!' Beli Ram snorted. 'Jinnah mian draws a line and declares Pakistan. But I am inside his precious Pakistan and he doesn't want me. So, I draw a circle around my house and declare it Belistan!'

'Oye, Beli, quit being a child!'

'Is Jinnah not being a child?' Beli Ram waved his hands in the air. 'Anyway,' he narrowed his eyes, 'how do you know for sure? Kishan Singh, who you will admit knows more than the two of us, hurried back from Ambarsar some days back. He had probably heard from his sources that Laur would go to India, which is why he returned.'

Mehmood frowned. Beli had probably sighted Kishan Singh and assumed the rest.

'Which is why I say we go see the line for ourselves. Then we will know whether to cross or stay. It is early morning; enough time to go till Muridke, check and come back.'

Mehmood tried to reason with Beli. 'You think you can see this line?'

'Well, if you can't see the line, it can't be much of a line then, right?'

'Oye, Beli, these literate people do everything with pen–paper. Even the division of land. The newspaper carried the map and it clearly showed Laur in Pakistan, Ambarsar in India. Jinnah and Nehru have split the two great cities of Panjab between them.'

'But why wait when we can cycle to the river to see for ourselves?'

'Again, you're at it. Folks can't see the line because nobody has *drawn* the line on the ground. Which is why running here–there is pointless. I'll go to the station, as I said, to arrange your ticket. You sit tight, inside your house.' Mehmood lowered his voice. Since the announcement of the border between India–Pakistan, the Hindu mohalla was emptying faster than a leaking pail.

Beli Ram looked uncertain. 'But—'

'Pehnchod! Have you gone deaf?' Mehmood snapped. 'Aren't you hearing stories of what is happening in the city? The gurdwara on Temple Road was stormed just yesterday. They burnt everything down, even the Sikhs who were inside for prayers. My neighbour has been carting stuff home daily. Cloth bundles, a mountain of utensils wrapped in an old sheet, even an aluminium canister of pure ghee and a sack of almonds! Loot! Looting Hindu shops and homes in broad daylight.'

Beli Ram was shaking visibly. 'I have another idea.' He tapped a finger against his mouth. 'We get to the riverbank and see. You can't divide a river now, can you?'

Mehmood started to propel Beli back towards his house. 'We stay quiet and—'

But Beli continued to stare ahead, and Mehmood followed his gaze. Mad Billo was in the banyan tree, swinging her legs and singing. Her family, refusing to take her back in, had thrown her clothes out. Billo took refuge under the banyan on the concrete plinth, strung up a few kameezes into a tent, slept in the open – while folks sweated inside their homes – and perched in the banyan tree often. Beli said Billo would knock on the door of her ex-home to use the latrine. Refused, she took a dump right outside. They hurled abuses at her, but she only laughed in response. After many days of removing turds from their chabutara, they let her use the latrine daily. Beyond which, she showed no interest in the house.

Beli Ram was looking feverish. Mehmood touched his friend's forehead, but Beli slapped his arm away.

'You know, Mehmood,' he whispered, 'some days I can't make out if the woman in the banyan is Billo or the churail.'

The churail was a good story, but Beli clearly believed in it. And, in his current state of mind ... Mehmood shook his head. 'Let's go, Beli,' he caught his friend's elbow. 'Listen, when a bogey from one train is shunted to another track to attach to another train, temporarily, what do you do? Hmm ... Jump on the tracks to investigate? That's death. Your bogey needs to get to Ambarsar for some time. You stay here until I return with some concrete news. Hunh?'

Beli Ram refused to budge. 'Haven't you heard Mehmood, they are killing all passengers on trains headed to Ambarsar?'

Mehmood sighed. 'But some are still managing to get away safely. Which is why I need to go out and get the right information: which train, which bogey, when?'

He worked the tip of his moustache as Beli chewed his mouth, head downcast.

'When do I return?'

'As soon as Laur gets its sense back.'

'Will you come with me?'

'So you can put me on a train back to Laur from Ambarsar?'

The absurdity of the situation made them laugh. They linked arms and walked to Beli Ram's house. At the door, Beli turned to take leave of Mehmood, but his eyes strayed to the banyan.

'You know Mehmood, the mohalla men complained that Billo had taken over their evening spot. They smashed her tent and sat down for their hukkah and chitter-chatter. But Billo ... She climbed the banyan and laughed at them, and sang about parlay coming and red rain and brothers who drink blood ... Scared, the men all fled.'

56
Delhi (August 1947)

From the window of his bedroom, Vallabh watched a mynah frolic in the earthen bowl of water by the garden tap. In the heat, it was not enough to be able to drink water, the bird needed to cool off. Perhaps he should follow the mynah's example, his blood was on a boil—

A familiar clink meant Mani had entered – the bunch of keys at her waist heralding her presence.

'Father,' Mani's brow was creased, 'shouldn't you be resting?'

His spastic colon had flared up and he had almost fainted. Doctor Kanuga had advised rest and reading of only light or humorous stuff. Which had made Vallabh laugh.

He acknowledged his daughter's concern by nodding. 'Junagadh has acceded to Pakistan, Mani.'

He pursed his lips. Jinnah had accepted tiny Junagadh's accession with a firm eye on Hyderabad. With Hyderabad sallying to Pakistan, how would they build a nation out of India? And Jawaharlal had received reports saying that Pakistan was making preparations to enter Kashmir in large numbers. Vallabh was hurrying the steps to integrate India: laying telephone and telegraph lines between Jammu and Pathankot, dispatching a Panjab High Court judge to the court of Maharaja Hari Singh of Kashmir to be his next prime minister, opening independent channels of communication with the three feudatories of Junagadh, granting Hyderabad a special three-month grace period to help the Nizam make up his mind on accession. And yet, he could feel time and events overtaking him …

Manibehn sat on the edge of the bed, fingers interlaced in her lap. 'Vidya Shankar says you are to tour Old Delhi this morning?'

'Reports have come in of threats to the Nizamuddin dargah.' The shrine had become a sanctuary for Muslim refugees. And fear had settled in its Muslim neighbourhood, Nizamuddin Basti.

Stepping away from the window, Vallabh walked slowly to his study. He placed a hand on Mani's head as he went. 'Let me go to the saint before we incur his displeasure.'

∞

Accompanied by his private secretary, Vidya Shankar, Vallabh walked through the narrow lane of the medieval settlement of Nizamuddin. Bordered by shops on both sides, which sold incense, embroidered silk cloths, rose perfume, and petals, this was one bustling part of Delhi. Not that day.

A sullen resentment hung in the air, faces were pinched with fear, and none took note of him. The dargah was visited daily by thousands of people, Muslims mostly, but since the saint did not discriminate, people from other faiths – Hindus, Sikhs, Christians – too flocked for his blessings. But Delhi was seized with the madness of the time. Some Sikh and Rajput soldiers had attacked Muslims instead of protecting them. Fearing they were losing control over their own soldiers, Vallabh had replaced them with the Madras Regiment. And taken to learning the situation on the ground for himself. The battle against lawlessness must be won.

They completed a walkabout of the dargah, weaving their way through women and men who sat on the marble floor, reading the Quran, conversing softly, praying; devotees tying threads to marble screens; children scampering about. Vallabh entered the sanctum, where the smell of rose was heavy in the air, a blanket of rose petals adorning the saint's grave. Joining the men circumambulating the grave and seeking blessings, Vallabh asked the saint to keep intact the communal harmony of Delhi. Outside, he spoke to the custodians, whom Shankar had sought out, and reassured them.

Forty-five minutes later, Vallabh concluded his meeting with the police officer in charge of the area.

'Anything untoward happens, and you will be held responsible.'

Continuing with the tour of the city, they reached Faiz Bazaar police station. As the two men stepped out of the car, the air whistled and cracked sharply. Shots had whizzed past, narrowly missing him and Shankar. They ducked and made for the station. Inside, a grim home minister took stock of the situation. The shots were coming from an adjacent building, he was informed.

'Stop it then!' Vallabh ordered.

'The building is under Muslim control, sir,' the police officer said.

'What kind of explanation is that?'

'Sir, it is impossible to silence the snipers without blowing up the building.'

Delhi had already caught Panjab's infection, with refugees from West Panjab streaming into the city, beelining his residence, petitioning him with tales of woe. Vallabh had issued shoot-at-sight orders for rioters, and publicly threatened partisan officials with punishment. He had formed the Delhi Emergency Committee and tasked it with three goals: protecting Delhi's Muslims; organizing camps for frightened Muslims leaving their homes in Delhi and the neighbouring areas; setting up camps for devastated Sikhs and Hindus arriving from Pakistan.

Vallabh's eyes bored into the police officer. 'I will not tolerate Delhi becoming another Lahore.'

'Sir,' the officer nodded. 'With all due respect, it is impossible to silence the snipers without—'

'Blow it up.'

57
Delhi (August)

A keening broke through the mist of his sleep.
Jawahar bolted up. The sky outside his window was still dark. He swung off the bed, his feet fumbling for slippers. The calendar on his desk showed 18 August 1947. Which was yesterday. He made his way down the corridor, softly, to avoid waking the rest of the household: Indu with her boys; Nan, who was visiting; and the few refugees they could accommodate inside. Pushing open the netting door, he stepped out.

The pre-dawn morning had a hint of cool, which would evaporate in an hour. The heat was killing those whom brothers weren't. And the monsoons had withheld their bounty, sullen at the bloodied ground. Tents had sprung up in the lawns of his bungalow – as if an army was readying for war. Yet, the army in this camp was bedraggled, belimbed, bereft. Was Bapu right then? The line was meant to be only on paper, but it had morphed into the bloody battle line of brothers. Two millennia later, the Mahabharata was being re-enacted. Just as Bapu had feared …

Ahead stretched the rows of tents, as many as could be squeezed in the bungalow grounds. Similar tent cities had also sprung up in the homes of Maulana Azad, Vallabhbhai, and others. Pots and pans and dead embers of cooking fires marked each tent, the business of feeding bellies when homeless. Skirting the garden, he walked in the direction of his room, hoping to locate the person whose lament had awoken him.

A figure sat huddled in a white mulmul dupatta outside a tent, sobbing. He addressed her softly. She refused to look up. He urged her to go lie down, rest, before dawn broke. Her muffled sobbing persisted. He put a hand on her shoulder. Her head shot up. Uncombed hair spilled out from under the dupatta, her eyes full of the hatred he had encountered in the last few days as partition convoys had begun disembarking in Delhi. This was not a freed people. This was a people who had been cast out.

'Got it?' The woman snarled. 'Got your free Hindustan? Got to be Raja? You drove the angrej out so you could sit on the throne. Congratulations! But I prefer the English. With them, at least we had our home.' The woman dug her face back in the folds of her dupatta and resumed sobbing.

Jawahar stood there, his toes twitching in his slippered feet. He wanted the woman to continue to berate him. He touched her shoulder again. 'Bibi, go rest inside.'

The woman stood up, resting one hand on her heavily swollen belly, the other supporting her back. She locked eyes with him. 'I will name her Nimi.'

'Nimi,' he acknowledged. 'Nice name ...'

'She's a girl, I know.'

Jawahar nodded. The thought of the baby's gender had not struck him.

She patted her belly. 'Her father wants a son, but I know ...
This is Nimi. We lost one Nimi, but god will give us another.'

Around them, the camp was beginning to stir. The rosy hue
of twilight was streaking across the eastern sky. Birds had taken
up their chatter.

'When the men in our colony heard that Pindi would be part
of Pakistan, they decided to leave. But our colony was mixed,
Hindu–Muslim–Sikh living side by side. There was no problem
amongst us, but the searing wind was blowing. One day, a mob
of armed men descended, and threatened to kill all Hindu and
Sikh families. The maulvi of our colony, a sheikh, he held a
Quran in his hands and faced the crowd, and said they could
begin – but only over his dead body. After which, the mob left,
but we knew we had a few hours to decamp.'

Her eyes were hard as she reminisced. From the corner of
his eyes Jawahar saw a young woman who sat beside a pail
furiously scrubbing her forearm. Her long braid was matted.

'I stuffed jewellery under my kameez, in my salwar. As we
rushed about wondering what to take with us, our neighbour's
daughter crept into the courtyard. She was my doll, the one I
played with after finishing my chores – her mother and I would
sit and sift grain or embroider together. The men were gathering
what weapons they could ... knife, axe, sword ... We were to
leave in a truck. Nimi started crying and, to distract her, I sent
her to the kitchen to fetch something. As she toddled back,
a man rushed in, brandishing a gandasa. You know a gandasa,
Panditji?'

The woman's eyes moistened again abruptly. Meanwhile,
the young woman near the pail looked like she would scour
her limb away as she persisted with her maniacal cleansing.

'Gandasa is a thick stick, mounted on one end with a curved
blade. To harvest sugarcane. This man was a local lout, and, in

the commotion, he had become a hero as he organized the kafila of confused people. He had arranged the truck. Even suggested we kill our Muslim neighbours as we leave.'

She gulped now, the words getting stuck in her throat. The smell of smoke and brewing tea was in the air. A shout rose from one tent. Hearing which, the woman at the pail started, her large eyes petrified. She had gone completely white. Except for her inflamed arm.

'Before I could blink, I saw that blade sticking out at Nimi's back – its steel edged with red. Nimi did not cry; she did not shout. Only, she was astride the gandasa and the lout was striding out with her, carrying her aloft. Her blood was on the packed-mud floor of our house … the same floor where I had rocked her to sleep in my lap so many afternoons …'

Edwina said it was the stories she witnessed and heard in the refugee camps that got her out of bed every morning. Jawahar though felt like he would crumple under the weight of these stories.

'Panditji,' the woman touched his shoulder, 'you know, the blood of children is a different colour? Nimi's blood was bright red … Like a … like a fresh tomato. Not the colour of cherry that I have seen adults spill on our way here.'

58
Laur (August 1947)

Kishan Singh's house was locked for three weeks now – a big padlock hanging on the front door. He had put it there himself. Surinder and Narinder had not ventured out since Pammi went missing. With curtains tightly drawn and the barest candlelight, Kishan Singh was giving everyone the impression that they had fled.

Kishan though crept out before dawn every morning, via the back door, and returned only after dark. He spent his days scouring the labyrinth of the old city, wandering the boulevards of the newer sections, trudging through the dirt roads on the outskirts. But he learnt nothing about Pammi's abduction. People cautioned him: A daughter so dishonoured was as good as dead. But Kishan persisted. So routinely did he break curfew that the police simply ignored the madman.

However, even in his crazed state, Kishan was certain he had foxed the remaining residents of the colony. The barricade at the entrance had been dismantled, the city was under curfew and who would recognize him when his own mirror didn't?

The sun had burnt his face, grief had hollowed his eyes, he wore dust and dried saliva.

How then had the bundle arrived at his back door?

Kishan found it pre-dawn as he was about to slink out. He took it inside to open. A white cloth of coarse fabric and a folded sheet of paper with a message scrawled in Urdu.

'For your kafan, after we get your daughters.'

Kishan sank to the floor. He would not venture out that day.

Hindu and Sikh families fleeing the colony had urged him to do the same. 'Think of your remaining daughters.' Iqbal virji had sent frantic summons to get to Lyallpur: There was safety in numbers and if they had to leave, they would do it together.

But how could Kishan leave Pammi behind? Who would comfort her when she returned?

Now this.

Hakam Singh had warned him. Of Muslim treachery. Of the need for self-defence. And, sure enough, after Pammi was abducted, Ahmed Niazi had ventured to Kishan's house with a proposal to marry off Narinder and Surinder to his sons, Asad included, and join the two households. Kishan Singh could convert. That way everyone would be safe. Even in his distraught state, Kishan had registered the betrayal.

He fingered the traditional Muslim burial cloth before him. Was Ahmed Niazi behind this kafan? Or some other Muslim goon making Laur kuffar-free. Either way, the time had come to retrieve Hakam Singh's parting gift.

❦

A light breeze had picked up as if to remind Lauris of all they had missed that summer. With minimal traffic, birdsong was loud in the air. Beli Ram wanted to linger, but curfew would begin soon.

Mehmood and he were hurrying home from Lahore Junction when a loud roar snapped them to attention. It came from the end of the lane. Sure enough, flames were leaping skywards. And a frenzied crackling filled the air. Both men dashed towards the fire.

People were pouring out from their homes, some watching the blaze from their thresholds, others racing down to Kishan Singh's house. Onlookers ringed the railway clerk's home in growing circles. The men closest to the gate had covered their noses with their palms or turban ends. Yes, a smell of burning flesh ... Then a shout and extended arms pointed to the rooftop of the house.

A figure had emerged. Beli Ram and Mehmood narrowed their eyes, trying to discern who it was through the billowing smoke and blaze. Someone gasped, and exclaimed, and the words got picked up and buffeted across the surging gathering. In the man's hand was a revolver that he was brandishing about. And in the other hand was a cloth he waved.

'Come! Come!' The figure shouted.

'Why, it is old man Kishan!' Beli exclaimed.

Except, he looked like a giant atop the corner of his rooftop, arms flailing, strands of hair flying in the breeze.

'Fetch the wedding procession now! What are you awaiting?'

Mehmood and Beli Ram turned at that moment to look at each other.

'You wanted to take my daughters! You think they are all ready for marriage – come now, and fetch them! And here's the kafan you sent for me. I am ready too.'

Another round of whispers broke out. As the fire roared in the lawn, the smell of charred flesh intensified. Apparently,

Kishan's Muslim neighbours had proposed he marry off his two younger daughters to their sons. That way, they would all be related and Kishan's safety was assured. Mehmood watched Beli Ram's stricken face, and wrapped an arm around his shoulders. The faces of the onlookers wore a curious assortment of expressions, horror, panic, and the anticipation of circus goers.

'BRING on the marriage parties!' Kishan was roaring above the sizzling fire, thrusting his revolver as he lunged at the air. 'You can bring your grooms now.'

'Yes, he seemed okay with the suggestion ... He kept listening, kept nodding ... We thought he'd agreed ...' the whispers floated through the air.

People started to cough as the acrid smell laced their throats and nostrils. But they were rooted to the ground, their eyes on the man who promised a fitting end to the unfolding drama.

'Pehnchod, what kafan is this?'

'The marriage pyre is lit. I have lit it myself. What is keeping the grooms out? Hurry now, boys. Don't you want to join your brides?'

With one last roar, old man Kishan cocked the revolver at his head. A shot rang out. He hovered over the edge for a few seconds, then toppled over, falling into the pyre blazing in his lawn. A loud crash, the flames clambered upwards in black-tipped red fingers, sparks sizzled in the air like glow worms. Fed, the fire crackled lustily.

Abruptly, it was all over.

'In this men's game of tit for tat, why should women have to suffer?' Thus had Tara questioned her sepoy. Before she herself became a casualty. Now Narinder and Surinder joined the swelling ranks of women whose bodies became the battlefield in the ongoing battle between men.

59
Delhi (September 1947)

The telephone rang. Jawahar listened, his face darkening –
monsoon clouds having forsaken the skies for his brow of
late. Slamming the phone down, he tore out of the house.

In his car, he snapped to Khaliq, 'Connaught Place!'

Perched on the edge of his seat, neck craned, his eyes scanned
the horizon furiously. The roads, which usually bustled, were
mute. Government workers, bus–taxi–tonga drivers, shop
owners, many of them Muslim, were all staying safe at home.
The violence of Panjab had seeped into Delhi, reports of rioting
were arriving hourly. Apparently, a gang of Sikh refugees from
eastern Panjab was organizing a revenge operation on Delhi's
Muslims. They were sighted noting down addresses of Muslim
residences, and were now targeting homes, dragging people out,
killing them. The Sikh squads were being answered by Muslim
gangs in turn. Delhi's ammunition dealers were largely Muslim,
as were the blacksmiths, who had converted their workshops
into bomb and bullet smithies. Tit for tat. Feuding brothers
who needed no lesson – they had an epic to guide them.

As the car rounded into the circular road that was the city's premier shopping district, Jawahar sighted policemen, staffs slack in hands, gossiping idly. While a man scrambled with ladies bags on both his arms. Behind him came another, his arms cradling – what? – cartons of fountain ink? And then, several men tumbled out, an assortment of goods in their arms, cosmetics, wool shawls, yarn, more handbags ...

'Stop!' Jawahar barked and jumped out as the car slowed. He hit the ground running. His jog brought him face to face with a posse of policemen who were catching the action.

'WHAT are you doing?' he shouted. 'Do you not see the looting? Why are you not stopping them?'

The men – lean, languid – shifted, examined the ground, made feeble attempts to lift their staffs.

'What?' he thundered.

'Sir,' one of them spoke up, 'the Muslims got their Pakistan, that is where they are headed. What is wrong with our Hindu brothers using the stock which will get left behind?'

'Fool!' Jawahar rasped. 'Hindustan is the home of all Indians, Hindu, Sikh, Mussalman.'

Meanwhile, a clamour had erupted as several men dragged multiple cartons out from a store ahead. Jawahar grabbed a baton from the limp hands of one policeman, ran to the thicket of men and started thrashing them.

From the car, the elderly Khaliq watched, debating whether to join Jawahar or not. His goatee would single him out as a Muslim, which might not help. The looters, noticing the achkan-clad man of medium height and patrician features, recognized him for Pandit Nehru. They dithered, unsure, then scampered off, taking with them what loot they could.

60
Laur (September 1947)

At Lahore Junction, coolies were ferrying corpses, not bags, as cleaners swept blood from bogeys onto tracks. The last train that had arrived had not a single passenger left alive. Putting Beli on a train would be sending him into the jaws of death. But leave Beli must. The city had so swiftly emptied of Hindus and Sikhs, one would think they were birds, not humans, that would set to building nests afresh …

Mehmood twirled his whiskers until an idea struck. Upon which, he went to the house of Shammi Joseph to plead his case. The erstwhile lively mohalla was eerily quiet as Mehmood requested to loan Shammi's rickshaw. It was Shammi's source of livelihood, his prized possession, and, in a city where looting was the new order of the day, Shammi worried he would never sight his vehicle again. He was still debating what to do when Lata Joseph waddled up to them with some difficulty.

'The god who ferries Beli Ram to safety will also bring your rickshaw back.'

Now, Beli Ram hastily packed as Mehmood practiced his rickshaw-pulling skills. It was a while before he could coordinate the pedals and handles to steer the vehicle. But the lane was empty except for a shadowy figure in the banyan tree. Beli locked the wooden door and, clutching his bundle, dragged his feet to the rickshaw.

'What's that?'

Mehmood was placing bottles in the coir basket he had attached to the rickshaw handle.

'Never mind.'

Mehmood motioned for his friend to sit and handed him a thin towel. An unsure Beli Ram perched on the rickshaw and watched Mehmood wrap his head cloth such that it covered his mouth and nose.

'But why?' he asked when Mehmood motioned for him to do the same.

Mehmood held up a reassuring palm, patted his kurta pocket, and hopped onto the rickshaw. As they rode out of the lane, the bundle of his belongings in his lap, Beli Ram wistfully eyed the home he was leaving. From the banyan, a silent Billo watched them go. She would be the last one left. If only they had treated her right, Billo would not have joined the churail in the banyan tree and made them all flee. Beli Ram sobbed into his bundle. Mehmood grunted as he pedalled. A light rain began to fall. And from the dry, deprived earth arose an aroma of first rain that would linger in Beli Ram's heart, entangled forever with the loss of home.

∽

The strength required to pull a rickshaw was surprising Mehmood. His limbs ached, and he wiped his eyes of sweat and drizzle frequently. Except for two donkeys copulating beneath the clock tower, the roads were empty because of curfew. And Mehmood was sticking to alleys and lanes wherever possible. Beli had stopped sniffling; the only sound coming was the creaking of pedals.

Mehmood was hoping to get to the banks of Ravi in time to catch the large kafila heading to India from Lyallpur. Akali leaders had asked the farmers to evacuate the canal lands in a group. Iqbal Singh, the elder brother of Kishan Singh, was one of the kafila leaders – Mehmood had heard at the station. Surely, they would take Beli Ram in? Rounding onto Bani Hata, Mehmood braked sharply. Behind him, Beli Ram slid forward in the seat and swore.

Ahead, a posse of armed men obstructed the lane, their weapons glinting in the light of a half-moon. Shooting a quick glance behind at Beli Ram, Mehmood instructed him to cover his face. He secured his safa such that only his eyes were seen. Meanwhile, the men were advancing. Mehmood's hands were in the coir basket. When the men were near enough for him to see their eyes, Mehmood plucked the glass bottles from the basket and smashed them at their feet. Fumes erupted and a pungent odour cascaded down upon them. Bearing down upon the rickshaw, Mehmood pedalled furiously. He could hear the goondas coughing and shuffling behind them. His own eyes were itching, but Mehmood did not let up until he was on the dirt road that led to the riverbank.

∽

It looked like a unit of the angrej army.

Trucks and tractors in the front and at the rear, loaded bullock carts in the middle, armed men on horses flanking each side –

the convoy proceeded with not a single man or animal straying out of line. At the head of the kafila were white-bearded Sikhs, some even wearing the medals they had won in the wars they had fought for the angrej. In their hands were kirpans and rifles and spears.

From behind a thicket, Mehmood and Beli Ram watched awestruck.

Iqbal Singh, whom they had seen at the station when he visited his younger brother, was easy to identify. His long white beard was in splendid contrast to his blue turbaned and clothed self. In his hand was a shotgun.

'Okay, Beli,' Mehmood prodded his friend in the back. 'Go join them.'

Beli licked his lips nervously. 'What if they shoot me?'

'Raise your arms,' Mehmood demonstrated the action he had seen in a war film once, 'as you approach them. Tell them you are a Hindu fleeing the Muslims of Laur.'

'Adiya!' Beli Ram slapped a hand on Mehmood's shoulder, his eyes glistening with tears.

From his kurta pocket, Mehmood removed several ampoules of bromine and put them in Beli Ram's hands. 'These will do the same magic those bottles did. Rab rakha!'

The two friends embraced tightly. Then Beli Ram slung his bundle over one shoulder, choked back his tears, and walked away. At the edge of the thicket, he turned around one final time.

'Mehmood, brother, I will meet you yet again.'

61
Delhi (September 1947)

'If India is granted freedom, power will go to the hands of rascals, rogues, freebooters …'

Winston Churchill's words rang in Jawahar's mind as he read the latest cable from Sampuran Singh, India's deputy high commissioner in Lahore.

50 THOUSAND HINDUS AND SIKHS ARE DAILY BUTCHERED BY THE MILITARY AND POLICE HERE. NO HIGH COMMISSIONER CAN SAVE THEM. ALL HINDUS AND SIKHS IN WEST PANJAB WILL BE FINISHED.

Jawahar could feel the bile rising from his stomach. He had not slept properly in months, the exhilaration of freedom had died within days, the horrors were mounting daily, and it looked like a newly independent India was readying to carry out the prophecy of the one man who had vehemently opposed the country's independence.

Admittedly, there was an element of hysteria in the telegram, but the reports of Muslim gangs blocking Hindu and Sikh caravans at river crossings to prevent them from escaping to India were too many to ignore. The Western press was having a field day reporting the macabre incidents of communal violence out of East Panjab. How conveniently they had forgotten that this bloodbath was a legacy of the same ideology of hatred that the Muslim League had used over the years to justify the creation of Pakistan.

Jawahar watched Vallabhbhai walk up the driveway, Defence Minister Baldev Singh in tow. He had requested an urgent meeting on the deteriorating communal situation.

Greetings over, he handed them a pamphlet. Originally in Gurmukhi, he had had it translated to English.

Oh, Sikhs! Read this and think yourself, what have you to do under the circumstances? In your veins there is yet the blood of your beloved Guru Gobind Singhji. Do your duty!

'The Sikhs had clearly been the aggressors,' Jawahar fumed.

'Sikhs are the most well-organized of the attackers,' Vallabh conceded. Yet, he refused to put the Sikh leaders behind bars.

Jawahar flung his arms out. 'If the Sikhs continue this way – expelling Muslims out of East Panjab – Tara Singh will get his Khalistan–Sikhistan one way or another. And India, another partition.' Distaste, like acid, filled his mouth.

'We have to tread carefully. The Sikhs are thirsting for revenge against the Muslims. Putting their leaders in jail will be like adding oil to fire,' Vallabh reasoned.

'We have to keep in mind,' Baldev Singh said quietly, 'that the Sikhs have also lost the most. And the provocation is never-ending.' From his file, the defence minister produced a pamphlet. It had a picture of Jinnah, sword in hand, and an exhortation below.

*Be ready and take your swords! Think you, Muslims, why we
are under the kafirs today? O, kafir! Your doom is not far and the
general massacre will come.*

'And RSS leaflets are all over the streets of Delhi, urging all
Hindus and Sikhs to attack all Muslims and to terrorize the city.
The whole country is going mad!' Jawahar hissed and began
pacing his office, hands locked behind his back.

Just the other day he had come across a Hindu man with a
cart loaded with loot, certainly Muslim. When he questioned
the man, his reply was chilling in its cold clear logic: 'They
have their Pakistan, we will have our Hindustan.' Jawahar's
mouth was set in a grim line. As long as he was at the helm,
India would not become a Hindu state. The majority of the
city's ammunition dealers and blacksmiths were Muslim, and
intelligence reports warned of a Muslim uprising. As if to
balance that equation, Vallabhbhai had issued licenses to many
new Hindu arms dealers in Delhi. As home minister, the tough
Sardar was in a tough situation, but this was no way to solve the
problem. It would only escalate the tension. Jawahar returned
to the situation at hand.

'A quarter million refugees are marching towards Lahore
and there is no way to get to Pakistan except through the city
of Amritsar. But the Sikhs are not letting any Muslim kafila pass
through ...'

'I am in regular touch with Master Tara Singh,' Vallabh said.
He wished Jawaharlal would forsake his lofty ideas and see the
ground reality with clear eyes. The vengeful Sikhs and Hindus
in Amritsar were the very same who had been driven out of
their homes in West Pakistan. Was Jawaharlal not aware of their
fear and resentment? Not everybody had his vision of a secular
nation – least so, when stories of Muslim atrocities in Pakistan
were blowing like a storm in Delhi. 'I will go down to Amritsar

and address the Sikhs myself. But I would like you to do one thing: Stop trying to break up riots on your own.'

Vallabh paused and Jawahar turned towards him – the two locked eyes with each other.

Each knew what was being referred to but left unspoken: Rangoon. A few weeks ago, assassins had gunned down the Burmese Prime-Minister-in-waiting and some of his Cabinet. A disgruntled British Army officer was implicated. What if, in the face of the mounting chaos and disorder, the British-led military decided to overthrow the infant Indian government?

However, if one way to contain the violence was to jump in the fray, Jawahar was not going to stop doing it. Neither was his family, by the looks of it. Returning from Mussoorie, Indu's train was stopped at Shahdara on the outskirts of Delhi. Leaning out of the window, she sighted a mob in pursuit of two men. With instructions to the boys to stay in the carriage with the ayah, she leapt out. Jumping into the thick of action, she, with some other passengers, managed to reach one old man and surround him, keeping him safe. The other, meanwhile, had gotten away with the mob in hot pursuit. Eventually, she turned up at home with the elderly man and sacks of potatoes hauled from Mussoorie. Food was scarce and the refugees in the tents outside had to be fed.

No, he would not let the thought of assassination distract him from what he needed to do. India had not wrested its freedom after long years of struggle only for Indians to kill each other. No!

Jawahar placed his hands firmly on the table, and addressed his home and defence ministers. 'We are dealing with a situation which is analogous to war, and we are going to deal with it on a war-like basis. But, unless we keep to some standard, freedom has little meaning.'

62
Delhi (September 1947)

Thick dust. Impenetrable. The plane hovered above it. If it tried to pierce through, it would be dangerously close to the cavalcade crossing the plains below. Heat and the lack of rains had sucked the soil dry, and the migrating columns were churning dust in their wake. They flew on until the dust cover thinned.

Jawahar sighted a column that stretched on interminably. Bullock carts piled high – he narrowed his eyes – with kitchen utensils, string cots, assorted household chattel; men pulling cattle; women with babies in their arms and tin trunks on their heads; children walking with the tread of elderly; all coated with dust, in raggedy clothes, barefoot, trudging, trudging, trudging. The sun, merciless above them.

What promised land were they heading to? Wasn't free, independent India supposed to be that promised land?

A grim Jawahar estimated the kafila was a few miles long at least. It was proceeding with sluggishness, and even the sound of the plane overhead did not stir one creature – man or beast.

He inhaled sharply, dust filling his nostrils. How had he failed to notice? In the relatively clear stretch of airspace they were in now, he realized that there were two parallel columns, not one – each heading in the opposite direction. Marching with slow deliberation, east, west, the convoys were together yet apart, the distance of several feet between them serving for no man's land. Here then was the boundary line of India and Pakistan. Not the one drawn by Cyril Radcliffe on a piece of paper. This living, leaving, heaving humanity in migration across the plains of Panjab, where they had cohabited for centuries in heterogenous communities, fleeing to the safe homeland of their coreligionists – this was the true Boundary Line.

As his throat filled up, his heart lurched. From the corner of his eye, he'd sighted a woman being dragged out of a kafila. He turned in his seat, bending to look closer. She resisted, digging her feet into the ground, but several men were pulling her like a bedraggled doll across to the bank where thick reeds grew. She vanished. Sitting up, he scanned the spot in the column from where she was taken. Nobody moved in pursuit, nobody seemed to have noticed her disappearance – or nobody had the energy left to care. A scuffle to the side and he saw the woman dash from the reeds, her hair loose, her chest bare, as she struggled up the incline that would take her back to the kafila. But the loose topsoil betrayed her. And thick burly arms were upon her once again, grabbing her, pulling her by her hair, and she vanished from sight again.

Jawahar turned to the pilot, who wagged his head sorrowfully. The plane sortie was undertaken with the clear instruction that it would not be asked to land. The British pilot could not risk his life, and would certainly not be held responsible for jeopardizing the life of India's new Prime Minister.

The plane clattered on. From the passenger seat, Jawahar attempted to thwart physics by focusing his eyes on the dust cover, hoping it would laser through. Several minutes later, partial visibility resumed.

Dead cattle. A once-colourful dupatta mingling with the dust. A naked child splayed on the back of a large black buffalo. Vultures in a row on a bare-branched tree, watching the passage like hooded assassins, waiting to pick on the first to fall. A woman seated by the side of a column. Her chador fell from her head and spreadeagled behind her until it was one with the soil. She was caked with dust as she sat cross-legged, her arms embracing a body. It was the body of a grown boy, perhaps an adult, for the limbs spilled out of the woman's lap, the legs folded on one side, the arms limp. She herself sat upright, head bowed in loving attention to the contents of her lap, one hand cradling the dangling head, the other turned up as if in question. She appeared frozen in time.

Over millennia, the mighty Indus had deposited the alluvial soil of Panjab. In this soil had flourished one of mankind's earliest civilizations. And now, the soil was so disturbed, it had taken flight even. Jawahar breathed deeply, the soil of Panjab laced with the flesh and blood of Panjabis filled his nostrils, mouth, and eyes.

To instruct Arjuna in his duty, Krishna revealed his form as the destroyer of worlds, the one that burst into the sky with the radiance of a thousand suns, that shattered time even. And Arjuna realized he was beholden to one thing alone: The call of action.

The stirred-up soil of Panjab had revealed that a new history had begun, and a struggling new nation could overcome her difficulties – or go under. And Jawahar realized he was beholden to one outcome alone: That the much-loved motherland, the ancient, the eternal, the ever-new India rise.

63

Delhi (September 1947)

Wailing loudly, a woman was showing Edwina the scars on her arms, face, neck, before she tore her shirt open and pointed to her chest where crescents were tattooed. Edwina crouched on the ground to hug the woman, patting her back, smoothing her hair, whispering. Pamela found her like this as she made her way through the refugee tents. She was working in the Map Room as PA to Major-General Pete Rees, head of the Military Emergency Staff, but Mummy needed help with the refugees that just kept pouring in. Several camps had been set up in Delhi, all of which needed her attention – including the 5000 refugees on the Governor General's estate. Additionally, food was short, and Mummy had put the house on tight rations of spam and cabbage.

As Mummy made to rise, another woman clasped her feet and mumbled. The tangle of women around her was piteous, as was their weeping, and Pamela wondered how best to make herself useful. Glancing around, she sighted a woman sitting on her haunches beside a pail. As she headed towards her, a naked child dashed about, and a man pointed to his shaven head and moaned. Likely a Sikh dishonoured in West Panjab. She nodded sorrowfully and kept walking.

The woman did not raise her head at Pamela's approach or her greeting.

'Are you alright?'

Stupid question! No one was all right in the refugee camp. Pamela swatted a fly and tried to ignore the grim unsanitary smell pervading the tents. When seeking inspiration, she mimicked her mother – so Pamela crouched low. The woman's face was cradled in her folded arms.

'Hello, I am Pammie.'

The woman twitched, and lifted her head ever so slightly. She was young.

Pamela smiled. The girl's eyes blinked furiously. This would take a while. Pamela removed the large bag she was carrying and sat on the floor, the grass decimated by too many feet. The girl's eyes flicked to the bag and lingered. Inside was knitting yarn, Mummy's initiative to prepare for the tough winter months ahead. Pamela plucked the ball of yarn out and offered it to the girl. 'Mind you, the dye comes off on your fingers.'

But she continued to look in the direction of the bag. Hmm … Also visible was a book that Pamela had been reading: *The Mill on the Floss*. As she took out the paperback, it struck Pamela how the girl on the book cover sat with her face hidden in her hands much like the young refugee before her. 'Here,' she held out the book.

The girl lifted her head, but her eyes remained glued to the book.

'Go on!'

She bit her lower lip, which trembled.

A wail rent the air and the girl dove back into herself – shivering and moaning.

'Hey, hey, hey,' Pamela scooched forward and embraced the girl. 'It's okay, it's okay.'

When the girl had calmed down, Pamela sat back again. Her companion was no older than her, and Pamela was loath to think of all she had suffered. Perhaps she should have got Neola along – he would have served for distraction. But the camps were overcrowded; besides Neola was incurably inquisitive and might have wandered off into unwanted territory. Neola reminded her of Shamsher Singh, who was in quite a state of late. The relatives he was expecting from Lahore never showed up. Which might be a good thing considering the daily horror on trains, but Shamsher had also been informed that his eldest niece had been abducted. The poor chaprassi was beside himself with worry. Pamela sighed. What was the name of the niece now … Frowning, she tried to recall their conversation … The name sounded like hers … Pamela … Romila? No, that was one of the teachers at the estate school. Pamela … Pam … Pammie … Pammi … Pam-mi! Yes, Pamm-mi!

The girl's head shot up.

Pamela realized she had spoken aloud. Was that the girl's name too? 'Pamm-mi?' she repeated.

The refugee girl's mouth wobbled and she blinked back tears from her large eyes.

A thought seized Pamela. Shamsher Singh said his niece was studying in college. This refugee was educated, she was drawn to *The Mill on the Floss*, an English classic, which was a college textbook too. A book about the loss of innocence …

'Pamm-mi, are you from Lahore? Is your uncle here, in Delhi? In Viceroy House? Shamsher Singh?'

Hearing which, the girl started to wail loudly.

Pammie held the girl's hands tightly. This could be a coincidence ... Could be not ... Besides, Shamsher Singh could solve the riddle easily.

༄

When Lady Sahib's driver conveyed an urgent summons, Shamsher Singh clutched the two letters he had received from Kishan Singh, and rode to the refugee camp set up in Pandit Nehru's house. En route, he repeated a prayer to Waheguru.

Lady Sahib and Miss Sahib were with a young woman, who was weeping, tears streaking her grimy face, her long matted braid hung over one shoulder, as other refugees crowded around them, sharing scraps of information about the girl.

'She had come from Lahore.'

'We thought she was dumb; she just cried and never uttered a word.'

'She scrubbed her arm all day long – see how it's branded in Urdu!'

Shamsher Singh picked his way through the refugees crowding around the Vicereine and Pamela.

'Ah, Shamsher,' Lady Sahib beckoned him, 'come.'

Shamsher Singh gulped down the anxiety clawing at his throat. He removed the photograph Kishan had enclosed with his letter. Seated on a bench, Kishan in the middle, two younger daughters to his left, the eldest to his right – all were smiling into the camera. He studied the delicate features of the eldest: sharp nose, large eyes, long hair.

'You have identification,' Lady Sahib noticed the photograph in his hand, 'good!'

Shamsher looked from the photograph to the young woman who sat with her eyes downcast. The fair lily of the family picture looked crushed. 'Pammi ... puttar,' he said hesitantly.

She raised her head and looked at him. There was a flicker in her wounded-animal eyes. Perhaps she saw a resemblance, perhaps she remembered him from when she was younger ... 'Pammi puttar,' he repeated, his eyes welling up.

She tried to smile, her mouth wobbled, her face scrunched and she burst into fresh tears.

'Oh, puttar, you are home ... You have come home.'

Squatting beside Miss Sahib who held both Pammi's hands in hers, Shamsher Singh began to stroke his niece's head. Tears ran down both their faces.

64
Indo-Pak Border (September 1947)

The kafila had been on the road for two weeks. Beli Ram's plodding feet had churned so much dust that he was marking the growing distance from home by accumulating the soil of birha on himself. Soil which starched his clothes, spiked his hair, painted his face.

Since the route to Ambarsar was lined with murderous Muslim gangs, the kafila was headed to Ferozepur instead. They were almost at the Sutlej river when night fell quickly. A rainless summer had finally passed, and the short days of Patjhar were upon them. As the men on horseback took guard positions, others set about to cook meals, feed the animals, wash, and sleep. Beli Ram had attached himself to Iqbal Singh's family, who were kind enough to store his lone bundle and feed him. He helped in turn by collecting deadwood for fires and lugging cooking vessels from the truck to stove and back again.

The riverbed was as dry as the cough their dust-filled lungs expelled. So the kafila turned to its meagre ration of water. Meanwhile, a commotion had begun at the rear. Some men were complaining about the location and pointing to the clutch of trees in the distance. Since it was night-time, all Beli Ram could see were shadowy trees, leafless mostly ... but strange trees ... large clumps festooned on the thin branches ... Somebody claimed it was a churail ... no, several churails in the trees, which set off a collective clucking and the two families right at the end loaded their bullock carts and started to move ahead to a new spot.

An elderly woman, hands stacked on her back, scolded them. 'What do you expect? All those women who have died giving birth to Pakistan! They squeezed it out of their bodies, didn't they? Now their spirits are strung on the trees of Panjab ...'

Because there was little space left near the riverbank, or to gain distance from the berating bibi, the families trundled down the riverbank to park their bullock carts on the dry bed.

'Oye,' one of the kafila leaders shouted, 'why set camp on the river?'

'Dry as a crone, isn't she?' a young man laughed as he untied a string cot. 'With so much space, pehnchod. At last, I shall sleep without my neighbour's fart in my nostrils and ears!' His laugh rang out as he happily unpacked to set up camp at night.

That bothered Beli Ram. Rivers were their lifeblood. Despite a few showers in the last few days, the vanishing rains had hurt them. Now, to set up camp on their famished selves seemed like a travesty. Beli crossed his arms and touched his earlobes. Little fires dotted the camp like glow worms. There was a smell that he couldn't identify – maybe it was his own unwashed body? – but woodsmoke rode over the camp, exhaustion took over, and he fell asleep.

Beli Ram awoke pre-dawn, the sky slowly shedding its inky dark, a few stars still twinkling in the distance. A good time to take a dump before the kafila awakened. Bunching up his lungi, he made his way to the thicket near the camp's rear. The land sloped and a large ditch opened up. A pond that had dried in the summer. Beli picked his way through the dark to find a suitable spot. He was terrified a snake would sting his naked bottom just as he released a hot turd on its sleeping self. Finding an adequate space, he was relieving himself when the smell, indeed stink, that bothered him the previous night resurfaced. He wrinkled his nose. Was it *his* stinking shit?

Coaxing his bowels took a while and a rosy hue started to streak the horizon. That reminded him of Laur, his one-room home, his ablutions, the walk to the station where he would grab tea and kulcha with Mehmood—

Beli cried noiselessly, sniffled as he deposited his dump and stood up. Blinking, he was walking up the slope when something caught his eye. A corpse, several corpses, hacked bodies frozen in death, limbs awkwardly jutting out, atop which vultures hopped. Several large birds sat in the trees – too full to eat?

Beli gagged.

Trembling, he raced up the slope, slipped, and rolled down. Dismembered bloodied corpses piled like rotting fruit. Baking in the unrelenting heat. The sickly sweet smell filled him. Beli choked on the bile in his mouth. The beady eyes of a vulture rested upon him. Its neck bobbed. That fearsome beak would tear him to pieces in no time. Scrambling, tearing at the ground, Beli clambered for cover.

∽

Shaken, he sat on the riverbank and watched the sun rise slowly. Around him the kafila was beginning to stir. The families camped on the riverbed lay sprawled. Today, they would cross the border and reach Hindustan. Reach safety. The river was the boundary line, Iqbal virji had said. So what would change once they crossed the river? Would the people look different? Speak different? Eat different? Only their gods would be different ... Which left Beli unconvinced. These gods were like boundary lines, everyone knew about them, but no one had seen them—

A roaring sound.

The kafila? Beli swivelled. Was that some animal— no, there, it sounded again, a roar ... a steady growing roar ... He sprang up and looked in the direction of the sound. It was coming from beyond where the riverbed curved where— Oh! Rabba! A wall of water was coming up the river. Beli screamed, waved his arms, hopped up and down. The roar drowned him out, but some caught his frantic flailing and looked towards the river. Horses and buffalos had begun neighing and bellowing. Shouts, screams, scuffles. The river roared above them all.

The wall of water swept up the campers on the riverbed, gathering men and animals in its gallop. The foaming torrent would breach the riverbank soon. Beli scanned his surrounding for elevation. He sighted a tree and dashed to it. 'RUN! RUN! RUN!' he alerted the kafila.

The horses tethered to the tree had sensed danger, rearing and snorting, their large eyes bulging with fear. Beli's hands chafed as he struggled with the ropes, fingers slipping and sliding. Finally, the horses were free and Beli lunged for the tree trunk. The river was in his ears as he gripped and grabbed and pulled himself up with difficulty. Wedged in the branches at a sufficient height from the ground, Beli turned towards the kafila. There was utter pandemonium on the ground. The released horses were flying away. Were people gathering their things? Tying up pots and pans and cots? The water would drown them any minute—

'Run! Run! Ruuun!'

Could anyone hear him above the raging river, which was starting to spill its bank? A petrified Beli tucked himself within the tree. How high would the water rise? How angry was the river? He scanned the horizon. The water was a thundering, frothing beast. Across the kafila, in the clutch of trees, vultures perched on treetops. They had ceded ground to a superior predator.

Water clutched at the feet of the refugees. As Beli watched anxiously, a young boy noticed him festooned in the tree. Catching his eye, Beli yelled.

'Run!'

Acknowledgements

Lahore/Laur is the land of my elders. It is my virsa. In the riverine border town where I grew up, Lahore had been left behind on the other side of the Sutlej in 1947. But like any true love, it never left us. Its fragrance was in my father's language, my uncle's stories, my mother's Pak dramas, in the ghazals floating every evening in our house, transmitted by PTV. It was present in my town's countless tales with the same denouement: Partition.

All my writing has been an attempt to bring to paper stories I grew up with, stories that spoke of an undivided land and time, stories that I didn't find in the books I read. The Partition Trilogy is, I hope, a culmination of that search. Partition is our virasat, our collective legacy, and the trilogy of books is an attempt to put faces on the ones who loved and lived and lost in that cataclysm. Including our leaders who faced multiple dilemmas as the charger of time galloped to 15 August.

I owe an immense debt to the libraries that have supported my two-decade quest as I have researched this period. Beginning with the Singapore National Library, followed by the Hong Kong Public Library, and now the New York Public Library (NYPL). Libraries and librarians are invaluable, something that has been brought home to me with renewed clarity as the pandemic lockdown halted my regular library visits and the NYPL came to my rescue. Phew! My gratitude to all the writers and historians who have written about this period, some of whom I've been able to mention in the bibliography.

Jhaphis to Prasanna, my first reader, my husband, my love. It takes a particular skill set to read a manuscript at its rawest first draft and provide feedback without wrecking either manuscript or marriage. Hugs to Minoshka Narayan, who not only read the manuscript but also did initial research for the trilogy when she was a high-schooler, and the books were just an idea in my head. Love to Sunita Malik, old friend and Sardarni, who's always had my back. My daughter, Malvika, who nourishes me with cha and chats, and lets me claim Nyx as my assistant and support animal.

My gratitude to the entire team at HarperCollins India, especially my wonderful editors, Udayan Mitra and Prema Govindan. I could not ask for better collaborators in my storytelling.

A very fine storyteller from Panjab, Bulleh Shah, said of Lahore that it was the city of a million doors and windows: Daal dass khan shehr Lahore andar ... As you read/listen to the song, you realize that the poet is using Lahore as a metaphor. Here's to Lahore then, and stories and storytellers, who show us ourselves in the stories they weave.

Select Bibliography

Azad, Maulana Abul Kalam. *India Wins Freedom: An Autobiographical Narrative*. Bombay: Orient Longman, 1959.

Bourke-White, Margaret. *Halfway to Freedom*. New York: Simon and Schuster, 1949.

Brown, Judith M. *Nehru: A Political Life*. Yale: Yale University Press, 2003.

Campbell-Johnson, Alan. *Mission with Mountbatten*. London: Hamish Hamilton, 1951.

Carter, Lionel, ed. *Partition Observed: British Official Reports from South Asia*. 2 vols. New Delhi: Manohar, 2011.

Chaudhuri, Nirad C. *The Autobiography of an Unknown Indian*. London: Macmillan, 1951.

—— *Thy Hand Great Anarch!: India, 1921–1952*. London: Chatto and Windus, 1987.

Chopra, Prabha, ed. *Sardar Patel and the Partition of India*. Delhi: Konark, 2010.

Collins, Larry, and Dominique Lapierre. *Freedom at Midnight*. New York: Avon, 1975.

Corfield, Conrad. *The Princely India I Knew: From Reading to Mountbatten*. Madras: Indo-British Historical Society, 1975.

French, Patrick. *Liberty or Death*. London: Flamingo, 1998.

Gandhi, Indira, and Jawaharlal Nehru. *Two Alone, Two Together: Letters between Indira Gandhi and Jawaharlal Nehru, 1940–1964*. Edited by Sonia Gandhi. London: Hodder and Stoughton, 1992.

Gandhi, Rajmohan. *Patel: A Life*. Ahmedabad: Navjivan, 1990.

Gopal, Sarvepalli. *Jawaharlal Nehru: A Biography*. 2 vols. London: Jonathan Cape, 1975–1979.

Guha, Ramachandra. *India after Gandhi: The History of the World's Largest Democracy*. New York: HarperCollins, 2007.

Hajari, Nisid. *Midnight's Furies: The Deadly Legacy of India's Partition*. New York: First Mariner Books, 2016.

Hodson, H.V. *The Great Divide: Britain–India–Pakistan*. Karachi: Oxford University Press, 1971.

Hutheesing, Krishna Nehru. *We Nehrus*. New York: Holt, Rinehart and Winston, 1967.

Khan, Yasmin. *The Great Partition: The Making of India and Pakistan*. New Haven and London: Yale University Press, 2007.

Khilnani, Sunil. *The Idea of India*. 1997; London: Penguin Books, 2003.

Khosla, G.D. *Stern Reckoning: A Survey of the Events Leading Up to and Following the Partition of India*. New Delhi: Oxford University Press, 1989.

Krishna, B. *Sardar Vallabhbhai Patel: India's Iron Man*. New Delhi: HarperCollins, 1996.

Mathai, M.O. *My Days with Nehru*. New Delhi: Vikas, 1979.

Menon, V.P. *The Story of the Integration of Indian States*. London: Longman, Green, 1956.

Menon, V.P. *The Transfer of Power in India*. 1957; New Delhi: Sangam Books, 1981.

Moon, Penderel. *Divide and Quit*. 1961; London: Chatto and Windus, 1964.

Moraes, Frank. *Jawaharlal Nehru: A Biography*. New York: Macmillan, 1956.

Morgan, Janet. *Edwina Mountbatten: A Life of Her Own*. London: HarperCollins, 1991.

Mountbatten, Pamela. *India Remembered*. London: Pavilion, 2008.

Nehru, Jawaharlal. *The Discovery of India*. Delhi: Oxford University Press, 1985.

—— *Selected Works of Jawaharlal Nehru*. 1st series. 15 vols. Ed. Sarvepalli Gopal et al. New Delhi: Orient Longman, 1972–1982.

—— *Selected Works of Jawaharlal Nehru*. 2nd series. 55 vols. Ed. Sarvepalli Gopal et al. New Delhi: Jawaharlal Nehru Memorial Fund, 1985–.

Pandey, Gyanendra. *Remembering Partition: Violence, Nationalism and History in India*. New Delhi: Cambridge University Press, 2003.

Shankar, V. *My Reminiscences of Sardar Patel*. Vol 1. Delhi: Macmillan, 1974.

Talbot, Ian. *Divided Cities: Partition and Its Aftermath in Lahore and Amritsar, 1947–1957*. Oxford: Oxford University Press, 2006.

Talbot, Ian, and Gurharpal Singh. *The Partition of India*. Oxford: Oxford University Press, 2002.

Von Tunzelmann, Alex. *Indian Summer: The Secret History of the End of an Empire*. Henry Holt and Co., 2007.

Wolpert, Stanley. *Shameful Flight: The Last Years of the British Empire in India*. Oxford: Oxford University Press, 2006.

Ziegler, Philip. *Mountbatten: The Official Biography*. London: Collins, 1985.

About the Author

Manreet Sodhi Someshwar is a bestselling author of six books, including the award-winning *The Radiance of a Thousand Suns* and the critically acclaimed *The Long Walk Home*. Hailed as 'a star on the literary horizon' by Khushwant Singh and garnering endorsements from Gulzar for two of her books, Manreet and her work have featured at literary festivals. Her articles have appeared in *The New York Times*, the *South China Morning Post*, and several Indian publications. Manreet lives in New York City with her husband, daughter, and cat.